WINGS

AND

STONE

Marijon Braden

If you're interested in finding out more about this book, please visit my website at www.marijonbraden.com

To send me an email, mj@marijonbraden.com

ISBN:9780985985431

CONTENTS

For my daughters

PART ONE

SUMMER

CHAPTER ONE

RUNNING. RUNNING. I COULD HEAR them behind me, but I knew I was far enough ahead that they couldn't catch me. The cobbled path turned ahead, but I was good. Jumped the gap. Still safe. Running hard. The trick was not to lose focus. The minute I faltered, they'd be all over me. I knew that. Ohmygod—where did that come from? I slid underneath. Still safe. Still running.

The next turn was sharp and I took it too fast, tripping just a bit, but it was enough. I could see them now, angry, reaching. Another gap—good jump—and I tried to not get too jittery. I remembered what was ahead. If I wasn't very careful, I could go down hard.

"Carrie, can you empty the dishwasher?"

My mother's voice called from upstairs and I was done. As I fell, the monkeys were all over me. How annoying. Why does she always have to interrupt during Temple Run?

"It's Sara's turn," I yelled back. I turned off the game and put some music back on. I loved my phone. Best. Birthday. Gift. Ever. From Dad, of course. If it were up to Mom, I'd be sending up smoke signals.

"It's not my turn," my sister said as she came down the steps.

"Yes, it is," I said. I signed onto YouTube, trying to find the singing cat video I'd found. "I did it last night."

"No, you didn't. We ate at the mall last night, remember? And I did it the night before that. You'd better go, she's in a huff," Sara said.

"She's always in a huff," I muttered. Sara sat on the couch, closed

1

her eyes, and started playing the flute. But without her actual flute. Like when people play Air Guitar. Except that Air Flute is not nearly as much fun to watch.

"Why do you do that?" I asked.

She stopped and shot me a look. "I always do this. You've seen me hundreds of times."

"Yeah, but why? I mean, how can it be of any help?"

She shook her head, irritated as usual. "It's all visualization. I can hear the notes in my head."

"Carrie, empty the dishwasher," Mom called again, her voice a little sharper.

"But how do you know the notes are the right ones? How can you tell if you're sharp or flat or whatever?"

She shot me another look, got up off the couch, went into her room and slammed the door. Good. I found the YouTube video. It was hysterical. I was watching it for the third time when Mom came down the stairs.

Annoying again.

"Carrie, I just asked you twice to empty the dishwasher."

"No, Mom. You asked me once, and then you told me once. Not the same thing." I was looking at the phone and she grabbed it out of my hand.

"Now, Carrie."

"You can't take my phone."

"I just did. You'll get it back when the dishwasher is empty."

"It's not yours, you know. Dad gave it to me."

"Yes, but I pay the monthly charges. As soon as you start handing over sixty-three dollars a month, it will be yours."

"Why are you so mean to me all the time?" I yelled. "You never take Sara's phone away."

"Sara has figured out that doing something the first time I ask will save her and I both a lot of aggravation. When are you going to learn?"

I made a face. "Perfect Sara," I said.

Mom shook her head. "Hardly perfect. And you're smarter than she is. Why haven't you figured this out yet?"

She turned and went upstairs. I crossed over to the desk and turned on the computer. Found YouTube again. After a few minutes,

I could hear Sara come back in.

"Mom said I was smarter than you," I told her.

"Yeah? Then how come I have a phone and you don't?"

Sometimes I wished I lived alone. In a cave. With Internet, of course.

It's always been Mom, Sara and me.

And Dad. Sort of. I mean, he's around. I don't remember a time when he lived with us, but I know that Sara does. He remarried when I was eight. He only lives three towns over, so we can see him most weekends, and he shows up when he should—concerts, track meets, awards, you know, all that important stuff. The problem is that he's got a new family that sucks up most of his time—my two little brothers—so he's always going to a soccer game or a t-ball game or some other game.

Mom is a high school teacher. Thank God not the high school I'll be going to. She teaches Math so she's not just smart, but kind of brainy. And geeky. She's got her master's and keeps talking about a doctorate.

I'm sixteen and I'm not tall like Sara, or curvy like Mom, and I have brown hair and eyes and too many freckles, but my best friend Becca says I'm pretty, and Damien, this really cute guy in my French class last year, told me I was a beautiful star. And he said it in French, so it sounded SO much cooler.

I'm not a girly-girl like Sara. I don't coordinate my outfits before I leave the house, or get hysterical over my hair not looking perfect. I'm not a musical prodigy, but I am smart. And I play soccer. I've been playing a long time and I'm very good at it. So good, in fact, that the high school coach saw me at soccer camp this past July and asked me to play on the girls varsity team this fall. Me, Carrie Fleming, running with the big dogs.

Sara is eighteen and drives Mom's ten-year-old Subaru that was passed on to her when Mom bought a new one last year. Sara, however, does not like to drive, especially at night. Mom and I have no problem with that. Both of us have ridden with Sara at night and we completely understand. Sara is the perfect example of that old saying that just because a person CAN do something, doesn't mean they SHOULD.

Besides, I think Sara likes the idea of being chauffeured around.

I just walk everywhere. Or run. I have a great playlist that I listen to whenever I run. The high school coach had a long talk with me, about how I had to run every day during the summer to keep in shape, so I'm not fat at all, and my legs are really long and beautiful. I hope that I can get a scholarship too, so I can become a veterinarian. I love animals, and we have a cat and two dogs. I'd have horses and a goat if I could. But Mom said no. Many, many times. So I'll just have to wait.

I used to wish that I could have ten dogs, and Mom would say "Careful what you wish for." I asked her what that meant, and she told me that sometimes, a wish comes true and it's not what you'd expect. That if I did have ten dogs, I'd have to walk them all the time and clean up a whole lotta dog poop, and then I'd have to brush them, and trim their nails, and take them to the vet and I'd never have time for anything else. I can see her point. Ten dogs might not be such a good idea after all.

And when Prince William got married, we all watched the wedding and Mom even cried a little, and Sara said she wished SHE could marry a prince of something so she could buy whatever she wanted and have people around her all the time to do whatever she wanted.

Mom laughed and said "Careful what you wish for." I couldn't imagine a downside to that at all.

But, as usual, she was right.

I hate when that happens.

The best thing about Mom being a teacher is that she gets the summers off. When we were little, we'd do all sorts of fun things, like go to the shore for a week with her girlfriends and their kids. But three years ago Sara got a job as a mother's helper every afternoon, and we just sat at home. Sara went to band camp, and took extra classes in the mornings. Classes in the summer. Really? I practiced soccer drills while Mom sat in the sun and read all day. The following year, Sara got a job at the country club. It's a fancy place that's close enough to walk to. Sara would never dream of working at a not-fancy place. Sara was a waitress in the banquet room, so every time there was a wedding or birthday, she had to work, which was practically every weekend, and she had music stuff during the week, so I took over her mother's helper job, and Mom spent another summer tanning and reading. I tried to warn her about skin cancer, but she wouldn't budge.

When this summer rolled around, Mom was already arranging the pillows on the outside chaise lounge, so I went down to the country club and got a job working with Sara. The people are nice and because of the whole Sara-not-driving thing, we can usually walk to and from, and if we work late at night, Mom comes and gets us. Because I was new, I didn't get to wait tables, just bus them and generally help fill water glasses, but the pay is okay and the tips are good. I was still running every day, got to swim at the club, had a great two weeks of extreme soccer, hung out with Becca and all my other friends and still usually got to sleep in pretty late. All and all, a fairly decent summer.

I was even looking forward to starting high school, even though I'll be starting as a sophomore. Our school district is weird. There are lots of kids in our town. We have eight elementary schools, two middle schools, and one huge high school. Half the town is normal. You go to elementary school until fifth grade, middle school until eighth grade, then high school. But the other half of town—my half —is different. You don't go to middle school until sixth grade but you still stay there for three years. They don't even call it Middle School. They call it Junior High School. Which means you spend your freshman year there. Totally sucks, right? The school board has been trying to change it for years, but the parents on our side of town keep fighting it. I guess they don't want their sweet, innocent kids thrown into the Big Bad High School as helpless freshman.

I was hoping to have a lot of classes with my friends, and besides soccer I was going into Honors French. I love French and want to get to spend a semester in France when I'm a Junior. Sara could have gone last year, but for the past couple of years, she's played flute in this orchestra of high school kids from all over the state , and wanted to do that again instead. Seriously stupid move, IMHO, but she's really into her music. I also think that if she went to France, she might run into a real princess, which might pose all sorts of challenges to her idea of who is royalty and who isn't.

The point is, I'm very good at French. I actually started learning when I was in pre-school, some program they were just testing out, but I liked it, and Mom kept finding classes and tutors. So I speak much better French than most kids who just took it in school. Which is why I started talking to the cute guy at table three at the end of the Hatton/Mayfield wedding in August. It was a full dinner wedding, cocktail hour, live band, the whole big deal. And over two hundred people. That's a lot of prime rib with baked potato or stuffed sole with rice pilaf. Bride was gorgeous, blonde and sweet with a clingy dress and a headpiece that looked like something Princess Kate would wear. The groom, well, not so good-looking, but I heard he made lots of money.

The wedding was over. The place was supposed to be empty, but, as usual, there were a dozen or so stragglers, people who didn't get that it was time to leave so the underpaid staff could clean up and finally go home. Table three had been cleaned off, but there was one lone man sitting there, sipping wine. He wasn't old at all, maybe a few years older than Sara, and he was really cute. Longish, curly dark hair, amazing blue eyes, dark skin and a very white smile. I told him the party was over, but asked if there was something else I could do for him.

"I don't speak much English," he said, rather sadly. But he had an accent that sounded French, so I asked him again in French, and his whole face lit up.

He started talking, and he was speaking French, but it sounded different from what I was used to hearing. Like when I read *Canterbury Tales*, and I knew it was in English, but it sounded so strange. That's the way he talked, so I asked him to slow down, and he did, and we had a nice little conversation.

Me: Is there something I can get for you?

Him: No, thank you, I'm having this lovely wine.

I thought, wow, he looks too young to be drinking.

Me: Where are you from?

Him: Rouen.

Well, that explained the wine. I know they drink wine in Europe all the time. But still.

6

Me: That's where they burned Joan of Arc.

Him: Among others.

Me: Did you know the bride or the groom?

Him: Neither.

Me: Whom did you know?

Him: No one.

Me: Then how did you get in here?

Him: I saw the lights and was thirsty, so I came in and sat down and had some wine.

Now, this was a serious breach of just about everything. First of all, he had to have gotten past the main gate, where every person who comes through has to show a membership card, employee I.D. card or in the case of an event like this, an invitation. Once past the gate, there's the clubhouse door guys who double checks the I.D.s, etc., and then there's another guy at the entrance to the ballroom checking again. He could have come in from outside, which didn't make sense either because there's a huge fence around everything. The point was, he should not have been there, and he was going to be in serious trouble if any of the staff figured out he was a gatecrasher.

"You can't be here," I told him. "You needed an invitation. But if you get up and leave now, you won't get into any trouble."

He was pretty drunk, I think. Or really sure of himself. He wagged his finger at me. "No, I won't leave. After all, I am a Prince in my own country, these people should be honored I am even here." He drained his wine glass. Then he said, in pretty bad English, "The wine is good. I stay. Besides, I have found my wife here, and I must wait for her, yes?"

I breathed a sigh of relief. So, his wife was the guest. Well, okay then, maybe he wasn't in trouble after all.

"Where is she?" I asked.

He motioned with his hand. "There, see? The beautiful one with the hair of copper and eyes like the green of the sea."

I looked. He was pointing to Sara.

Sara is beautiful. Really. Even though I sometimes think she's a real brat, I have to admit she's beautiful. Her skin is clear and she's got this amazing blondish-reddish hair, long and curly but not frizzy, and big green eyes and she's tall and has a pretty hot body.

She knows how good she looks, but it's no big deal for her. She thinks she's above everyone else. Seriously. Being the oldest, she grew up believing our father when he called her his little princess. Most girls, by the time they hit six or seven, have figured out that the term "princess"was not a real designation of royalty, and just get on with being non-royal. But not Sara. So she's never surprised when boys follow her around and do things for her without even her asking. She just laughs at them and keeps on playing the flute. She wants to play in a real orchestra someday, but to do that she has to go to a really good music school, and that means she needs a big scholarship, so she says she doesn't have time to date boys.

But boys always seem to find time for her, even boys who claim to be princes.

I said in English, "She's my sister."

He looked heartbroken. "Sister? She has taken vows?"

I was confused for a second, then explained, in French again, "No, she's not a nun. She's my SISTER. And she's not married to you"

"Not yet. I have not asked her. But she is my destiny."

Destiny? Was he kidding? But it gave me an idea.

I went over to Sara, who was clearing off the head table, and tapped her on the shoulder. When she turned, she narrowed her eyes at me, like she did every time I showed up in her face when she didn't want me to be there.

"What?" she snarled.

"See that cute guy at table three?"

Her eyes went over my shoulder, and when she saw him, she actually kind of smiled. "Yeah? Who is he?"

"He's a crasher and I think he's drunk. He's all alone, and he doesn't speak English very well, so I don't want to get him in trouble. Can you help me get him out of here?"

She shifted the tray to her other hand. I knew what she was thinking. Sara didn't bother with guys. At all. She'd never even had a serious boyfriend. But she liked them, I knew, and she especially liked the cute ones, so there was a chance she'd say yes.

"Why should I?" she asked.

"He says he's a prince."

"Let me get rid of this tray," she said, and went off into the kitchen.

I grabbed a few centerpieces waiting for her, but when I turned,

Doug, the manager, was scowling at French Guy. I hurried over and tugged on Doug's sleeve.

"Ah, he's with Sara and me. He's going to walk us home as soon as we're done. Is that okay?"

Doug made a face. "I thought he was some drunk who didn't want to leave." He glanced around the banquet room. "We're almost done here. Have him wait out in the hall, and you and Sara can leave in a few."

I smiled, then sighed with relief, and hurried back to table three.

"Listen," I said in French, "if you wait out in the hall, I'll get Sara and we'll both walk you out, okay?"

He frowned. "In the hall?"

"Please. Otherwise, there could be trouble."

His face changed completely. He looked suddenly very strong and capable, not drunk at all. "Of course. There can be no trouble." And he walked quickly out into the hall.

Sara came out of the kitchen, looked around, and hit me with her not-happy face.

"Where is he?"

"Out in the hall. Doug thinks he's with us, so let's get out of here soon."

But Doug wasn't the only person to notice French Guy. I mean, besides being good-looking, he'd been dressed in black, with high, polished leather boots and a silk vest over a shirt that had a ruffle around the wrists, like a pirate's shirt. Not your usual wedding guest attire. So in about two minutes, all the rest of the help wanted to know who was hanging out in the hallway and why, so rather than lie, I just shrugged and told the truth.

"He's a prince with a huge crush on Sara and he's walking us home," I told them.

Well, that's all they needed. By the time we were ready to leave, ten minutes later, everybody was calling Sara "Princess", and she was calling them serfs, and the whole thing was actually kind of funny. So we punched out, and instead of going out the kitchen door, Sara and I walked through the banquet room, into the main hallway.

He had been lounging in a chair, but jumped to his feet when he saw us. He faced Sara, reached for her hand, and kissed it.

"My name," he said," is Prince Lucien Hugo Gargouille, and I am at your service. Please, call me Luc."

I translated, and Sara smiled prettily. "Prince? How cool. Well, I'm Sara Elizabeth Fleming. This is my sister, Carrie. I think it's time to leave now."

Luc nodded, and said in English, "I know who you are."

Sara made a noise. "Really?"

He nodded. "Yes. I saw you in New York."

Sara's jaw dropped. So did mine.

Sara had been invited to play with a student orchestra last June. She had gone into New York City and spent two days rehearsing with other high school musicians from all over the country. On a Sunday afternoon, before a concert by the London Philharmonic, the student orchestra performed three pieces. Sara had a solo. Only one other student had been chosen to solo, but even I, who didn't know anything about music, knew that Sara had stolen the show. Mom and I were so far away from the stage I thought we'd never see or hear a thing, but when Sara stood up and played, she shone in the spotlight, and her music soared out over the audience like a golden bird in flight. There was an eruption of applause when she was done, and I knew that, besides being a total pain-in-my-butt sister, she was also a star.

"You were at Lincoln Center?" she asked.

Luc nodded. "Yes. My Family has box seats there. When I heard you play—"

He grabbed her hand again and held it against his chest. "I could feel you. Here. In my soul."

Sara caught her breath. "Oh."

I giggled. "I think he's got a bit of a crush on you, Sara. Careful."

Doug stuck his head out the door. "Hey, you guys okay?"

Sara snatched her hand back from Luc.

"We're good," she said. "Just leaving." She threw me a dark look and marched out the front door.

Sara was practically running down the front steps to the driveway, so I knew she was upset, because she never ran anywhere. Then she stopped and whirled around, and Luc practically ran into her.

"Are you stalking me or something?" she demanded.

Luc frowned and looked at me. I translated quickly. His face softened in the darkness.

10

"When I saw you play your flute," he said, as I translated, " I could feel your passion, your love of the music. You moved me. So, of course I made inquiries, yes? It took a while to find you. We have been very discreet, because I did not wish to scare you away. I would do nothing to distress you. Believe me."

"So, you are stalking me?"

Luc reached for her hand again, speaking slowly so I could translate. "Sara, I am a prince among my people. I have chosen you, of all the women in the world. Because you touched me, not just with your beauty, but also with your spirit. I meant no offense."

I could tell she was starting to bend. One way to Sara's soft spot is through her music. She turned away and started walking down the drive to the street. Luc followed, right behind her.

"Your family has a box at Lincoln Center?" Sara asked. I could tell that impressed her.

"Yes," Luc said in English. "I spend much time in New York. I often go to concerts. And the opera."

She kept walking, but turned to look at him. "Opera? There aren't many guys your age who are into opera." Luc smiled. "I am much older than I look," he said.

We'd reached the end of the drive. The street was pretty empty, but there were a few cars. We never felt uncomfortable walking home late at night. The neighborhood was safe and we were just minutes away. But it looked like Luc was getting ready to follow us home, and I didn't like that idea too much. Neither did Sara.

"Listen, Luc, it's been great meeting you. And I'm glad you liked my playing. But Carrie and I need to go home now, and maybe you should be heading out too."

Luc glanced at me and I translated.

"You do not wish me to walk you home?"

Sara smiled. "Thanks, but no thanks."

He shook his head. "But, I cannot leave without you. Don't you understand? You are to be my wife."

Sara was looking for me to translate, and when I did, she made a face.

"Tell him, I can't marry him now, I'm too tired. We'll have to wait 'till tomorrow."

When I told him, Luc suddenly looked very serious. Then he said,

11

slowly, and in English, "You must promise. You must promise to love me forever."

Sara nodded. "Sure. Whatever you say."

"No." He grabbed both of her hands and looked into her eyes. "Say the words."

Something very strange happened. All the night noises stopped. The crickets, the traffic. It was all of a sudden real quiet. Sara gulped. Her eyes got really big.

"I promise to love you forever."

There was a ripple in the night. There was no other way to describe it. It was as though the earth quivered, there was a quiet humming sound, and then everything went back to normal. The crickets, the car noises, it was all back. Luc kissed her hand again, took a few steps back, and he was gone.

Sara and I looked at each other.

"Next time, get rid of your own prince," she said.

As we walked home, I could tell she was in a pretty good mood, and that the whole "Prince" thing would be cool for her, something she could talk about for the next couple of days, before going on to the next joke.

Boy, was I wrong.

Chapter Two

MY DOG, MOON, MAY BE the world's cutest dog. She's a cocker spaniel, black and white spotted, with big, brown eyes. She's my responsibility, which means I feed her, walk her, and do all that other stuff, and she loves me best and sleeps with me all night. But every morning, when she needs to go out, she doesn't wake me up. She goes upstairs because Mom is always up early even when she doesn't have school. Moon hangs around upstairs for a bit, trolling for any scraps of food that may have appeared overnight, then comes back down and snuggles back with me until I decide to get up. And that's why she's not just cute, but practically perfect.

So it wasn't her fault I woke up early the morning after the Hatton/Mayfield wedding. It was my phone. I had programmed it to play the theme from the Harry Potter movies every time I got a text. It seemed like a great idea at the time, but that morning, after the third go-round, not so much. I reached over and grabbed it, squinting. Kevin had sent me three texts in a row, all the same: *Just saw FB—wherz ur crown?*

How annoying.

Kevin is my oldest friend. He and I were born two months apart. His mom and my mom met while walking their respective babies around the exact same neighborhood at the exact same time every day, so I grew up spending a lot of time playing with him when we were little. Thanks to him, I found out that there were toys to play with that weren't fashion dolls with hundreds of plastic accessories, or stuffed animals that were pink and fluffy, which was all I knew because that's all Sara ever played with. Now that we're older, we still hang out together, although he's into on-line role-playing games, and even though he's really cute and one of my best friends, that's all he is. I could never have a boyfriend who posted his new avatar on Facebook every time he leveled up.

I got up and went out to the computer. Our house is a bi-level. When you come in the front door, you can go upstairs, where the living room and kitchen and the main bedrooms are, or you can go downstairs. Sara and I have our rooms down there, and share a huge bathroom., We have our own big living area where we have a computer, TV, Xbox and Wii. It's perfect because all our friends can hang out there, it's fairly private, and Mom lets us alone. Boys aren't allowed on our rooms, of course, but they can hang out with us in the rec room. The desktop is there, and now that Sara has a laptop, it's all mine and I don't have to worry about sharing. Sharing with Sara usually means that she can use everything whenever she wants, and if I want to use anything, I have to seek her out to ask permission. See what I mean by spoiled brat?

There's a Facebook page for the country club, where they post pictures from all their events. There was a great one of Sara, and someone had Photoshopped a crown on her head. It was SO funny. I wondered if she'd be pissed off. I mean, last night it was fine, but Facebook? Maybe not.

So I texted Kevin back, then checked e-mail. . I found a message from the high school track coach, inviting me to start doing drills with the team five days a week starting Monday at the high school track. I was really psyched about that, and emailed him back right away.

I was posting to my Facebook page when the doorbell rang. Moon ignores the doorbell. She's a very quiet dog. Besides, she thinks everyone she meets is her next best friend. But Mom's dog, Fred, a Westminster terrier who thinks he's a killer guard dog, was yapping away really loudly, so it was hard to hear who Mom was talking to, but I suddenly realized the guy who was at the door was speaking French.

Oh crap.

I ran up the steps and practically pushed Mom into the wall.

It was Luc. Oh, double crap.

"What are you doing here?" I asked him in French.

He beamed at me. "I am here to marry your sister," he answered, thankfully, also in French.

Perfect.

"Mom, this is Luc. We met him last night. He's here to see Sara." I was opening the screen door and herding Luc downstairs. "He's kinda new in town."

Mom was looking at me funny. She was holding Fred and frowning. Like I said, she's way smart and is also pretty good at detecting bullshit, which at that moment was about hip deep in the foyer.

"Last night? Was he at the wedding?" she asked.

"Yes. Well, not really. He was lost and kind of wandered in. I'll get Sara."

"Does he want coffee?" she asked.

Luc turned and smiled at her. "Yes. That would be lovely," he said in English, and I could see Mom melt a little. This guy oozed charm, and she was falling fast.

I pushed Luc down on the couch and went into Sara's room. She was buried under the blankets. Her room gets really cold when the air-conditioning is on. I shook her a few times and she finally growled at me.

"Carrie, this had better be really good."

"Luc's here."

She frowned at me. "Who?"

"Luc. The guy you said you'd marry today, because you were too tired last night? He's here to take you up on the offer."

She sat up. "Here? In the house."

"Actually, on the couch."

"Why did you let him down here?" she hissed.

"I didn't want him sitting around waiting with Mom."

She made a face. "Smart move. I'll be right out. I need to pee and brush my teeth."

"Well, you can't sneak past him, so at least put something cute on."

I left her, and sure enough, there was Mom, sitting with a cup of coffee for him and a cup for herself. Fred was on her lap, ready to pounce at the slightest provocation. Moon was sitting at his feet, wagging her stumpy tail. As usual, it took her thirty seconds to fall in love.

"He's from Rouen," Mom said.

I tried to smile nonchalantly. "Yes, he told me."

"Are you going to Mansfield High?" Mom asked him.

Luc frowned. "What is Mansfield High?" He was speaking English very slowly.

"The high school," Mom said. "Are you a student there?"

"Oh no," Luc said chuckling. "I am not a student. I spent already many years at University."

"Oh? You look very young," Mom went on.

God, she is SO nosy sometimes. All the time. Why can't she just leave things alone?

Sara popped out, fully dressed. White denim pencil skirt, flowered tank top. "Hi. Gotta brush my teeth. Be right back." She darted into the bathroom. Luc looked confused, but I was pretty amazed. I'd never seen Sara get dressed that quickly before.

Mom was still trying to pry information out of Luc. "Is your family here?"

Luc shook his head. "Yes, but I am here with my, um—"

He looked at me. "How do you say advisors? I'm here with my Family's attorney and all our generals. And a banker from Paris, yes? We are seeking financing for the war," he told me in French.

Generals? Attorney? War? He was here for a war? "Lawyer, Mom. He's here about some legal issues. Listen, don't you have, you know, stuff to do?"

Mom looked at me and shook her head. "My daughter," she said to Luc, "thinks I'm being a pest. It was a pleasure meeting you."

He stood up when she did and bowed again from the waist. I could tell she was impressed. I would have been too if not for the whole war thing. She left and he sat back down, drinking more coffee. Sara came out, smiling at him.

"Sara, can I talk to you a minute?" I was going to try to give her a heads up, but, as usual, she was clueless.

"Later. Hi, Luc. How, uh, did you find out where I live?"

"My lawyer. I told you, we made inquires," Luc said, speaking

English very carefully. "Now, about the wedding."

"Yeah, well," Sara made a face. "I'm sorry if I gave you the wrong idea, but I'm not marrying you. I don't even know you. Besides, I'm going to college and then playing with an orchestra somewhere. I can't marry anybody. But you're really cute, and you seem to be a real gentleman. If you want, I'd love to go out to dinner sometime."

He frowned. "I don't understand."

Sara looked at me. "Can you translate?"

I did, but Luc was still frowning. "You said the words," he told her. "You said you would love me forever."

"I know, but I just did that so you'd leave us alone. It didn't mean anything."

Luc looked apologetic. "Perhaps you need some time to think," he said in French. "You spoke the words. Such a vow is not taken lightly by my people. They all heard you, and they are waiting now."

Sara put her hands on her hips as she listened to me translate, then tilted her head at him. "Your people? What are you talking about?"

"The Family Gargouille." he said, in English, as though that would explain everything.

Sara looked at me. "This is your fault," she said. "He was your lost puppy. I was just doing you a favor. You need to get rid of him."

She was right. I was the one who dragged her into this. Although, he had picked her out already, and I had a feeling that he would have found a way to meet her one way or the other.

I spoke in French. "Luc, listen, I think you need to go slow. She needs to get used to the idea. Why don't you give her a few days to mull things over? This is a big deal, you know?"

He nodded and answered me in French. "Yes. A very big deal. And my lawyer should be involved. I shall return in a week."

He smiled brilliantly at Sara and leaned over to kiss her cheek. She giggled, blushed, and had no idea I had merely stalled for time. He bounded upstairs, waved at us from the doorway, and was gone.

Sara rolled her eyes then went upstairs, probably in search of breakfast. I was hungry too, but more worried. Who was this guy? What was all this talk of wars and generals and a mystery lawyer who could track people down at nine o'clock in the morning?

I sat back down at the computer and started searching for his name. I wasn't sure of the spelling, but the closest thing I came up with wasn't about a royal family at all. It was about a dragon that was tamed by a saint, killed and turned into a gargoyle, which had nothing to do with a war, but did happen in Rouen. 1500 years ago. So I gave up and went upstairs for breakfast.

Mom has this really strict rule about eating in our house. If you need a utensil, like a spoon, or a vessel, like a glass or bowl, then you have to eat at the dining room table, or at least the breakfast bar. She says that's so we can all eat together as a family. Stupid rule, because you can eat chips out of a bag, which means you can take the bag downstairs, but need a glass for the soda, which has to stay upstairs. Or you can eat a bagel downstairs, but if you spread it with cream cheese, you have to go upstairs. The only exceptions are if we have four or more friends over. We're also not allowed to have our phones, computers, or even a book when we eat. We have to either sit in silence or actually talk to each other.

Sara drinks coffee with Mom, but I really don't like the taste, so I made some hot tea and cereal, and then told Mom all about the soccer coach and how he wanted me to start practicing on Monday. Usually she gets pretty excited about stuff like that, but she was looking at me funny so I knew something was coming up about Luc. I kept talking for as long as I could, but I finally stopped, and she sighed very loudly.

"Your sister told me all about what happened with Luc last night, and while I appreciate the fact that you didn't want to get him in trouble, you seem to have put Sara in a very awkward position," she said.

I glanced over at Sara, who was pretending not to care by eating her peanut butter toast very slowly.

"I know. And it's really weird. I mean, he said he was a prince and all, and this morning? He was talking about generals and advisors and a war, but when I Googled him, all that came up was stuff that happened hundreds of years ago with gargoyles."

"Gargoyles?" Sara said. "Are you kidding? I finally meet a guy who's at least cute and may be a prince and he's really a gargoyle? He couldn't be a vampire or werewolf or something sexy?"

"Sara," I said, 'it's not like vampires and werewolves are real, you know?"

"Oh? And gargoyles are?"

"I'm not saying he's a gargoyle. I'm saying that's all I could find. I'm probably spelling his name wrong. But it's not all my fault, you know. You're the one who said the words."

Mom looked back and forth between us. "What words?"

"It was really strange," Sara said. "He said I had to promise to love him forever, and everything got real quiet. I felt like it was just he and I standing there, and so I said it, that I'd love him forever and—" She looked at me. "'What happened? Did you feel it?"

"Yeah, I felt it. I thought I was imagining it. It's like the whole world shook."

"Yeah," she agreed.

"And there was a sound."

"Like a hum or someone singing."

"Yes. And the air shimmered."

Mom looked at both of us and shook her head. "Listen, girls, I know he's pretty hot, but really."

"No, Mom, honest, it was SO strange. And you think he's hot?" Sara made a face. "Yuck."

I rolled my eyes. "Sure, Miss 'I'd love to go out to dinner sometime'."

She wrinkled her nose at me before leaving the table. Mom shook her head again and went back to reading the paper.

And that was the end of Luc. I thought.

CHAPTER THREE

OUR STEPMOTHER IS A LAWYER. She has all these important clients, so she's never around to do anything. That's actually a good thing, because I don't like her and neither does Sara. That's because she hates us. No, I mean it, she does. She expected Sara to babysit the boys all the time for free, but Sara said no. Sara says no to stuff all the time, but this was kind of a big NO. I'm younger, so I didn't get asked right away, but when I did, I said no too. Because I could. And because Sara said no first, so it didn't feel so weird. So she hates us.

I love the fact that Dad didn't make us babysit the boys for her sake. He's pretty brave.

Her name is Heather. She's a blonde and lots younger than Mom. She's skinny too, even though she had two kids in three years. She wears pencil skirts with her suits and drives a Mercedes.

Heather, just as a point of information, has absolutely no sense of humor. At all. I don't understand how Dad can stand to spend so much time with her.

My half-brothers are named Dante and Henry. Dante is six, and he's pretty cute, and Dante would be a cool name if it weren't for that *other* Dante, the Italian poet one, which completely ruins the originality factor.

Henry is just a bad name for a kid, period. I mean, who names their son Henry? He's just five, and a complete dork, and it's probably because of all those people yelling "Henry" at him all the time. Heather picked out the names, of course. She is so lame.

Dad picked us up and took us to Dante's t-ball game. The games are actually fun to watch. Dante is a pretty sharp player for such a little kid. He's already got a certain grace. You can tell he's a natural athlete. He'll probably grow up to play with the Yankees. Heather is hardly ever at his games. And when she does show up, she brings her laptop for God's sake, and only looks up once in a while to yell or cheer. I hope Dante knows that all moms aren't like that.

Sara spent most of the time with Henry in the next field, helping him with soccer drills. Henry hates soccer, I think, but he loves Sara, and she played soccer through middle school and was pretty good, so they practice together a lot. Henry doesn't like to practice with me anymore, and I don't blame him. I get very competitive and forget he's a little kid, and I would yell at him if he missed the ball. Besides, it's a smart move on Sara's part, because she doesn't have to spend much time trying to talk to Heather, and as much as Sara doesn't like getting sweaty, she doesn't like talking to Heather even more.

Dad and I still talk all the time. His name is Matt. He's tall and thin, with light hair and pale green eyes. He's pretty easy-going, and laughs all the time. Sara doesn't talk to him as much as she used to. But Sara's always been quieter than me, and between her music and being universally adored, she doesn't feel the need to talk to anyone.

Sara is Dad's favorite. I don't mind. I mean, she came first. And then there was all that "princess" stuff, which was probably not in her best interest, because he just made it harder for her to believe that she can't have whatever she wants whenever she wants it. I think she was more upset when Dad left than I was. So they're not as close as they used to be.

We were having a pretty nice day. Heather had closed her laptop and was talking to another parent in the front row, leaving Dad and me alone. I didn't mention Luc to Dad, and I know that Sara didn't either, but I was thinking about him. He was one weird guy. Then I started thinking about his lawyer, who "has ways.". And then I noticed the tall, dark man sitting across the field from us, on the other team's bleachers. He was dressed in a black suit, red tie, and aviator sunglasses. He wasn't watching the ball field at all. His head was turned in the direction of the next field. He was watching Sara and Henry.

"Hey, Dad, do you know that man? The one in the suit?"

Dad squinted. "No. What the hell is he doing in a suit? It must be eighty degrees out here."

"So, you've never seen him before? Do you think that's strange?"

Dad shrugged. "What's strange? He's probably the uncle of some kid on the other team."

"But he's not watching the game."

Dad was quiet for a minute or two. "You're right. He's watching Sara. Is something going on with her?"

I shrugged. Other than the fact that a mysterious Frenchman who may or may not be involved in a covert international coup wanted to marry her, no.

Dad nudged me with his elbow. "What?"

"Nothing, Dad. Honest. Did I tell you? I start practice with the high school team next week."

"Hey, Carrie, way to go. Let me know if you need a lift anywhere."

"Dad, I can walk there, remember?"

"Yeah, I know. But it would be a good excuse to see you during the week."

I shook my head. "I'd have to book you at least a week in advance to fit into your schedule." With Heather working so much, it fell to Dad to chauffeur the boys everywhere.

Dad smiled. "I'd make time, you know that."

I nodded and drank from my water bottle. Dad has his own business, designing and maintaining commercial web sites, so he works from home and is pretty flexible about when he has to actually sit down and work. Which is a very good thing for Dante and Henry. Heather is always having last minute meetings in court and is hardly ever home.

"Mom is thinking about getting her PhD," I told him. I knew that he and Mom talked about us all the time, but I wanted him to know how she was doing. I think he still cared about her.

"Figures. Your mother loves being a student."

"Yeah, I know. I don't get that."

He looked at me over his sunglasses. "I always thought you were like her. Don't you like school?"

I shrugged. "Yes. I'm looking forward to going again this fall. But starting out as a sophomore is kinda scary. I mean, half the kids have been there a year already."

"Nah, don't worry about it. You're a good kid. You'll be fine."

I looked back across the field. "He's gone."

"Who's gone?" Dad asked.

"Suit guy. He's gone."

"He probably had to get back to the funeral home," Dad said, and we both started laughing.

Mom drove me to practice Monday afternoon. I didn't do my usual morning run, and when we got to the track it was hot. The smart thing would be to have practice first thing in the morning, but that's when the guys practice for track, football, whatever—so us girls have to sweat it out big time. But that was okay with me. I was so excited to meet my fellow teammates.

Who, as it turned out, were perfect bitches. As I came up to the group, one of them—short, dark ponytail, yellow shorts—turned to me and said, "Who do you think you are, playing with us? You belong on JV. What makes you think you're good enough for us?"

I was stunned. I gulped once and looked at everyone. Not one friendly face. I didn't think about how the rest of the team would react. I was just excited to be picked for Varsity.

The thing is, I knew most of the girls. I'd been playing soccer for a long time, and so had most of them, and I'd crossed paths with them at a summer soccer camp, a soccer banquet—somewhere. So they knew me. They knew I was a good player. And they still didn't want me.

But my Mom is a tough lady, and watching her all these years taught me to stick up for myself. I knew if I backed down now, I'd be miserable forever, so I put on my hard-ass face.

"Who do I think I am? I'm the girl YOUR coach thought was good. Good enough to play with all of you. It doesn't matter if I think I'm good enough or not, because he does. Maybe things are different here in high school. Maybe here it's okay to question your coach, and go against his wishes, but me, I do as I'm told."

That shut her up. They all looked a little embarrassed for a second. Then a tall girl came forward.

"I'm Kate. I'm the captain. If Coach says you practice with us, then fine. You're here and we're here, so let's go. But a lot of girls wanted to get your place on the team. We have a pretty good junior varsity team. We had girls that did great last year and wanted to play with us but weren't put through. So you'd better be good."

To be honest, I wasn't planning on being a show-off. I was going to keep my head down and try to be friends. But two hours later, after scoring about ten points off their best goalie and making more steals than I could count, I was tired, sweating like a pig and so close to tears I was afraid to talk. They were all looking at me a little differently. I'd never worked so hard in my life. I pushed myself too hard, I could tell, but I didn't care.

I was getting ready to call Mom to pick me up when I heard somebody call my name. I looked around, and there was Kevin, sitting way up on the bleachers. I waited for him to climb down, and we walked off the track together.

"I just wanted to see how your first practice went," he said. "You showed them."

Kevin is pretty tall, but not gangly and awkward like lots of boys his age, and he's got dark hair that's kind of long and falls over his eyes so he's always shaking his hair out of his eyes to see. He's got light blue eyes and all the girls think he's cute. I do too, but first and foremost, he's my friend. He's such a good friend that he walked to the track to watch me practice because he had probably figured out that those girls would hate me. And he was right.

I was starting to cry. "They don't want me there. I'm as good as any of them, and they don't care. They're just mean and awful."

Kevin grabbed my duffel bag from me and threw it over his shoulder. It wasn't all that heavy, it only had socks, a towel and some water bottles in it, but it felt like it weighed a ton.

"They're just jealous," he said. "You're so fast and coordinated, and they see it, and they don't like it, but so what? After you start winning for them, you'll be their best friend."

He didn't try to pat me on the back or anything. In fact, he pretended not to notice I was crying, which is why we're friends.

We walked towards home. Kevin lived around the corner from me. It was only about two miles, and it was mostly downhill. We just walked along until Kevin asked me about Sara and the whole "Princess" thing. I told him everything, about Luc and his lawyer and the generals. I even told him about the guy at the t-ball game.

"So, Luc is a nut-case?" Kevin asked at last.

I shrugged. "Maybe. He seems nice, very charming, you know? Or maybe it's just the accent. Sara will probably go out with him if he asks. She loves the idea of him being a prince. You know how she is about that stuff."

"How about you? Would you go out with him?"

I snorted. "Listen, Luc is all about Sara. He probably doesn't even remember what I look like. He was...smitten. That's it. He was smitten."

Kevin laughed. "You sound like a romance novelist. Smitten. Great word, by the way."

"Yeah? I'll remember to use it on my college essay. Thanks for walking me home."

"No prob. You looked good out there. Don't let them get you down. Want me to come tomorrow?"

"Better not. All I need is for them to think I've got a fan club, then they'll really hate me."

He just nodded. We were turning the corner onto my street, and I suddenly felt tired. I needed a shower and just wanted to stretch out somewhere, so I wasn't paying attention to much, when Kevin said, kinda worried, "Did somebody die?"

I looked up, and there was a long, black limo parked across the street from our house. I squinted against the sun, and I recognized the driver. Same black suit, same red tie, same sunglasses.

He was talking on a cell phone, and as he looked over he saw me and quickly shut the phone. He made a face. He had recognized me. He knew who I was.

"It's him," I whispered. "From the t-ball game. He must be watching our house."

Kevin cleared his throat. "Just keep going. Let's get into your house and tell your Mom."

We walked up the driveway and to the front door. Kevin seemed very cool. My heart was pounding so hard, I thought the whole neighborhood could hear it.

We went inside and I bounded up the stairs. Mom was in the kitchen, chopping up a pile of vegetables. She cooks a lot. Kevin's mom was also there. They were drinking wine and laughing. She looked up when she saw me and put down the knife.

"What?"

"Somebody is following us."

She moved towards the phone. "Did he follow you from practice? Was he on foot?"

"No. He wasn't at practice. He's sitting in a car out in front of the house."

She stopped. "What? Then how is he following you?"

This was going to be hard to explain. Being a Math teacher, my mother has a very logical mind.

"Mom, he's not following me. He's following Sara. He was watching her at Dante's t-ball game yesterday, and he's out front right now in a big black car."

"Sara got home from band practice over an hour ago. I drove her myself. I didn't notice any big black car."

God, she could be so dense. "Mom, he would have been following you. It's his job to be practically invisible. Of course you wouldn't notice him."

"If he's practically invisible, why do you keep seeing him?"

Okay. Good point.

"Could you please just go look?"

She nodded, and we all went to the living room. We spent a few seconds starting out the picture window. No black car. Anywhere.

"It was there. Honest, Auntie M," Kevin said.

My mother's name is Margaret, and since we've all known each other forever, Kevin calls her Auntie M and I call his mom Aunt Beth.

"What did you see, Kev?' Aunt Beth asked.

"A big black car. New York plates. A man sitting in it is a dark suit, dark hair and a red tie."

New York plates? Wow, he's observant.

"The same man in the same suit was at the game. Call Dad. He'll remember."

Mom frowned, but went back and grabbed the cordless house phone off the wall. Why she insists on a landline is beyond me. She walked into the other room. Aunt Beth pecked Kevin on the cheek. "How was practice?" she asked me.

I shrugged. "Sucked. The girls hate me 'cause I'm only a

sophomore. They don't think I should be there. I out-ran half of them, and they never even gave me a hi-five."

Aunt Beth sighed. She and Mom are practically the same—same height, weight, age, same blondish hair and brown eyes, but Mom is good-looking, with a great smile and bouncy hair and her eyes practically sparkle. Aunt Beth is just plain—limp hair, sad smile. But she's the sweetest person you'd ever want to meet and Kevin's dad is crazy about her. So is Kevin. So am I. I trust her just like I trust Mom.

"They're probably jealous," she said.

"That's what I told her," Kevin said. He had his hand in the cookie jar and was pulling out Oreos. He handed one to me then went into the fridge and found the milk. He's at our house a lot, and knows his way around. "I also told her once she started winning games, they'd all love her."

Aunt Beth sighed again. "Maybe. Teen-aged girls are tough." She'd know. Kevin has two older sisters, twins, both freshmen in college.

Mom came back and hung up the phone. She looked thoughtful. "Your father agreed there was someone at the game, just like you said. Are you sure it was the same man?"

I nodded, my mouth full of cookies and milk.

Mom took a deep breath. "Okay. Keep your cell phone handy. If you see him again, call the police, then call me. I don't know what's going on, but I don't like it. I'll go down and let Sara know." She chewed her bottom lip. She did that whenever she was thinking. "Could this have anything to do with Luc?"

Well, duh. I mean, here we were, living boring, normal lives, when suddenly a gorgeous Frenchman who may be involved in some sort of international skullduggery shows up and wants to marry Sara, and the next day we're stalked by a Man in Black.

"Maybe," I said.

I looked over at Kevin. He winked. I wish I could do that.

27

Chapter Four

TUESDAY'S PRACTICE WAS MUCH THE SAME, but I was in a good mood going in because I spent the morning with Becca. She's been my best friend since pre-school, and she looks exactly the way I wish I looked. She's got white-blond hair and blue eyes, and she's tiny, with one of those solid, strong-looking bodies that cheerleaders have. She's also got a great sense of humor. She'd been on vacation with her family the week before, so I had to fill her in on a lot of stuff—Luc, the Man in Black, soccer—how my life was suddenly complicated.

"It's not complicated," she told me. "It's just finally gotten interesting."

"Finally? And what does that mean, exactly?"

She rolled her eyes. We were sitting on swings at the children's playground, about three blocks from my house, eating grapes. She popped one into her mouth and chewed.

"Listen, you're my BFF, but even I have to admit you're a little soccer-obsessed. Not that that's bad, exactly. I mean, it's better than being boy-obsessed, or drug-obsessed, but it kind of limits conversation in large groups, you know?"

"So, I'm boring at parties?"

"No. Well, first of all, we don't go to parties."

I nodded. "True. But I was kinda hoping that would change."

"Me too. And now, you'll have all sorts of cool things to talk about besides what's happening on the Girls Soccer Team. That's a good thing."

"Is it really cool to have some psycho stalk your sister, and an old guy in a suit follow you around?"

"How many other people do you know have that going on?"

"True again. Can this possibly mean I'll be finally one of the cool kids?"

She shook her head. "No. You've got me and Kevin dragging you down. Kevin is great, but too geeky. And I'm just a lump."

I threw a grape at her. "You are not a lump!"

She grinned and threw one back. "I don't do sports, I'm not smart like you, I'm not a music or drama person—what am I? A hot blonde with a smokin' body, but that will only get me so far."

"Next year, when Sara's gone, you can be Class Beauty and have a million guys fall at your feet."

"I could do that. I'll have to ask your sister how and why she manages to ignore them all."

I made a noise. "She's so wrapped up in her flute, only Prince Charming would make an impression."

"So, isn't this Luc guy supposed to be a prince?"

The grapes were gone. I turned the plastic bag upside down, and bits of stems fell to the ground. "Maybe. But the whole thing is creeping me out."

She hopped off the swing. "You're overreacting . Seriously. But if he is a prince, then you could live with them in a palace or someplace. That would be very cool. Then not even I could keep you out of the Cool Kids Club."

I so love Becca Howard.

But my great mood crashed and burned when I got to practice and none of the girls even said hello. I did manage to learn a few more names, not because anybody introduced themselves, but because I heard them calling back and forth to each other during drills. Then the coach came by, watched us all for about ten minutes, called Kate over and had a brief talk with her. About me. I could tell because they both looked over at me, and the coach looked pissed off. I waved at them both. Then Coach came over, welcomed me, and left.

Kate announced they would be running the Culver Lakes loop the next morning. Then she formally introduced me to everyone, saying they should all make me feel welcome. Then she gave me a look that could curdle milk, as Mom would say. I was on her list for sure.

The Culver Lakes loop is legendary in the Mansfield school district if you're into sports. Culver Lakes is a very rich community that backs up against the high school parking lot. Someone years ago mapped out a route through Culver Lakes that was exactly five miles and mostly uphill, with one long, slow descent at the end. It was supposed to be brutal. Anyone involved in high school sports ran it on a regular basis. Urban myth said it made defensive linemen weep.

After practice and a shower, I went to the country club with Sara and worked a cocktail party. No sign of the Man in Black. No mysterious cars. Sara was not thrilled by the idea that someone was following her. I don't think she believed me. Just the same, she called for Mom to pick us up instead of walking home after nine.

The next morning, I ran the Culver Lakes loop. It almost killed me. It almost killed all of us. Finally, we were acting like a team, because we were all so tired and miserable and sweaty and bitchy that everyone forgot who hated whom. I love running, but this was ridiculous. My legs hurt so badly when we finally reached the downhill part at the end that I just wanted to lie down and roll back to the school. I called Mom for this one, and she came and picked me up.

"This is child abuse," I declared, slamming the car door. "No one should be forced to do this."

"No one is forcing you," said my mother, who always said she loved me but I sometimes doubted her sincerity.

I stared down at my thighs. "My legs are still trembling. Look. I may never be able to walk again."

"Oh, I doubt that. I'm sure you'll be just fine."

"No, I will not be fine. This was the worst practice ever."

"You've only had three," she pointed out.

"I don't care, I hate it."

"Want to quit?"

I thought about that. Yes, I felt like I could never run again, but no one had said anything terrible to me, in fact, one or two of the girls actually laughed at a few of my jokes.

"Maybe. No. I'll see how I feel tomorrow."

Mom smiled. "That's my girl."

We drove up our street, and there was a blue van parked on the side, and as we passed it, I saw that the Man in Black was sitting in the front seat.

"Mom. Don't look now, but the guy is here. The one who's following Sara. He must have changed cars so I wouldn't notice him. He's sitting in that blue van over there."

She parked the car in the driveway and turned off the engine. She glanced in the rear view mirror. She could see the van.

"Sara is home," she said. She looked at me hard. "Are you sure about this?"

I nodded. "It's him. I swear."

"Okay," she said. Then she got out of the car, slammed the door shut, and walked right over towards the blue van.

Was she kidding? She could get hurt. What kind of a woman goes after a full-grown man in a van?

A pissed-off mom, that's who.

I bolted after her. As she approached the van, the engine started up, but she ran right in front of it and slammed both of her hands against the hood really hard.

The man inside yelled at her. "Are you crazy?"

"Yeah," she yelled back. "I'm the crazy woman who lives in this house. What are you doing here?"

She ran around to the driver's side and jerked the door open.

I was right behind her. The Man in Black looked stunned. His jaw dropped and he pulled off his sunglasses, staring at Mom.

She stared back. It was like she was holding her breath. They stared like that for almost a whole minute, and then she all of a sudden realized where she was and kind of shook herself.

"Have you been following my daughter?"

She didn't sound nearly as mad as she did before, which was a good thing, because I wouldn't wish my Mom's anger on anyone. Not even a creepy guy in a black suit.

Only he wasn't at all creepy. In fact, he was quite handsome, maybe my Dad's age, with very kind brown eyes and longish brown hair and a strong face.

"Oh," was all he said.

31

Mom drew herself up. "That's not an answer."

He sighed. "No, Ms. Collier, it's not."

That was weird. I assumed he had some connection to Luc, and Luc knew our last name. But how did this man know that my Mom took her maiden name back after the divorce? How did he know her name was Collier?

She was thinking the same thing. "How do you know who I am?"

He took a deep breath, and turned the van engine off. He pulled the keys out, shaking them in his hand.

"I know quite a lot about you and your girls." He spoke with a faint British accent. Posh. "I represent His Royal Highness Prince Lucien Hugo Gargouille. Since your oldest daughter, Sara, is betrothed to His Highness—"

"Wait a minute." Mom shook her head. "Sara isn't 'betrothed' to anyone. And who is this prince?"

"Luc, Mom," I said.

She looked at me. "Luc is really a prince?"

I shrugged. "I didn't believe him. He was saying some crazy things."

"And what about this betrothal thing?" She was watching me closely.

"When Sara said those words. We told you, remember? It was like a vow. I guess that's what he means." Sara was so going to kill me.

Mom rolled her eyes. "I'm sure no one is going to take a thing like that seriously. She only said it because he was drunk. She wanted to make sure he'd leave. She was trying to keep him out of trouble."

"Yes. I know exactly what happened. His Highness has explained that the vow may have been said under less than straightforward circumstances. But it was said. That's the thing." He took another deep breath. "I think we need to talk about this. Perhaps we can get out of the street?"

Mom stepped back. "Sure. Come on in the house."

"Thank you." He turned around and said something, then got out of the van. The back door of the van opened, and a kid jumped out. He looked a lot like Luc, the same curly hair and blue eyes, but younger, nearer my age. He was dressed in faded jeans and a black tee shirt, and he was way cute. He grinned at me and nodded.

The man cleared his throat. "Allow me. My name is Gregory

Abbott. You can call me Abbott. Everyone else does. As I said, I represent the Family Gargouille. This is Jean-Christophe Gargouille, cousin to His Royal Highness and sixth in line to the throne. Jean-Christophe, this is Caroline Fleming, and her mother, Margaret Collier."

"I'm Chris," he said. He bowed over my mother's hand and kissed it, just as Luc had kissed Sara's hand. If nothing else, the cousins were a class act.

"I'm Carrie," I said. I was suddenly aware of the fact that I was dressed in faded gray shorts and a tee shirt that was blotched with sweat. I was still wearing my soccer cleats and shin guards. My face was probably still beet red. And my hair was a mess. Perfect. Cute Guy and the Little Match Girl.

He didn't kiss my hand, or even bow, but his grin broadened. "Soccer?"

I nodded.

"Running drills?" he asked.

I nodded again.

"That must suck in this heat,' he said.

I nodded again. "Big time." Then I grinned back at him. And then we all went into the house.

Mom made coffee. Mom's big on making coffee. I swear, if aliens were invading the earth, and lasers were destroying everything around us, and we had to gather together all the things necessary to run up into the mountains to escape extinction, the first thing Mom would do is make coffee.

So, we all sat around the dining room table while Mom poured everyone coffee. Well, just herself and Sara and Abbott. Chris and I had iced tea. But she seemed very calm and not at all rushed, which pissed me off because I was DYING to know what was going on, and I could tell that Sara was too, but we had to sit and wait. Mom will not be rushed.

Fred was going crazy over our two guests. He's usually annoying, but then he calms down. But he sat at Chris's feet and yapped for so long that Mom picked him up and threw him into her bedroom and shut the door. Moon, of course, remained oblivious.

Finally, like, twenty minutes later, we were ready to talk. Mom took a deep breath, folded her hands in front of her on the table, and smiled at Abbott.

"Were you following my daughter?" she asked.

"Yes," he said at once. " I, or one of my associates, has been following Sara since Sunday morning."

He stopped talking, took a gulp of coffee, set the mug down and waited.

Mom nodded. "Why?"

Abbott narrowed his eyes. "I've been trying to figure out the best way to explain to you what's been going on. Obviously, this is a new situation for you, and I assure you, it's new for me as well. Never in the history of the Gargouille Family, has something like this happened before. Usually, the person who becomes betrothed to the heir has been chosen after careful investigation and consideration. In fact, he or she has generally been known to the Family already. What His Highness has done is unprecedented, and has created a myriad of complications."

Wow.

Mom sipped her coffee. "You keep referring to Sara as 'betrothed.' She is nothing of the sort. She barely knows Luc and she has done nothing to indicate anything more than a passing interest in a date. Why all the time with the 'betrothed'?"

"Yes." Abbott nodded. "Yes, I know, but you see, Ms. Collier—"

"Please," Mom interrupted, "call me Maggie."

A look flickered across Abbott's face, and he smiled. "All right. You see, Maggie, certain words were spoken, and those words—"

"Yes, I get all that," Mom interrupted again. "But seriously, you're going to hold her to something said in a moment of, I don't know, sympathy or whatever? She only said it so that Luc would leave. She didn't mean it."

"But the words were spoken," Abbott repeated, his smile fading. "They were heard. And the moment they were heard, the entire Family knew it. Since that moment, I've had all of my resources checking out your daughter. Your entire family, for that matter. We know just about everything there possibly is to know. I was watching her myself because I wanted to see if I could get some sort of sense of her, of what sort of person she was. It is very important to know what we're dealing with."

"So, what did you find out?" Sara asked. I looked at her in surprise. This whole thing had captured her imagination, I could tell.

He looked at her. "You are an excellent musician, and that appears to be your main focus. Very admirable. To be a great musician, that kind of dedication is vital. You have very strong family connections. Also admirable. You are well thought of at your job, in school, and by your peers. You have few bad habits and no dark secrets. That is most assuring." He smiled. "You seem to get along well with other people. You're friendly and unafraid to engage others in conversation. An excellent trait. In fact, as the fiancée of the heir to the House of Gargouille, you are acceptable. There is usually a two-year engagement, during which time all the resources of the Family will be at your disposal. However, the engagement period—"

"Stop it," Mom said impatiently. "Stop talking like this is a done deal. It is not."

"Wait, Mom." Sara leaned forward, her eyes bright. "What do you mean by resources?"

I had been watching Chris. He suddenly grinned.

"What Abbott here means," Chris said, "is that the Family is filthy rich. You'll have your own bank account, credit cards, and a personal staff to help you out. And my cousin isn't a bad guy. He's a bit slow on the uptake, but I've heard he's pretty fun on a date."

"Sara," Mom snapped. "Don't be ridiculous. You're not marrying Luc. So what if words were spoken? This isn't some kind of fairy tale, this is the real world, and mere words don't have that kind of power."

Abbott looked very serious. "I was afraid of this. I need you all to listen very carefully to what I'm about to tell you. This isn't a story that is often told, but it's all true."

He took another long drink of coffee, then began to speak. "Thousands of years ago, there dwelt a Family in the heart of what is now France. They were a strong and powerful Family, and they had control over a vast kingdom. Under their protection were scholars, farmers, priests and warriors. In times of great danger, those under the banner of Gargouille, transformed. Their shapes changed, they sprouted wings, and grew in size. In this way they always defeated their enemies. Such is the stuff of legend.

"Sometime in the mid-seventh century, when the Church was trying to establish itself among the pagan peoples of the world, a bishop named Romanus, in the city of Rouen, thought that one way to assert authority over the region was to defeat the strongest kingdom around, which meant Gargouille. The Family had existed peacefully for centuries, their people living happy and productive lives, but they had no interest in this new God. When they heard of this threat, they sent the mightiest of their warriors to meet Romanus. The warrior changed into a dragon, and was sure of victory, but Romanus had the power of God behind him. He used a crucifix to subdue the dragon and brought the creature to the center of Rouen, where it was burned alive. The head and neck of the creature remained intact, as its own fire breath had tempered it for centuries. The head was then mounted on the wall of a newly built church as a sign of the might of God.

"When the Family heard that their dragon had been killed, they realized they could not fight against such power. The head of the Family went to Romanus and swore undying loyalty. Romanus didn't quite trust the Family, who for ages past had been a rule unto themselves. So as a gesture of good faith, the Family pledged their entire kingdom to the service of the Church. The warriors, scholars, all of them, changed into their fighting forms and flew to the tops of the churches to defend the house of God against all evil."

"Gargoyles," I blurted. "You're talking about gargoyles. When I Googled Luc's name, that's all I could find."

Abbott nodded. "Yes. Gargoyles. Members of the immediate royal Family still have the ability to walk about freely in human form, and although they are still very long-lived, always choose a mortal to marry. That is how the bloodline remains strong. Which is why it is so important that Luc find a suitable bride and continue the Family line." Mr. Abbott sat back and looked at us expectantly.

Sara snorted. "Oh, this is cute. I'm engaged to a gargoyle. Just perfect." She looked at me. "And it's all your fault. Thanks, Carrie."

"It's not my fault," I said hotly. "Luc found you without me. I just —"

"Hold it, both of you," Mom said. She tilted her head at Abbott. "Do you really think, in this day and age, anyone is going to believe such a cock-and-bull story?"

Abbott sighed. "Yes, well, I know it sounds absurd, which is why we're prepared to show you a little something that may change your mind. Go ahead, Chris."

We all looked at Chris. He stood up and backed away from the table. He bent his head and crossed his arms in front of him. I could see his jaw clench. The air smelt like smoke.

He started growing. His ears became large and pointed. His skin turned the color of sand. Huge wings sprang from his shoulders. His face became lion-like, and a mane of fur sprouted around his face. When the top of his head reached the ceiling, he dropped onto all fours. Talons sprouted from his front paws and his mouth became a snout full of teeth. He turned his face to us and snarled.

My mother turned white, her eyes wide. Sara whimpered. My mouth dropped open.

Then he sat back on his haunches, folded in his wings, and tucked his massive head down. The details softened, blurred together. Fur and feathers turned to stone.

He had become a gargoyle.

Chapter Five

ABBOTT LEANED FORWARD. "I HOPE you can appreciate," he said softly, "why we don't want this to get around."

Mom stood up. She was staring at what was once Chris. "Get that out of my house," she whispered. "Now."

The air smelt like smoke again, and, in a blink, Chris was back, slender and curly-haired. "I'm so sorry, Ms. Collier," he said. "I never meant to frighten you. But you have to believe Abbott. You must understand how important this is."

I heard a sob, and turned to find Sara's eyes were streaming tears. "I'm engaged to something like that?"

"No," Chris said quickly. "Well, yes. Technically. But Luc has never Turned. He's never had to. He's heir to the throne. He's got enough going on."

"Maggie," Abbott said gently, "please sit down. Everything will be fine."

Who was he kidding?

But Mom sat down anyway. So did Chris. We all just sort of looked around at each other for a minute. Sara sniffed and Mom gulped down what was left of her coffee. Somebody had to say something.

"So, Chris," I said, "Why don't you have an accent like Luc? You sound like you were born and raised here."

He looked at me gratefully. "Actually, I grew up in Vermont. My parents sent me to live with some good friends right after I was born. I have visited France often, and can speak the language, but I'm most comfortable speaking English."

I nodded. "Well, that answers that. I've got another question. Are all the gargoyles in the world like you?"

"Excellent question, Carrie," Abbott said happily. "Most of our people are those on cathedrals or buildings built before 1900. It became more difficult as time went on to work with modern buildings, but we've managed to be represented on most architecture throughout the world. As these churches and such went up, the Family would choose guardians, Turn them, place them where needed, and then put to Sleep."

"Sleep?" Mom asked. Good for her. She was trying to pretend this was just a normal kind of conversation.

"Yes," Abbott explained. "Sleep is when they change to stone. Only members of the royal Family have that power. Some gargoyles, who are related by blood to the Family, can change back and forth at will. Chris, here, is an example. But most need to be put to Sleep, and, when needed, Awakened. Called to duty, as it were."

"Duty?" Mom asked again. She was trying. I hoped that soon she could move up to more complex sentences.

"Yes," Abbott said. "Called on to defend against evil."

"Is that what Luc was talking about, then?" I asked. "When he said he was here about a war?"

Abbott and Chris exchanged a look. Chris rolled his eyes. Abbott cleared his throat.

"Did Luc mention a war?" he asked, very innocently.

"Yes. When Mom asked him if his Family was here, he said he was with generals and advisors. He mentioned a war." I glance at Mom. Her eyes narrowed.

Chris snorted in disgust. "My cousin can be a real idiot," he said. He looked at Sara. "Do you think you can teach him to keep his big mouth shut?"

Sara had stopped crying, but her mouth was in a thin, tight line. She nodded a few times, very quickly.

"Yes." Abbott smiled reassuringly. "It looks as though there is a bit of trouble brewing, but this sort of thing has happened before, and it usually comes to nothing."

Mom folded her arms across her chest and leaned back in her chair. "You know, Abbott, you might as well just tell us everything."

"All right." He smiled again. "Will you call me Greg?"

"Sure," Mom said. "You know, Greg, you might as well just tell us everything."

He stopped smiling. He glanced at Chris, who lifted his shoulders once, then let them slump.

"Well," Abbott began, "you must understand that fifteen hundred years ago, when the Family pledged to protect the Church from evil, it was because there was evil. In a very real and physical form. I'm not talking about bad men and women who did terrible things, although people like that did and still do exist. Evil is…" He rubbed his fingertips against the side of his head. "Evil is just as real as gargoyles. There are things that are not of this world who exist here despite all our efforts. We can keep them under control, but every once in a while they find a way to gain power, and during those times, well, the world can get a little tricky. Take the Dark Ages. That was a tough one."

"Oh?" Mom tilted her head at him. "Are you suggesting that there are demons or vampires or whatever running around that we need to be worried about?"

"Yes. There are. Demons and vampires, that is. Everything else has been pretty much exterminated. There are probably some genii about, just in the Middle East, and there are selkies still in Europe, but they're fairly harmless, I should think. Here it's mostly demons and vampires."

He said it very matter-of-factly. Like it shouldn't be hard to believe. But, really, we just saw a teenage boy become a giant lionized gargoyle, turn to stone, and then back again, so I guess vampires shouldn't have been such a leap.

"Wait a minute," Sara said sharply. "Vampires aren't evil. They are trying to live among humans, aren't they? They don't drink blood anymore, right?" She looked around hopefully. "I mean, there are all kinds of stuff about them now, and I thought they were fine living with people."

Sara, who hated reading as a little kid, had discovered the teen-fiction version of vampires a few years ago and fell in love. As far as I could tell, she owned every vampire series in book form out there, as well as DVDs of every movie and TV series that involved sexy, young, well-dressed Vampires In Love. She thought they were

Romantic with a capital R.

A flash of anger passed over Chris's face. "Don't let all that fool you," he said harshly. "Vampires are evil. They feed off of human blood. They kidnap people and hold them prisoner, sometimes for years, keeping them alive just to have a fresh supply of blood. I know that in the past few years, it's all about how the poor, misunderstood vampire just wants to live a quiet life, but that's a crock. They're vicious. They have no souls. Remember that."

Sara's jaw dropped open.

Abbott cleared his throat. "We think it's all part of their plan," he explained. "Slowly, insidiously, the message has gotten out that there is nothing to be afraid of. If and when vampires reveal themselves, instead of people running for their lives, they'll probably ask for an autograph. Chris is right. They are evil. They are what we fight against, by any means necessary. And that may mean the war that Luc spoke of. It's gotten serious."

We all sat there in silence. Then, a sweet, familiar tune began, filling the air. Abbott looked around, frowning.

"Seriously? Harry Potter?"

Chapter Six

IT WAS MY CELL PHONE. I dug my hand into the pocket of my shorts. "Sorry," I mumbled. I turned it off quickly, then looked to see what had so rudely interrupted us. A text from Becca.

Check ur mail—schedules :)

"Mom," I asked, "did we get the mail yet?"

"What? Carrie, we're in the middle of something here."

"Yeah, I know," I said. "But schedules are here."

Mom shook her head. " Schedules?"

"Sorry," I said, then shot out of my chair and was out of the house and down to the mailbox in seconds. I glanced through the mail quickly and there it was, my class schedule for my first year in high school. I opened it with trembling fingers.

Lunch seventh period? Were they kidding?

I texted Becca back.

Just got it Come over.

I walked slowly back into the house, trying to make sense of what I was looking at. I needed to get on Facebook right away.

As I climbed the stairs, it was obvious that the whole mood had changed. Mom was putting coffee cups in the sink, and both Chris and Abbott were on their cell phones. Sara was still sitting at the table, but she was looking mighty pleased with herself.

"What?" I asked.

Mom shrugged. "Well, since we found out everything, Luc doesn't want to wait to see Sara, so he invited her over to have dinner with him. I've been asked, as well. It looks like there's still lots to talk about."

"I just got my schedule," I told her. "Do I have to come with you? Can't I stay here? Becca is coming over, and I want to see Kevin, can't I just get a pizza or something?"

She looked over at Abbott. What did his opinion matter, anyway? But he snapped his phone closed and came over. "Carrie, there's no reason for you to come with us. I understand that you have been a very good translator, but that won't be necessary, as I am fluent in French myself. We'll just be over at the Hilton. But I'd feel better if Chris stayed with you. Would you mind?"

I glanced at Chris. Becca would absolutely eat him up. "Sure, that's okay. But, like, do I need a bodyguard or something?"

Chris had put his phone away as well and joined us.

"No," he said. "But we'd like to have somebody with your family whenever we can."

Mom had her worried face on again. "Then we do need protection?" she asked.

"Merely a precaution," Abbott said smoothly.

"How are you going to keep an eye on us at school?" I asked.

Chris shrugged and grabbed the schedule from my hand. "I'm enrolled this fall," he said. "I'm a junior, but it looks like we have World History and Honors French together."

I stared. "How did you manage that?"

He grinned and shrugged. "We're a powerful Family, remember? We usually get what we want."

Okay then.

The screen door slammed open and Kevin came bounding up the stairs. He looked at Chris and Abbott and made a face.

"Sorry, I don't mean to interrupt, I just—"

"It's okay," I said, thinking fast. "Kevin, this is Abbott and Chris. Um, Abbott is a friend of Mom's and Chris is his, um, nephew. Chris is going into Mansfield this year, so, we're, you know, comparing schedules. Becca is coming over."

Fred, still trapped in the bedroom, started barking madly again. Fred loved Kevin.

"Listen, Kev, can you grab the dog so he'll shut up? I'll meet you downstairs in a minute."

Kevin gave Chris a long look, then nodded. He disappeared down the hallway, came back with Fred tucked under his arm, and went downstairs.

Mom shot me a look. "That kind of quick thinking bothers me a little," she said.

"Well, I'm guessing we're all sworn to secrecy, right? I mean, I don't think lots of people know what's going on, not that they would believe it anyway." I said.

Abbott nodded. "You have just become a member of a very select club," he said dryly. "Sworn to secrecy doesn't begin to cover it." He looked at Mom. "Ready?"

She looked flustered. "Shouldn't we change? I mean, dinner at the Hilton—"

"Not to worry. We'll go directly up to the suite and have dinner there. Sara?"

Sara was beaming. Room service at the Hilton. With a Prince. She could be so shallow sometimes.

Mom dug some money out of her purse. "Here, order a few pizzas, and try to get a salad. There's nothing wrong with trying to eat healthy, you know."

I rolled my eyes. "Okay, Mom, sure. Have fun."

They all buzzed around for another minute or so, then left. I looked at Chris.

"What are you afraid is going to happen?"

He sighed. "Luc is a good guy, but he got a little over-enthusiastic about finding Sara, and started asking lots of questions and getting all sorts of people looking for her. So news of his, well, interest was pretty widespread in, uh, certain circles. I just hope the wrong people didn't hear anything, that's all. I'd rather that your family stay under the radar for as long as possible."

"Wow. He had people looking for her?" Kevin was SO right. Luc was most definitely a nut case.

Chris shrugged. "He's a little impulsive."

"Ya think? Wow. So, would a vampire come after us?" What a cool idea. I mean, chased by a vampire? As long as I didn't get caught, of course.

"I don't know. I hope not. They are nasty."

"You've met one?" God, this guy was amazing.

44

"Well, yes. I was eight, so I couldn't do much but run. Now, if I had to, I'd be able to put up a fight, but I'd rather not."

"Where was this? Here?" Were there vampires here in New Jersey? Oh. My. God.

Chris shook his head. "No. Gettysburg. Right after the first day of battle. They swarmed, you know? All those dead and dying on the battlefield, it made them a little crazy."

I stared at him. "Gettysburg?" I was starting to hyperventilate. "How old are you?"

"I'm seventeen. Honest. But we don't age like other people, and not at all while we Sleep. After the Civil War was over, I went back up to New England. I was sitting on the corner of a quad at Yale on and off 'til last year. That's when I was Called. So I woke up and went back to Vermont. Last week, Luc said he wanted me down here so I could keep an eye on Sara. Having a younger cousin in high school turned out to be pretty useful."

"Oh." What could I say to this guy? He'd BEEN IN the Civil War. He'd been encased in stone for the past hundred and fifty years. How did he manage to seem so cool?

I almost asked him, but the door banged open again. It was Becca.

"I've got lunch seventh period. That so sucks," she yelled.

"Me too. Down here," Kevin yelled back, so she scampered downstairs.

Chris looked at me and grinned. "Doesn't anyone knock before they come in around here?"

I shook my head. "They've been my friends for a long time. They're like family."

Chris sighed. "You're lucky. I've never really had friends. It's tough when you're always turning to stone."

"Yeah. I bet. Well, you can hang with us. We're pretty cool. Just don't tell them when you were born, okay?"

"Deal."

"Chris?"

"What?"

"What do they look like? Vampires?"

He thought for a moment. "They can't use magic, but they have a kind of power, some people call it Glamour, and they can use it to look just like a normal person. Vampires are vain, though, so it's usually a very good-looking person."

"Then how can you tell that it's a vampire?"

"I can smell them." Chris shrugged. "It's a gargoyle thing."

"Oh."

We started down stairs.

"Chris?"

"Yeah?"

"What do they smell like?"

"They smell dead."

Like I thought, Becca found Chris to be absolutely fascinating. She kept trying to pump him for information. I gotta tell you, Chris was one cool liar.

Kevin had no problem with Chris once they started talking about football. Boys.

I was in two Honors classes, and my schedule was the worst ever. I spent over an hour on Facebook without finding more than ten friends who had any classes with me. I was going to be surrounded by strangers most of the time. Except for my very late lunch, which I had with Kevin and Becca. And my French Honors would have lots of upperclassmen in it, which would suck. But Chris would be there with me, which was a big plus.

He was looking cuter all the time.

Finally, Kevin announced that he was starving, so we ordered two plain pies and a small chopped salad to be delivered. We were all hanging out on the couch downstairs when out of nowhere, the cat, Smokey, jumped up onto the couch, looked around at all of us, then slithered down and settled on to Chris's lap.

Chris smiled and scratched Smokey's ears.

Smokey was my Dad's cat. After Dad left, Sara found Smokey at a shelter and brought him to Dad's apartment so that Dad wouldn't be so alone. Dad and Smokey got along just fine, but then Heather came along, and Heather was allergic to cats—of course—so Smokey had to go. Mom was more of a dog person than a cat person, but she felt sorry for Smokey and took him in, much to Fred's dismay. Smokey never got over his feeling of rejection, and became generally known around the house as the unfriendliest cat in the free world.

Kevin, Becca and I stared at Chris in awe.

"What?" he asked.

"That cat," I explained, "hates strangers. In fact, he doesn't like the people he knows very much either."

"I've never seen him sit on anyone's lap before," Becca said at last.

"Me neither," said Kevin. "Chris must be part cat."

If I had been eating something, I probably would have spit it out all over the floor.

Then the doorbell rang.

"Pizza," Kevin sang out and jumped up. I was right behind him.

"I need to get money," I said as I passed Kevin at the front door. I could see through the screen that the pizza delivery guy was new, a really handsome guy in tight jeans and tee shirt. Kevin had his hand on the door latch, and I was halfway up the stairs when Chris yelled.

"Don't open the door."

I stopped and turned back around. Chris had pushed Kevin aside and was standing in front of the door, staring.

"Carrie, don't let him in," Chris said, his voice very serious.

"Chris, it's just pizza. I mean—"

Fred had scrambled up the steps and was standing right next to me, growling, deep in his throat.

"Carrie. I know what it is. I can smell it."

"What?"

Suddenly, Moon was on the landing. Sweet, stupid Moon, who loves everyone. She was stiff, her teeth bared, a low rumble in her throat.

And then I knew. The handsome guy holding dinner was a vampire.

Chapter Seven

HE DIDN'T LOOK EVIL. IN fact, he looked pretty hot. Good-looking enough to be a TV- series vampire. I took a deep breath through my nose. All I could smell was melted mozzarella.

"Chris, are you sure?"

Chris looked quickly over his shoulder. "Carrie, get your friends out of the way," he said. The look on his face was scary.

"Kevin, come up here a sec, please?" I glanced around the kitchen, grabbed the cash off the counter, and pushed Kevin down the hallway as he came up the stairs.

"Carrie. What the hell is going on?"

I grabbed Fred and pushed him into Kevin's arms. "Kev, I can't tell you, but can you trust me? Please? I promise I'll explain later."

Much later. Like, in years, when we're both old and feeble and I can finally break my vow of silence.

I turned and started towards Chris, but, of course, Becca was there, trying to get a better look. I love Becca, honest, but if the pizza guy had flaming red eyes and blood was dripping from his fangs, all she'd notice was his dimples.

"Becca, up here. Now. It's important. And get Moon, okay?" Becca dragged my dog up the steps by her collar and was not looking happy. I grabbed her and pushed her towards Kevin. Then I inched downstairs, finally standing next to Chris, looking through the screen at my very first real vampire.

He flashed me a smile that lit up the neighborhood.

"Hey, listen, my arms are killing me. I don't know what this guy's problem is, but can't I set these down somewhere? Inside?"

His voice was almost musical. And he made absolute sense. Of course, his arms must be tired. Why shouldn't he come in?

"Carrie, look at me." Chris spoke softly, and I turned to him. "Don't listen to him. You must believe me."

I held out the money. "But we're hungry. Can't we at least get the pizza?"

Chris shook his head, reached in his pocket for his phone, and dialed quickly. I watched him. Who would he be calling right now?

"It's me," he said shortly. "I'm at the girl's house. They found it. They're here." He snapped the phone shut and looked at the vampire.

"Toad is coming," he said.

It was just a flash, but I saw it. The vampire dropped the pizza boxes right on the porch. His eyes turned black. The whole of his eye. I mean, the white part went dead black. And he snarled. And yes, there were fangs. He backed off the porch and turned and ran.

I stared for a second. "So, I guess Toad is some internationally known vampire hit-man?"

Chris chuckled. "Kind of." He cautiously opened the door, grabbed the pizza boxes and handed them to me. Then he slammed the screen door shut. Then the solid front door. And then he locked it.

"So it's true? You have to invite them in? I thought that was just part of the legend."

Chris shrugged. "Most legends have a basis in truth."

Kevin popped his head out. "Is the big bad pizza man gone? Can we eat now?"

We stood around the breakfast bar and opened the first box. We all chewed for a few minutes in companionable silence. The dogs were happy and quiet, looking at us expectantly, waiting for that first crumb to drop.

"Are we going to find out what this is all about?" Becca asked at last.

Chris chewed calmly.

"Someday, Becca," I said. "I promise." I looked around. "What happened to the salad?"

"Garlic, probably," Chris said shortly. "He wouldn't touch anything with garlic."

"Garlic? Oh, so that what this is all about? The pizza man's a vampire?" Kevin asked.

"Yep," Chris said.

Kevin snorted. "I bet."

Chris shrugged.

Kevin sniffed. "Do you smell something burning?"

I did. I looked around frantically. There was a trail of smoke coming from the downstairs.

"We need to get out," I yelped.

Chris grabbed my arm. "If we leave, they'll get us."

"Who'll get us?" Kevin asked.

"Chris, the house is on fire. We can't stay. Besides, isn't Toad here?"

"Toad?" Becca asked. "There's a person named Toad?"

"He's on his way," Chris said. "We can't leave the house. We'll be sitting ducks out there. Besides, it's probably a trick."

"What kind of trick?" I yelled. The smoke was thicker now. I thought I could hear the crackle of flames.

Chris looked around then headed for the sliding doors that lead to the deck. "If we go out the back, maybe they won't be able to track us right away."

"What about Smokey?" I asked, glancing around. The dogs had raced out ahead of me, hoping for a walk.

"Don't worry," Chris said. "We'll leave the doors open. If the fire is real, the cat will get out."

We ran out the sliders, across the deck and down the steps to the backyard. I turned to look at the house. There was no smoke coming out from anywhere. No flames. Was it a trick?

"Keep moving," Chris ordered, and he moved across the yard. It was almost dark, and the backyard was all shadows. The dogs were running around happily, thinking it was playtime.

"We need to cut through and get back on the street," Chris said. "Let's go."

We all followed him across the grass, when suddenly Fred started growling again. I glanced over my shoulder. Six dark figures were coming from around the house, following us.

"Run," Chris yelled.

We ran. Kevin grabbed Becca's hand and we raced towards the

street. I could hear the dogs panting behind me. I was suddenly afraid, because the air was ice cold and there seemed to be smoke everywhere. I could barely see.

"It's not real," Chris screamed. "Keep running."

I dodged the forsythia bush by the sidewalk. I knew every inch of the neighborhood. I'd been running through these streets my whole life. So had Kevin and Becca. The vampires were so far behind us, they would never be able to catch us. I figured we needed to get to Kevin's house. Once we were back inside somewhere with the door closed again, we'd be safe. I swerved and pounded down the pavement.

I glanced quickly over my shoulder. I could see the vampires behind us, much closer than they should have been. How had they managed to move that fast?

Kevin and Becca were right behind me, Chris bringing up the rear. Kevin's house was at the end of the block. We'd be there in less than a minute. We'd make it, no problem.

And then the street opened up. I could see it cracking open, like an earthquake or something. The ground was shaking and I stopped short, panicked. The dogs kept running. Couldn't they see that the street was no longer there?

"It's not real," Chris screamed again, but it was real. It was right in front of me. I yelled for the dogs to stop, and whirled around. Kevin and Becca ran right into me. The ground to the left of us started opening up as well. What was happening? The vampires were so close that, even in the growing darkness, I could see that one of them was wearing a happy face tee shirt.

Chris stopped and turned to face them. The ground to the right of us was cracked and open. We were trapped. Chris stood still. I saw his shoulders lift. Then he started to change. As he grew, the vampires slowed. I heard Kevin swear under his breath, and Becca was whispering ohgodohgodohgod.

Chris dropped onto all fours and roared. He reached out and swiped at one of the vampires with a giant paw, and the vampire went stumbling to the side of the road. The others began moving, two to the left of Chris, two to the right, and one right in front. Chris moved towards one, but the vampire danced away quickly, like a video on fast-forward.

"You can't take us all," one of the vampires said. The sixth, the one who had been slapped away, was back on his feet. "Just give us the bride."

Bride? They wanted Sara. They thought I was Sara. They were after me. And there were six of them.

Chris snarled. Fred growled. Chris spun quickly and took another swipe, but missed. They were keeping just far enough away that he couldn't hurt them. And the three of us were stuck behind Chris, with no place to go but down a gaping hole in the earth.

Fred started yapping. What was that dog thinking? Then, from behind us, there was a low, whooshing sound, and a winged figure swept down. It was a giant frog, over six feet in length. It opened its mouth and bit off the head of one of the vampires. The body slumped to the ground and turned to gray ash.

"Yes!" Kevin yelled, pumping his fist in the air.

The remaining vampires turned and ran. They were gone in the blink of an eye. So were the craters that had surrounded us on the road. The pavement was smooth and unbroken. The smoke was gone, and the cold.

Chris turned to us slowly. He was back to his human form. Toad had landed on the road and was now a slightly plump, middle-aged man with thinning hair and glasses. Toad walked over to Chris and gave him a long hug. The older man leaned in close and said something to Chris. Chris nodded, and the two of them walked over to us.

"Are you all okay?" asked Toad.

We nodded. Becca was gray-faced. Kevin was glowing with excitement.

"Where are the craters?" Kevin asked.

"I'll explain in a minute. Now, get back into the house," Toad said, glancing around as he herded us back up the street.

Chris grabbed Toad by the arm. "They weren't Brunel," he said.

Toad nodded. "I know. I didn't recognize them."

Chris took a deep breath. "So, is the treaty intact?"

Toad shrugged. "I don't know," he said.

Becca grabbed my hand.

"What just happened?" she whispered.

"You have just become a member," I told her, "of a very select club."

Becca held my hand the whole time we walked home. She didn't say a word, just held on tight.

Kevin, on the other hand, wouldn't shut up.

"Did you see that? He turned into a lion. With wings. And that flying frog? He ate the guy's head. That was the best. Who are these guys? Why didn't you tell me about them? God, Carrie, this is so cool."

"No, Kevin. Those were vampires. Mean, evil vampires who would have sucked your blood. And I didn't tell you about them because I just met Chris three hours ago and I was kind of sworn to secrecy. I mean, you two can't say a word about this, okay? Not to anyone. You have to promise me."

"Yeah, sure. I promise. So, who are they anyway? Greek gods, maybe? Or from another planet?"

"Gargoyles," I said. Chris was walking ahead of us, and I knew he could hear us. "I can't tell you anymore. It's up to Chris to decide. Becca, are you okay?"

She nodded. She still hadn't said anything else. She was holding my hand so tightly that she was hurting me, but I didn't have the heart to tell her.

We went back in through the open sliding doors to the kitchen. There was no smoke anywhere, no sound of flames. The dogs were drinking noisily from their water bowl. They hadn't had that much exercise in years.

The pizza was cold. That didn't stop Kevin from picking up a piece and eating happily. "That," he said, "was the coolest thing ever. So were they really vampires?"

Chris looked troubled. "Yes. They were really vampires." He had his phone out again.

I reached out and grabbed his arm. "What's going to happen when Abbott finds out?"

Chris sighed. "You'll probably have to be moved. They know where you live. I don't know if we can keep you safe."

"But I start school in two weeks," I told him. "I don't want us to move. Mom has her job and Sara is in the All-State concert band. If we move, we'll lose all that. Can't you do something else?"

Toad looked thoughtful. "Well, we can tighten security. We knew this might happen. We had a plan in place that should still work. Not everyone has to know that you all were chased into the street. And that we had to Turn to rescue you." He looked at Kevin and Becca. "Is it even possible that you two can keep this a secret?"

Kevin made a rude noise. "If I say no, what will you do? Kill me?"

Toad looked at him steadily. "Maybe."

Kevin's face fell.

"I trust you two understand how, ah, unusual this is," Toad said. "A hundred years ago, anyone who witnessed what you two did would simply disappear. That's how important keeping this particular secret really is. These days, it's a bit harder to hide the bodies."

Kevin turned pale. "I won't tell a soul. Honest. Never. And you too, right Becca?"

Becca looked like her old self. "Not that anyone would believe us anyway. But sure, I can keep a secret, if you tell us what the hell is happening."

"Yeah," Kevin said, color coming back to his face. He was getting excited again. "What about the street. How did they do that?"

Chris closed his phone and leaned back against the kitchen counter.

"Vampires can't do real magic. That is, they cannot alter reality. They didn't start a fire in this house, or open up the road. But they're very good at getting into your mind and making you think things. That's Glamour. They can make you see things that aren't real. They projected onto your mind the images of the smoke, and the craters. Since your vision is the most trusted of your senses, you assumed that what you saw was real. But it wasn't." He looked very tired. "That's why they're so dangerous. They can manipulate large groups of people by just thinking about something."

"Oh." Kevin looked at Chris, then at Toad. "What you guys did. Was that real?"

Toad cleared his throat. "Yes, actually. We can do magic. But only amongst ourselves. Chris and I can Turn, become what you call gargoyles. We can also Sleep, that is, become stone. And we can make others Sleep as well, and call them back Awake. But we can't do anything to you, or to anyone else. Otherwise, we would have turned every vampire and demon left on earth to dust centuries ago."

"Demons?" Becca squeaked. "What do you mean, demons?"

Chris and Toad exchanged glances.

"As far as we know," Toad said carefully, "there has not been a demon seen in this country in over one hundred years. But they did and still do exist."

"Man," Kevin said reverently. "But why were they after Carrie?"

Chris shrugged. "They were probably sent to take Sara, and didn't even know Carrie existed. But it was Carrie that they found, so they just went after her."

"So," Kevin pressed on, "why would they be after Sara?"

"Okay," I said quickly. "Listen up. Remember the guy in the black suit?"

I told Kevin and Becca everything that Abbott had said. They listened carefully, Kevin grinning and Becca shaking her head in amazement.

I looked at Chris. "Anything else?" I asked.

"I think you covered everything. Abbott should be bringing your mom and Sara home pretty soon. We need to decide what to tell them."

Toad had been eating cold pizza and had not said anything for a while, but he cleared his throat again and looked at us.

"Sara has become a target. The Family needs to know that the situation has changed, and that her identity is known. We should be able to protect her, as well as Carrie and Ms. Collier." He looked hard at Kevin and Becca. "The two of you know more than is comfortable, but hopefully you'll just be an extra pair of ears and eyes in case something strange happens."

He looked at me. "Carrie, I'm glad that you behaved well under pressure and didn't collapse sobbing, like a blithering idiot. You'll need a cool head to keep things under wraps while making sure nobody odd gets close to your sister. I can understand your wanting to keep things as normal as possible. That's probably the best thing for all involved. I will talk to Abbott tonight. I will tell him everything. He needs to know. And I'm sure that adjustments will be made."

He slapped Chris on his shoulder. "Kiddo, you were great. I'm proud of you. You did everything right. I've got to go. But I'll be watching."

"Ah, Toad," I asked. "Who is Brunel?"

Chris and Toad exchanged glances. "They're a Clan," Toad said. "A very old Clan of vampires."

"How did you know that those six weren't Brunel?" I asked.

Toad smiled tiredly. "We can smell the difference."

"Cool," Kevin breathed.

"What about the treaty?" I went on.

Toad shook his head, still smiling. "Good listening skills, little girl. But don't worry. It has nothing to do with you." He waved and slipped out the back sliding doors. We all stared at each other. Chris looked tired. Kevin was still glowing. Becca came over and wrapped her arms around me.

"I want you to be safe," she whispered. "Do what you need to do to be safe."

"We'll keep her safe," Chris said. "Don't worry about that."

"So, is that guy Toad, like, the super-killer?" Kevin was looking at Chris with open admiration. "I mean, you guys were totally boss out there."

"Toad is a priest who has been studying how to defeat evil for hundreds of years. He's fearless. Those he trains are equally fearless. He's got a reputation."

"Chris," Becca asked slowly, her arms still around my neck, "I still don't get why they would want Sara."

Chris scratched the side of his neck. "Sara is now officially betrothed of the heir to the throne of the Gargouille Family. When she spoke the vow, it was like the cosmos recognized her as chosen. The Clans know that she is now a valuable asset to the Family, but she's not protected like the Family, and she cannot protect herself. If they, well, kidnapped her, the Family might be forced to negotiate for her release, and those negotiations might weaken their position."

"Yeah, but couldn't they just as easily grab Carrie?" Becca asked.

Chris's lips tightened. "They won't. Carrie is of no value to the Family, and the Clans know it."

No value? Really? "What do you mean, no value?" I growled.

Chris looked sheepish. "Listen, Carrie, it's not personal. I think you're great. But the Family has existed for hundreds of years with only one goal—to protect the world against evil. To do that successfully, they've had to make very hard choices. One of the most important things for them is protecting the future of the royal house. Only Royals can Awaken gargoyles. It's vital that the line continue. So if sacrifices must be made, then so be it. But I promise you—I won't let anything happen to any of you, okay? You have my word."

Becca sighed. "I trust him, Carrie."

Of course she did. After all, he was pretty adorable.

Kevin nodded. "Me too."

I should have expected that as well. Chris could turn into a huge winged monster. What's not to trust?

I looked at my two best friends and nodded.

I trusted him too. Because I had to.

CHAPTER EIGHT

MOM AND SARA CAME HOME about an hour later. Kevin and Becca had gone home, after much debate. I did not want them wandering around the neighborhood if it was teeming with vampires. Chris pointed out that if there were any vampires left in the neighborhood, they were probably terrified that Toad was still around, and that their interest had been me. Becca and Kevin were never in any real danger, according to him, but I was unconvinced. So he got on his phone again, mumbled, then assured me that extra protection was already in place, and that someone would be watching to make sure they both got home safe.

So Chris and I were downstairs watching SpongeBob when the door opened and Fred started barking like a crazy dog. Chris looked relieved. He hadn't said much as we had watched TV together. But then, he saved me from being kidnapped by a gang of vampires. What did he need to say?

Sara came bounding down the stairs, grinning from ear to ear.

"So, I guess you had a good time with Luc?" I asked.

She actually grabbed both of my hands as she jumped up and down. "Luc is amazing, completely amazing, and he absolutely gets me. He's a music lover and he understands how I feel, and he's SO supportive of me wanting to go to a great music school. And guess what? I have minions!"

I was drowning in a sea of sugary sweetness that was so unlike my sister it scared me. "Minions? What do you mean, minions?"

I looked past her and there, standing stiffly, were three young women, all dressed in identical black skirts and tee shirts.

"These are your minions?" I asked, staring.

"Yes. Aren't they great? I forget their names, they're French, but they're to stay with me at all times here in the house, and they have to do everything I say. Isn't that cool?"

"Where are they going to sleep?" I was a little stunned by the idea of "minions.".

"That's the thing. They're going to be sitting around asleep, you know, turned to stone, until I need them, or until they think I'm in any danger. They're also my bodyguards."

Chris had worked his way around to the women and was talking to them seriously. One of them actually rolled her eyes as she nodded her head towards Sara. Those poor girls. Condemned to babysit my sister.

"Mom and Abbott are upstairs. They want to talk to you. And Chris." Sara lowered her voice. "I think Mom has a thing for Abbott," she said.

"What?"

"Seriously. She was flirting with him. And he was flirting back. It was kind of fun to watch. Even Luc said something."

"What did Luc say?"

"Well, he said that I was the most beautiful girl he'd ever seen, and that he saw me from afar and knew at once we were destined. God, *so* romantic. He also said that we'd live in France, but that I could probably play with the London Philharmonic, isn't that amazing? Then he said—"

"Sara," I snapped. Oh, my God. "What did he say about Mom and Abbott?"

"Oh." She frowned. She did that sometimes if she had to think too hard about something other than herself. "Oh. I know. That he hadn't seen Abbott smile so much. Ever."

Perfect.

When I got upstairs, I could tell right away that Sara had been right. Mom was kind of glowing. She was talking to Abbott in a quiet voice, leaning towards him, smiling.

"Mom?"

"Honey, hi." She crossed the kitchen and gave me a quick hug. "I hear you had a very unwelcome visitor."

"Yeah, we did. But we're all fine."

"Thank God. Mr. Bishop told us what happened, but he's assured me that you were never in any real danger."

"Mr. Bishop?" I glanced at Chris.

"Toad," Chris said shortly.

Mom frowned. "Toad? How did that nice man get a nickname like that?" she asked.

Because, Mom, that nice man turns into a flying frog when he decapitates vampires. "Ask Chris."

Chris smiled blandly. "It's just a bad joke, Ms. Collier."

"Please, Chris, you must call me Maggie as well. After all, it looks like we're going to be spending lots of time together."

My jaw may have dropped open. "What?"

Mom smiled. "Let me show Chris and Greg out. We have things to talk about."

I went over and sat on the couch. Out the picture window I could see that the long black car was back. Moon jumped up on the couch and sat as close to me as she could without actually being on top of me. Mom came up the stairs and sat on my other side and I slid down so that my head fit just against her shoulder, and she laid her cheek against the top of my head and sighed. We sat there for a few minutes, and I could hear Sara's voice downstairs, and then a burst of giggles. Sara may be a snob, but she can charm when she wants something, and I could tell she was working her magic.

"So, we've got house guests for a while?"

Mom put both arms around me a squeezed. "Can you believe all this? How did this happen? I keep thinking I'm going to wake up tomorrow and it's still going to be Wednesday, you know?"

"Wednesday? Only Wednesday? I feel like it's been weeks since we met Luc."

"He's very charming, by the way," Mom said. "He sincerely thinks he's in love with your sister. And that kind of flattery and attention is hard to resist, particularly to a person like Sara. She's wanted to find a prince since she was two years old, and she's never given up. She may very well be swept off her feet."

"Are they getting married?"

"Not anytime soon, if I have anything to say about it. I feel like we've stepped through the looking glass, just like Alice. Nothing makes sense, but everything continues to move forward." She kissed the top of my head. "Were you scared tonight? Knowing there was a vampire at the door? God, listen to me. I can't believe that sentence came out of my mouth."

I hadn't been afraid when he was outside the door. I'd only been a little afraid when we were running through the neighborhood, because of the smoke and the cold. But when I saw Chris Turn, and knew that he was doing that because that was the only way to save us, I was terrified.

"Chris was here," I said. "And Toad came by, just to see how things were going. They're going to be watching us all the time, but it's only Sara that matters to them. They don't care about us."

"Yes, Abbott explained all that to me. And I made it very clear to him that if anything happened to you, I would take their precious Sara and they would never see her again, and their whole bloody 'vow' could go straight to hell. I think he believed me."

I smiled. I bet he did. "He seems nice, Abbott. For an old guy, I mean."

Mom chuckled. "He's great. And he's not all that old. And we are going to be seeing a lot of him, too, so I hope you get to like him. We'll also be seeing a lot of Luc. He'll be courting you sister. Their word, not mine."

"Wow," I said. "Should make for an interesting Prom."

She laughed. "Yes. It should."

"I bet Sara is going to be a very high-maintenance girlfriend."

"I'm sure. You know what her schedule is like. She's got performances this fall all over the state, and there's Philadelphia and St. Louis—I'm sure I've forgotten someplace. She has no intention of giving anything up, and she still wants to apply to at least six schools. Luc is willing to go wherever she goes. Poor Luc. She will lead him on a very merry chase."

"What if he catches her?"

Mom sat up and rubbed her hands across her face. "Believe it or not, Sara is a grown woman. In some countries, she'd be married with children already. If she chooses him, there's not much I can do to stop her. But I promise, I won't let anyone bully her into doing something she doesn't want to do. I don't care how old or important this Family thinks it is, they're not dragging my daughter into some marriage just because she said a few words in the moonlight. Although, they seem to be taking this very seriously."

"Like a binding magical contract?"

She laughed. "You and your Harry Potter. Yes, I guess just like that. But this is different. Harry and his magic lived in an imaginary world."

"Mom, magic is real. That's the thing. This is all real. It's not different at all."

She looked at me, her eyes big. "Oh, Carrie, what are we going to do?"

"Be careful, I guess. We have to be very careful."

Kevin and Becca were both in the bleachers the next day, watching me get ignored by teammates. Halfway through the scrimmage, after being blown off while trying to get someone to pass to me, Kevin started yelling very rude things. It probably didn't help my case any, but at least I had a few laughs. The girls on the team made a few very caustic comments, but some of them were smiling too.

After all, Kevin is pretty cute and can be very funny.

After the practice, as soon as the others were out of earshot, Kevin started in on what had happened the night before. I was still trying to process the whole thing—gargoyles, vampires, dragons and flying frogs all seemed impossible to get my head around. Almost as hard as imagining Sara with a handsome, suave Frenchman.

"So, tell me," Kevin said. "What did they all say after we left?"

"Well, Sara thinks Luc is way cool and she has minions."

"What?" said Becca.

"Three girls are assigned to be her, I don't know, babysitters, bodyguards, something. Their names are Isabeau, Fabienne and Amelie. I think Fabienne and Amelie are sisters. They did not seem thrilled with their assignment."

"Oh, that's not good," said Becca. "The last thing your sister needs is an entourage."

"Yeah, I know." I took a swig from my water bottle. We were walking home the long way, because the sun was brutal and the extra few blocks were shaded with huge oak trees. It was a perfect summer day—birds were singing, I could smell fresh-cut grass, and although I was tired I felt pretty good. I was with my two best friends in the world. In a few weeks we'd be in high school together. It could have been perfect, if not for the whole gargoyle/vampire war that may have been brewing.

"And then Sara tells me that my mother and the old guy, Abbott, were flirting with each other. Way too much information. This Family seems to think Sara is really going to marry Luc, but seriously, she's never had to do anything she didn't want to do her whole life, so I'm not too worried." I told them. "Oh, and Toad's real name is Bishop."

"That," Kevin said, "is a much better name for a person trained in the ancient art of vampire assassination."

I snorted. "What do you know about any ancient arts?"

"Nothing yet," he said happily. "But I'm going to become the best friend Chris ever had, and I'm going to learn everything I can, so next time anything happens, I'll be ready."

"Next time?" Becca shivered. "I hope there's never a next time. But I'm confused. How old are all these people?" Becca asked.

"I think," I said slowly, "that Abbott is just a regular old guy, maybe fifty. Chris says he's seventeen, but he was sitting around for, like over a hundred years. He was eight at Gettysburg."

Kevin stopped walking. "Gettysburg, as in the Civil War?"

I stopped and looked back at him. "Yeah. That's where he said he saw his first vampire. He said they swarmed the battlefield because of all the blood."

"Whoa," Kevin said softly. Becca looked pale.

"But those guys last night were so beautiful," she said. "How could they have been vampires?"

I shrugged and we started walking again. "Chris says it's part of their mind control thing, that they can look any way they want, and because they're vain, they're usually gorgeous."

"Perfect," Becca said. "Now, anytime I see a good-looking guy, my first thought will be that he's a vampire."

I laughed. "So, we make a pact. Only ugly boyfriends from now on."

"Are the girl vampires the same?" Kevin asked. "Because, you know, I like beautiful women. This could get tough."

Becca punched him on the arm. "The only beautiful women you need to know are right here, right now. So, it's one of us or your blood supply could be at risk."

"It was just so awesome," Kevin said. He'd been carrying my bag, and he started swinging it over his head. "When Toad flew down like that. I mean, I've never seen anything that cool, not even in the movies. And Chris just went—whoosh—instant smoke and wings. I'd love to see him do that in the middle of the cafeteria."

"Yeah, Carrie, what about Chris?" Becca asked. "How on earth did he end up going to the same school as you and Sara in the first place?"

"It's not a coincidence," I told them. "Apparently the Family is rich and powerful and they wanted Chris there to keep an eye on things, so—ta-da—he's there. He's also in two of my classes, which I guess is a good thing 'cause nobody else I know is. How did that happen, anyway? I'm going to be with a bunch of strangers all day. Totally sucks."

"Yeah, and seventh period lunch," muttered Kevin. "I'm going to be starving."

Becca made a noise. "You'd be starving if you had third period lunch," she said, and I laughed. She was right. Kevin was hungry pretty much all the time.

We turned down my street. I looked over where I had seen the black car on Monday. Was that only four days ago? "I keep thinking I'm going to wake up," I said. "That none of this is real, you know?"

Becca grabbed my arm. "I'm afraid," she said quietly. "Before last night there was high school and maybe not having a date to the spring semi-formal, or getting crappy grades for the first time. I was worried about not having cool clothes and getting bad acne and having a locker way over in the basement. But now there are vampires. I can't believe there are real vampires in the world that can run faster than anything I've ever seen, and that they might want to kill me."

I took a deep breath. "There have always been vampires, Becca. And we have always been protected from them. If we hadn't gotten our schedules yesterday, you wouldn't have been over the house at all and you never would have known any of this. I'm sorry, but it was just really bad luck. But I'm not afraid. We've got a flying frog on our side. I'm good with that."

Kevin gave Becca a hug. "Besides, I'm going to become the an expert vampire assassin. Doesn't that make you feel safer?"

Becca rolled her eyes. "I'm going to stick with the flying frog," she said.

The house was quiet. I knew Sara was working a luncheon at the country club. She didn't work during the school year, and neither did I. We both had way too many things going on, and Sara's schedule barely gave her time to sleep, let alone keep her job, so she was working as many functions as she could before school began.

"Mom?" I called.

Fred scurried over to sniff and wag his tail, but there was just silence. I went downstairs.

Moon was curled up in a corner of the couch. She lifted her head, yawned, and snuggled back in. I went into my room, dumped my bag, and came back out, heading for the bathroom and a shower.

"Hello."

I almost jumped out of my skin. One of Sara's watchdogs was sitting on the couch next to Moon.

"Where did you come from? You scared the crap out of me."

She shrugged. "Sorry. I just wanted to get down off the roof."

I sat down in the chair opposite her. "Roof?"

"Yes. It is my job to stay outside the house to make sure it is protected at all times. If one of my sisters is here, I stay on the roof." She shrugged. "The roof gets boring. When someone is in the house, and I am the only one here, I can come down to be with them"

I had to laugh. "I didn't know there were rules involved. You're Isabeau?"

She smiled. She was a very pretty girl. She had short, shiny black hair that swept across her forehead. White skin, big blue eyes. Striking. All three of them were. "Yes, I am Isabeau. And there are many rules involved."

"So, how did you three get babysitting duty?"

She stopped smiling, and tilted her head as she looked at me. "We have been chosen to protect the next queen of the Gargouille

Empire. I was in England, at University, when the request came. I could have said no. We all could have. We are of royal blood ourselves, cousins of Luc. If we had refused, there would have been others more than willing to take our place. It is a matter of honor. Would I rather be sitting in a pub right now, working on my poetry and flirting with a cute student? Yes, I would. But Luc will one day be our King. And Sara will be a powerful woman. It is a matter of pride that we keep her safe. It is what we were trained to do. But it will also be to our advantage, yes? We do not want to be students forever, and knowing the Queen may work in our favor."

"But she's such a brat."

Isabeau shrugged. "She is a beautiful woman. All beautiful woman have a fear in them that they will only be considered for what they look like, not for who they are. Some women become hard and bitchy. Some withdraw completely. Your sister may be a brat, but she is also struggling. Anyway, she was chosen by Luc. That's all that matters."

I had to think about that for a minute. Sara struggling? I found that hard to believe. But…

"So, like, where you perched somewhere? On top of a church?"

"I was at Oxford. I am a student. We do not spend our whole lives waiting to be Called. We must be trained. That happens when we are very young. Then we can lead normal lives. Most of us choose to become as educated as possible. Money has never been a problem, so we can go anywhere in the world and study whatever we want. Amelie was actually an apprentice in Paris, with the House of Chanel. We have given up a lot to be here. Oh, hello." Smokey jumped up on her lap and started purring like crazy.

"Are you a lion too?" I asked.

She nodded as she scratched behind his left ear. "Yes. All members of the Royal Family are lions. But some of us are other things as well. I am a lion, but I was trained by Toad. He trains us all."

"So, he's kind of like the guy in charge of security?"

She nodded. "Yes. But he is more than that. His grandfather was once the cousin of a king. His name was Charles, and he chose to become a priest, when priests were almost as powerful as kings. He studied the gods as well as the demons. When the dragon was defeated by the Bishop of Rouen, it was Charles who told the Family that this new God was too powerful to defeat. It was he who went to Rouen and pledged the Family to the church. He then spent years rising to power within the church. When his sons were born, they also became priests, but of one God, not many. Toad is his grandson. He rose to power as well, and became a Bishop of Rouen himself. But he still knows all about evil. Toad is a very dangerous man."

"He looks like a biology teacher."

She just looked at me. "You saw what he can do."

"Yeah. About that. Have you ever killed a vampire?"

She shrugged. "We have been at peace for hundreds of years, but our battle began a thousand years before that. We have all killed. Each generation is trained, just in case. Perhaps the next generation will never know what it is like to kill."

"What about Luc? Chris told Sara that he never Turned."

She kept her face impassive. "I have seen Luc in battle. He is ferocious. I'm sure Chris was trying to make things easier for Sara. Her position is an impossible one. Luc acted completely in the wrong. But there is nothing to be done now. I hope Sara learns to love him. Because she will be with him for the rest of her life."

Becca, Kevin and I were downstairs. We were playing Wii golf. We were also at war with Sara, who was practicing something and had asked us to keep it down so she could concentrate. I responded that maybe SHE should keep it down, because I kept shooting over par, and I needed to concentrate too. She slammed the door and blew into her flute, and we swung imaginary clubs and exclaimed loudly over every shot. It was starting to get a little annoying all 'round when the doorbell rang. I raced upstairs, and Luc was at the door, with Chris behind him.

"I am here," he said, "to ask your sister out for a walk."

A walk? Oh, this I had to see. I invited him in. He looked like he stepped out of a Ralph Lauren ad, dressed in loose, navy blue linen pants and a white silk shirt, sleeves rolled up, and unbuttoned halfway down his chest. He was very buff.

They followed me downstairs. I introduced him to Becca and Kevin, and yelled for Sara. She came out of her room in a huff until she saw Luc. Her mood turned in a heartbeat. Sometimes, she's amazing to watch.

"Luc? Hi. I wasn't expecting you," she said, smiling a little.

He bowed from the waist. "I was hoping to have you accompany me on a walk this evening," he said, very formally. "Your sister and her friends are more than welcome to join us. Chris will act as chaperone. And of course, Amelie will be with us as well."

Amelie had been sitting in the corner, her headphones on to drown out all the noise, but she sprang up.

"Excellent idea. It's beautiful this evening," she said.

Sara was kind of caught. She normally wouldn't walk anywhere, because she considers walking a form of exercise, and she hates exercise. But we were all standing around watching, so what could she say?

"That sounds great. I'll tell Mom we're going."

I would have thought that Luc would have wanted to be alone with Sara, and as we walked down the street towards the neighborhood playground, he walked next to her, his hands clasped behind his back, his head tilted towards her, listening to every word she said. Kevin, Becca and I walked behind them, trying to hear what they were saying. Chris and Amelie brought up the rear.

I dropped back and whispered to Chris, "You're really a chaperone?"

He nodded. "This is a pretty big deal," he said.

"Yeah, but…chaperone?"

He grinned. "Luc is a very old-fashioned guy."

I glanced at Amelie. "Are you a chaperone too?"

She shook her head. "No. I am here to protect Sara. Fabienne would be with me, if Chris were not. Two of us must be with her at all times."

I scooted back up to Kevin and Becca. "Are we enjoying our group date so far?"

Becca giggled. "I can't believe your sister is going along with this."

I couldn't either, but Luc must have been doing something right, because I heard her actually laugh.

When we got to the playground, Kevin, Becca and I headed for the picnic table. I expected Luc to do something romantic, like sit with Sara on the swings, or drag her behind the jungle gym for a little make-out session, but they sat with us. Sara was smiling. Luc was lit up like a Christmas tree.

"Sara tells me," he said, in slow, careful English, "that you play soccer, Carrie."

I looked at Sara. She had talked about me? How odd. "Yes. Center forward."

Luc nodded happily. "I played at University. Very exciting game. Chris plays as well, right?"

Chris had been hanging back by the slides, but came forward and sat with us. "Yeah. Just a little bit."

Luc nodded, then turned to Becca. "And you? You play soccer?"

Becca's mouth opened in surprise. "Ah, no. I don't play anything. I'm a professional spectator."

Luc frowned and looked at Chris, who translated swiftly. Then he grinned. "That is excellent also. And Kevin is your boyfriend?"

I shook my head. "No."

Luc pointed to Becca. "Her boyfriend?"

Becca giggled again.

"No," I said. "We're just all friends."

I kept glancing at Sara. I couldn't believe that she was sitting by, letting Luc spend one second of time talking to us. But she was still smiling, watching him carefully.

Luc shrugged. "Friends are all good, yes? Perhaps next time, we will all go to a café."

"Chris," I said, "maybe you could talk to Luc here a little bit about modern dating practices." From the corner of my eye, I could see Sara laughing silently.

Chris shook his head. "I've been perched on the corner of a dorm at Yale on and off for the past sixty years. My advice would be from observing the mating habits of the nerdiest people on the planet."

Luc jumped off the bench and stood, hands in the pockets of his pants. "Dating practices? What is dating practices?"

Becca caught my eye and we started to laugh. I could hear Amelie, curled up under an oak tree, laughing as well.

Luc ran his hand through his hair. "Did I make a joke?"

"No," Sara said. She was grinning. "It's just that sometimes it's easier to get to know a person when you're alone with them."

"Alone?" Luc looked like this was a completely new idea. "Are you sure?"

Kevin elbowed me. "Give the guy a break," he muttered. "Not everybody is smooth."

"Smooth?" Luc repeated. "Alone and smooth?"

Chris started laughing too, and began speaking rapidly in French.

"Hey," Sara said loudly, still grinning, "No fair. What are you guys talking about?"

I felt a sudden chill, and Chris and Luc both froze, and their heads turned in one movement towards the woods. Amelie appeared at Sara's side.

"What?" Sara asked.

Luc said calmly to Amelie, in French. "Take her. Do not leave her side."

Amelie put her arm around Sara. "We need to go home. Now."

Sara didn't get it. She was frowning and putting on her 'Oh, no I won't face, pulling against Amelie.

I looked around. There were six of them, coming out of the shadows. The sky suddenly lit up with lightning and rain poured down in a cold wall of water.

I yelled. "Go, Sara," and she ran, Amelie behind her. I couldn't move, even as I felt Kevin and Becca jump off the table and move away.

Luc and Chris stood, waiting. One of the vampires struck at Luc. Luc turned quickly, got his arm around the vampire's neck, and with a simple jerk, twisted the head, and the vampire turned to dust.

Chris had Turned. I had smelled the smoke, and as the sky lit up, I saw that he put himself between the vampires and the path that Sara and Amelie had taken out of the park. He lashed out with a vicious paw and one vampire was gone.

I looked back at Luc. The rain had soaked the silk shirt, and it clung to his body. He was fighting two of them at once. They were so fast, I could barely even see them through the pouring rain, but he moved like a dancer, all fluid grace, his hands and feet striking out in a series of flashes. It was like watching one of those old kung-fu movies Kevin liked so much.

I saw one go down, and at the same time, heard a roar. Chris was standing on the body of one of them, and I could see it try to move under the sharp talons. He leapt at the third vampire, and broke its neck with one snap of his jaw. Then he turned back to the writhing body on the ground and stepped on it again. It melted into the mud.

The rain stopped as abruptly as it started, and Luc stood, chest heaving, hands hanging by his side. He shook himself, and droplets of water flew out from his body. He ran his hands through his hair and took several deep breaths.

I hadn't seen what he did to the third vampire. I just knew that it was gone.

Chris had Turned back and ran up to Luc. They stood together, whispering furiously in French. Luc was nodding. He clapped Chris on the shoulder.

Then they noticed me, still sitting on the picnic table.

Luc smiled tiredly in the darkness. "You were supposed to go running home, like a good little girl," he said in French.

I shook my head. "I don't do 'good little girl'," I told him. "Why didn't you Turn?"

Luc shrugged.

Chris answered in French. "Luc is a better fighter than I am. Toad has been training him for much longer. Besides, for all his princely airs, Luc has basically a street thug mentality. He likes getting his hands dirty."

Luc put his arm around Chris and hugged him, pounding him on the back. Then he looked at me, pointing his finger and looking stern.

"You will not tell your sister of this, no? I do not want her to think I enjoy this too much."

"Your secret is safe with me," I told him.

PART TWO

FALL

CHAPTER ONE

I KNOW THAT NO ONE ever believes me when I tell them that I knew I wanted to be a professional musician when I was in the fourth grade. I mean, what ten-year-old kid makes that kind of decision?

But I did know. I knew the minute I played the flute in my first concert and I hit every note and the crowd applauded and I stood up and realized they were clapping for me, because I had done something right. Here was something I was good at. I knew that it was what I wanted to do with the rest of my life.

I'd been trying to find something to be good at for a while. There was dancing class—what a disaster. Soccer was okay for a while, but once Carrie started playing, and I saw how good she was, and how good it made her feel, I wanted to find something like that for myself. Art classes were fun, but there was no real spark. Then Mom made me sign up for band. I didn't know what I wanted to play, and honestly, I picked the flute because it was light and easy to carry. But then I started to play. My fingers just knew where to go. I could look at the musical notes and know, in my head, how they sounded. It was like picking up a magic wand. I felt in control, sure of myself and powerful, like nothing could stop me.

It was amazing. It changed my life.

Mom started worrying right away, telling me that there was more to life than just playing the flute. But was there? Was there really? Was there anything better than this feeling of flying?

I asked Carrie how she felt when she was racing down the soccer field, way ahead of everyone else, making that final kick into the goal and hearing everyone scream. She looked at me, thinking about it, before she grinned.

"Free," she said.

That's how playing the flute made me feel. Free.

I know I'm good. Every adult that I've come in contact with in regard to my music has told me that I have what it takes. I have the passion, the drive. I have the natural talent. They've also said that's not enough to make it, and I know that's true. So if I don't have a lot of friends, and never worked on the yearbook, or had a boyfriend, or went out drinking after football games—it's okay.

When I look into the future, I know it will be worth it.

Except now there's Luc, and—seriously—overnight, everything has changed. He thinks he's going to marry me. Is he kidding? Sure, after we all got together at the hotel, and Abbott explained about the Family and what being "betrothed" actually meant, it sounded pretty exciting. Luc is charming and said he understood completely about music school and playing in an orchestra. And the idea of having people around me for "protection" and to make sure I had everything I needed, well, that sounded pretty cool too.

But as it turns out, it's kind of a pain in my butt. The three girls who were supposed to be at my beck and call? They're cousins, and they were all having these amazing lives over in Europe when Luc called them and told them they were now supposed to be looking after me. I feel bad for them. They gave up everything and came over here and, I've got to tell you, their lives are pretty boring, watching me go to school and music lessons and out to dinner with my Dad. I couldn't remember their names, which were very French, like Amelie and Fabienne, and they looked exactly the same, so I called them One, Two, and Three.

One stayed perched outside the house next to the chimney, a tiny little winged lion. Two was right inside the front door, next to a potted plant. She had made herself so small, she looked like your basic garden ornament brought indoors. Three was on my dresser, which kind of creeped me out at first, because I knew she could see and hear everything. But Three also had been going to fashion school in Paris, and had actually worked at Chanel, and when I found out she could sew, I asked her if she'd mind making something for me, and—bingo—a sewing machine appeared the next day and Three spent her daylight hours designing and sewing some beautiful clothes for me.

What a perk. After that, I didn't care if she plopped on my pillow each night.

Mom got real bitchy about me asking OneTwoThree to help around the house. I've got chores to do, just like anyone else, I guess, but when I asked Two if she'd take out the garbage, Mom went through the roof and had a long phone conversation with Abbott, and after that OneTwoThree were forbidden from taking orders from me without Mom approving.

What's the fun of having minions if you still have to load the dishwasher?

Then there was the hoopla over me getting to and from school. And everywhere else. There are people out to get me. I mean, seriously trying to grab me. They had come after me in a playground, for God's sake. With Luc right there. Luc said later that they were not Brunel, which I didn't understand. I didn't care who they were or weren't. I just wanted to make sure they didn't try again. Carrie took the bus and if things had been normal, I would have driven myself to school, and all the other places I had to go, like to my music lesson, and different practices.

I hate driving, by the way. I spend my entire time behind the wheel with my hands clenched so tightly around the steering wheel that when I finally let go, my fingers are cramped. So after the playground incident, it was decided I'd have a driver named Garth, who was also some kind of ninja-vampire-slayer person. I was glad. But then Mom got all huffy about the car. Luc wanted one of the black limos that he and his Family use all the time. How cool would that have been? But no, Mom said we weren't "limo" kind of people.

Maybe not, but I could easily become a "limo" kind of person if somebody let me.

So we settled on a blue Volvo. God, what kind of cool car is a Volvo?

Carrie watched all of this with a glint in her eye and a smile on her lips. My sister is one of the smartest people I know, so I knew she'd figured out a whole bunch of stuff before I did. Whenever I asked her anything, she'd shrug and say, "Hey, you're the Chosen One," which may have been true, but I wish I knew what she knew.

I've always wished that. I know I'm not stupid, but I'm always missing things. When it comes to music, I'm totally focused, but the rest of the world somehow passes me by. That's why I've always wanted someone to take care of me. It's not because I'm needy or shallow, although I know that's what people think. I just need someone there to knock me upside the head when something important is going on so I won't miss it.

Carrie doesn't miss a thing.

So the first day of school, I jumped out of the Volvo, hoping nobody I knew would see me and ask why I was being driven in such a boring car. But I was wearing a great outfit from Forever 21, a short, printed skirt and a lacy sleeveless shirt with gladiator sandals and a gorgeous headband decorated with a lace rose. So I wanted everybody I knew to see me so they could love my look as much as I did.

I stood on the main steps, gazing up. Mansfield High School was built in the 1940's, so it's all brick and limestone, with long, narrow windows and turrets everywhere. Off the back of the building are a series of additions, built over the course of time to accommodate new labs, a media center, and new classrooms. But the front looks the same as it did seventy years ago. Almost.

"Have they always been there?" a voice next to me asked. I turned. Richard, whom I've known since the sixth grade.

"Have what always been where?" I asked back.

He pointed. "Those gargoyles up there. I've never noticed them before."

There were four of them, spread across the front of the building. They looked like dragons, so I knew that they had once been warriors, carefully trained by Toad, who had studied all the dark creatures of the world and knew how to defeat them all.

"They've always been there," I lied. "How was your summer?"

"Sucked. Worked my ass off. You?"

"Same." We walked up the steps and into the building together.

Luc had been teaching me a lot about gargoyles. We'd had a few dates in the past few weeks, but always with a "chaperone", usually someone willing to throw himself in front of a runaway train to save

Luc's life, but at least he stopped inviting Carrie and her friends. Our dates had been long walks or sitting over coffee, talking. Luc was a great listener. He didn't mind if I got carried away and start to babble, and he was very funny, always making me laugh. He'd also been teaching me about his Family. There's so much to know. I wish I could have had Carrie listen in, because I knew I'd never remember all that stuff. But I remembered about the dragons.

Apparently, there was a time in this world where magic was everywhere, and sprouting wings was not such a big deal. Years and years ago, when his Family ruled a kingdom in France, all the people in their kingdom could change into winged creatures. What the person was in real life determined what they turned into. Warriors became dragons. Priests became frogs. Members of the royal Family became lions. That's why there are different types of gargoyles. Bishop, the one Luc calls Toad, descended from one of the first kings, so he's royal as well as a priest. Toad has spent hundreds of years studying all sorts of evil things—vampires, demons, whatever, and according to Luc, was the best defense his Family had. Toad trained OneTwoThree, who are also descendants of the Royal Family. I was pretty well protected.

Luc explained to me that members of the Royal Family have always married regular people, and because the Family can live for hundreds of years, many of them had several spouses. But I was Luc's first. He'd never been married, and when he saw me at Lincoln Center he knew I was "The One." Hearing stuff like that, it's hard not to fall in love. Not that I was, but, God, he was so cool.

I started up the steps and felt a bump from behind. I knew that bump. I hated that bump.

"So, gorgeous," Jack said in my ear, "miss me this summer? I spent many nights thinking about you, long nights in bed, just—"

"Shut up, Jack," I muttered. "Stop talking like that. I hate it."

Jack Keller was on the football team, and he was one of those guys who couldn't understand why every girl didn't fall into bed with him. He'd been after me for almost two years, and I would run halfway around the school just to avoid him in the hall. I know, sexual harassment and all, but this guy was on the football team. He was a star tackle. He was way over six feet tall and solid muscle. Nobody was going to do anything to him for making vague, lewd suggestions to a girl like me.

"Come on, babe, this may be your last chance. We'll be going our separate ways next year, you'd be missing out on a big deal. And you are looking very hot. Great outfit. Did you wear that cute little skirt just for me?"

I looked up and down the hallway. It was crowded with students, all trying to get to homeroom, but I didn't see a familiar face.

"I've heard it isn't that big a deal," I told him, trying to walk faster.

"Hey." He grabbed my arm. "What the hell is that supposed to mean?"

"Ask Riley," I said. "Isn't she the one you were screwing this summer?" I saw Ethan Sullivan coming towards me. Thank God. Jack didn't have the nerve to bother me when somebody else was around to hear.

Jack let go of my arm and backed away, glowering. Ethan stepped up beside me. He was a junior, he had done an article on me for the school paper the year before, and he was a very sweet guy. He was kind of short, but cute, with big, brown, puppy-dog eyes and shaggy red hair.

"Hey, Sara, you look great. Perfect outfit, by the way. Jack still being a prize tool?" he asked.

Ethan puzzled me a little. I had thought that maybe he was gay, because he always complimented me on my clothes. And he had never hit on me. Not that I'm irresistible, but most guys who spent time talking to me wanted something. Ethan just seemed to like me. "Yeah. How was your summer?"

"Great. Interned at the *Daily Record*. No money, but great experience. How about you?"

"Just work. The country club again. And music."

"I hear your sister got tagged for varsity soccer. Do you think I could do an interview?"

I looked over at him. "On the paper again?"

"Yep. I plan to be editor by the time I'm a senior."

"I bet you'll get it, Ethan," I said. I thought for a minute. "You know what might be more interesting? Going to the other girls and asking how they feel about a sophomore, especially one from Northwood, playing with them. I bet that would make a good story." All of us who came from Northwood Middle School started in our sophomore year, which caused all sorts of problems. All the students who had come to Mansfield as freshmen thought we were invading their territory. I'd seen people get pretty tense over stupid stuff. Like playing a varsity sport.

Ethan looked thoughtful. "You're right. That would be good. Is there something going on there?"

I shrugged. Let him do his own homework. But I was pissed off at those girls giving my sister a hard time.

I turned into homeroom and Miss Caulfield waved at me. "Head down to guidance," she called out.

"Already?" What a pain.

"I think you've got a new counselor. Go."

I turned around and went back into the hallway.

My old counselor, Mrs. Wu, who I had absolutely loved, retired last June. I had thought that there wasn't going to be a replacement because of budget cuts, but it looked like I was wrong.

I slowed down as I got closer to the guidance office. Luc had warned me to let him know if any strangers suddenly showed up at school or work. He was worried about vampires. They could look like normal people. I had asked him about the whole sleeping in the daylight thing, but apparently that was not true. They had to stay out of direct sunlight, but could move around in the daytime just like anyone else.

The guidance secretary waved me in to Mrs. Wu's old office. A woman was sitting behind the desk. She was very beautiful, probably about fifty, with graying dark hair and big blue eyes. She motioned for me to sit down.

"Hi. Are you Sara? I'm Violetta Grant. I'll be helping you out this year. I must say, you've got an awful lot going on. It looks like we'll be scheduling auditions as well as interviews next spring." She smiled brightly. "It's good to meet you."

I held my backpack on my lap. I didn't know what to say. Luc said vampires were usually good-looking. So I just nodded.

Ms. Grant leaned forward. "Don't worry, Sara," she said in a low voice. "Luc knows all about me. Tell him we met, of course, but I'm on your side. Trust me."

Oh, what a relief. "I'm so glad. This is so hard, you know? I mean, it's my senior year, and there's so much going on for college, and I'm worried about money. I've got to apply for scholarships like crazy, and them the whole Luc thing? How am I supposed to concentrate on college when I'm worried about all this other stuff?"

She nodded. "I know. We all know. That's why I'm here. It took a lot of maneuvering to get me here, but it's my job to make the school part of your life as effortless as possible. I'm very good at this sort of thing. I've been doing it for a long time. Don't worry, Sara. I'll take care of everything."

I breathed a sigh of relief. Someone to take care of everything was what I really wanted right now.

Chris was spending a lot of time at our house, which was fine with me. I liked him. Abbott was also spending time there, but for an entirely different reason. He said it was to keep tabs on me, but I think it was because he had a thing for Mom.

That was also fine with me. Mom had been alone for a long time, and with me and Carrie out of the house soon, it was good she finally found someone. Besides, Abbott was an excellent cook, and I often came home to find him in the kitchen, a snow-white apron tied around his waist, chopping things. He said it was because if wasn't fair to Mom to have to cook for all the extra people, but I could tell he enjoyed it. And it impressed the hell out of my mother.

I took private flute lessons from a woman in Toms River named Carole Woodruff. She was an instructor at Rutgers University and, like many other instructors at Rutgers, she played professionally in New York City. She was second chair with the orchestra at the Metropolitan Opera House. She also took private students and charged a ridiculous amount of money for an hour lesson. I saw her twice a month, and it ate up all the money I'd made during the summer. The good news was that instead of having Mom drive me back and forth, or, worse, driving myself and putting every driver in the Tri-state area at risk, I could jump in the blue Volvo and be driven there. The bad news was that Two and Three had to come with me, and they had to sit on the floor outside Carole's condo, waiting with nothing but their phones to entertain them, while Garth sat in the car, eyes peeled for vampires.

When I apologized for having them sit and do nothing, Two just shook her head.

"We are grateful to do nothing," she said. "Anything else would mean you were in danger. Remember that."

That was just weird. I sat there when it was explained to me, and I nodded my head, but the idea that there are people who wanted to hurt me? I just could not get my brain around it. At all.

I had not been spending a lot of time with Luc. He was off doing king-things. He had a suite of rooms at the Hilton over in Parsippany, but he spent time in New York and London. It was just as well. I had auditions to prepare for, a college essay to write, and three concerts coming up, in addition to my regular lessons, so I wouldn't have been able to see him too much anyway. But he was becoming this vague, out-there kind of idea, this handsome guy who insisted that he loved me, and that we were going to spend our lives together. I didn't even know him.

"Who's Mrs. Grant?" I asked Abbott one afternoon. He was trimming mushrooms. He did it very methodically, using a small paring knife to carve away the brown spots and slicing the dried ends off smoothly.

He glanced up at me. "Mrs. Grant, I believe, is your new counselor."

"I know that. I mean, who was she before? She wasn't always a counselor."

I could tell he was deciding whether or not to tell me. Most of the time, when I asked questions, I was just given the brush-off. Carrie, on the other hand, was always having long conversations with Abbott about all sorts of things. I didn't get that.

"Mrs. Grant," he said at last, "before she was your counselor, spent most of her time being Queen."

I frowned. "Of what?"

He smiled. "Everything."

I got it. "Oh my God! She's Luc's mother?"

He nodded. "Luckily, Luc is very good at doing all the things that need to be done to keep the Family business running smoothly, so Her Highness has some free time. I think she wanted a chance to get to know you better. She likes you very much, by the way. She was quite worried about Luc's, ah, impulsiveness. But now that she's met you, she feels much better about everything." He looked at me very seriously. "I'd appreciate it if you didn't say anything to her. When she feels the time is right, she'll introduce herself to you."

"Wow." No wonder she felt so familiar. She looked like Luc. And Chris.

"Where's Chris's mother?"

"In Prague. The Queen has two sisters, both younger, of course, and with lots of children. As soon as Luc is wed, the rest of them will be free to marry, and hopefully they will have lots of children as well. It's very important that the line continue." He had been chopping an onion, and looked up at me quickly. "I hope you want to have lots of children."

"I'll be happy to have a dozen, as long as I can keep playing my music."

He scooped the onions into a frying pan. "That shouldn't be any problem. The Royal nursery is the happiest place on earth. Next to Disney, of course. You'll have plenty of help raising your children, I assure you."

"Abbott, how old is Luc?" I figured since Abbott felt like talking, I may as well go for broke.

He was thinking again. He opened the refrigerator, pulled out a bottle of wine, and poured himself a glass before answering.

"Luc," he said at last, "was born in 1831. Now, I know you understand about the Family aging very slowly, but Luc went to Sleep at a very young age. He was taken to Wales, where he remained hidden on top of a tiny stone church for a very long time. The Family thought he was in danger."

"Danger? What kind of danger?"

"He was the only heir at the time. That put him in a very vulnerable position."

"How?"

Abbott was looking at me again, still thinking.

"Abbott, I know I'm not as sharp as Carrie, but I'm the one in the middle of all this, and I should probably know everything I can."

Abbott nodded. "You're right. Okay then. Luc was Turned and hidden in one of the most remote corners of the world the Family could find. The Brunels had killed his older brother, Martin. The second son, Denys, was found drowned in a lake. It was never determined if it was accidental or not. But the Family line was suddenly threatened. So Luc was hidden away. Since that time, other children have been born, so the threat that the Family line would disappear was gone. But, at the time, it was critical."

I didn't know what to say. Luc had been keeping me entertained by stories of flying frogs and shepherds, fairy-tale stuff. This was real and hard and terrible.

"Sara?"

I turned and looked. Carrie was standing in the doorway, her eyes big and dark.

"Sara, are you okay?" She came over and bumped against my shoulder. "You don't have to worry," she said. "Things are much different now. Chris has been telling me all sorts of things. Luc is safe. So are you. Honest, we're all so well protected. Please don't worry." She glared at Abbott.

"Don't be mad at Abbott," I told her. "I wanted to know. Luc just makes me laugh all the time. He never tells me what's going on."

"That's because he really loves you," Abbott said quietly. "I know that it may be hard to imagine, in this day and age, that a man can fall in love with a woman just by watching her play Chopin, but Luc is genuine in his feelings for you. He wants to protect you. He still has a certain, ah, 19th century sensibility."

"Who are the Brunels?" I asked.

Abbott continued preparing dinner as he explained. "The Brunel Clan can trace their line back several thousand years. They have always been very powerful and troublesome. Other Clans treat them like royalty. And because of Martin's death, they are much hated by Luc and his Family."

"Are they the ones who came after us?" Carrie asked.

Abbott shrugged. "We don't know. Toad says not." He was shaking something in the frying pan that smelled wonderful. "They have always been the first to break whatever treaties have been established. We know that they have become very energetic the past several months." He poured some wine into the pan, then put the whole thing in the oven. He glanced at his watch. "Your mother should be home in about an hour. Dinner is done. I had originally planned to stay, but perhaps you girls would rather just be with your mom tonight?"

I shook my head. "No. Stay. We have things we need to talk about, and you should be here. I want Luc to meet my Dad. And I think if Luc expects to marry me, we need to spend more time together. I don't care what kind of sensibility he has, he's supposed to be my boyfriend, and we've never even kissed."

Carrie punched me in the arm. "Seriously? You haven't even kissed him? He's so cute! What is wrong with you?" she asked.

"We've never been alone," I told her. "There's always somebody lurking in the background."

Abbott grinned. "Didn't he tell you? You have to be a virgin."

"What? Are you kidding?" I stared at Abbott. "Tell me you're kidding."

Carrie crossed her arms across her chest. "Does he have to be a virgin too?"

Abbott nodded. "Yes. Of course, I realize it was much easier a hundred or so years ago. That's one of the reasons you're not allowed to be alone with him. Luc is just like any other man, and you are a beautiful young woman."

I should have been embarrassed, but I was more curious. "What happens if we have sex?"

Abbott had finished his wine and poured another glass. "I have no idea. I imagine the possibility has never occurred to anyone."

"What if I've had sex already with somebody else?"

Abbott's jaw dropped open. "Did you?"

I grinned. "This is a hypothetical, Abbott. I'm trying to have a conversation here."

Carrie sniggered.

"I don't know. It's never been an issue before. This is only the twelfth time in the past several thousand years that there's been a royal marriage. The last time was in the late 1700's, and the virginity of the couple was not at all in question."

Fred came racing through the kitchen, hurling himself down the steps.

"Your mother is home early," Abbott said. "I hope she's all right."

Carrie raised an eyebrow as she looked at me, smiling.

"Hello girls," Mom said, coming into the kitchen. She had her arms full of books and tote bags, but she kissed Carrie and I on our cheeks, and smiled big at Abbott. "You've made dinner again? You're going to spoil us, Greg. What have you all been chatting about?"

I took a load of books out of her arms and set them on the counter. "Abbott has been telling us about how I've got to be a virgin. Luc too. It's been quite enlightening."

Mom looked at Abbott, tilting her head to one side. "Have you been talking to my daughter about having sex?" she asked.

"Actually," he said gently, "I've been talking to her about not having sex."

"Ah. Well. I'm glad I came home when I did. What is all this about, exactly?"

"It's fine, Mom. Don't worry," Carrie said. "Listen, why doesn't everybody come to Varsity Night? It's next week, and Dad is bringing the boys, and Luc could come and meet the rest of the family. What do you think?"

I looked at her gratefully. Varsity Night was a big deal at Mansfield, the night before the football game with our long-standing rival, Morristown. All the varsity athletes paraded around the field, the marching band played, the cheerleaders put on a show—it was a big, noisy, fun night.

"That's a great idea, Carrie. In fact, it's perfect," I said. "We could all sit together, and maybe after we could all come here for pizza or something. What do you think, Mom?"

Mom reached for Abbott's wine glass and took a sip. "Sounds great. Luc and your father can meet on neutral ground, as it were. I'm sure they'll be fine. Greg, you'll come with us as well?"

Abbott nodded his head. "I'd be delighted."

Mom smiled. "Wonderful. I'm going to change now, and Greg, please pour me some more of that lovely wine. And then we're all going to talk about this whole virgin thing. Got it?"

Abbott nodded. "Of course."

Carrie and I looked at each other and started to giggle.

CHAPTER TWO

CARRIE TOOK THE BUS TO and from school every day. She could have ridden with me, I guess, but she never even asked. I could understand that. She had friends on the bus, and she was still a sophomore, so it wasn't weird or anything for her to still take the bus. And besides, I didn't think she'd like being driven around. She kind of liked to do things for herself.

But one night after dinner, she pulled me aside. Becca was behind her, and they both looked like they wanted something.

"Can you give Becca and me a lift to the mall?"

Mom was doing school conferences, and wouldn't be home 'till late. I hated driving at night, and I told her.

"I know." She lowered her voice. "I was thinking you could ask Garth to take you, and we would just, you know, tag along."

The mall? I hadn't been in weeks. With Three making clothes for me, and practicing so much, I hadn't thought about it. But it suddenly sounded like fun.

I ran downstairs. Two was on her laptop.

"I want to go to the mall," I told her. "How do we do that?"

She looked up and her face brightened. "An American mall? I'll call Garth and he can bring the car. It's easy."

"Good. Carrie and Becca want to come. Will there be room?"

She waved her hand at me—no problem. "He'll bring the mini-van. Plenty of room." She pulled out her cell phone and texted quickly. "He'll be here in ten minutes." She looked excited. "I haven't been to a mall in ages. I've been waiting for you to actually go somewhere besides school and music class." She looked past me and grinned at Carrie. "Thanks," she said.

Carrie grinned back.

I had an entourage now. It was silly, kind of, but Two and Three were with me everywhere I went, except school, because at school I had a whole other set of bodyguards. And Three was right—I hadn't gone anywhere. I didn't think it would be a big deal, but before we left the house, Three texted Abbott, Toad, even Luc, although Luc had just come back from London. It seemed like everyone had to know what was going on. Apparently Toad thought it would be a safe trip, because when we pulled into the mall parking lot, there were no gargoyles on top of Macy's.

It was fun to look everywhere. Carrie and Becca took off the minute we walked through the doors. Two and Three were right with me, Garth a few feet behind. I even had money. Luc had given me a wad of cash before he left, in case I needed anything. I didn't tell Mom, because I knew she would have had a fit. So I could pretty much buy anything I wanted. I'd never been able to do that before. It was way cool.

Whenever I saw something I liked, Three would shake her head and say, "I can make that." So I'd try it on, Two would take a picture of me on her phone, and Three would whip out a tiny notebook and scribble stuff down.

I looked at her. "How are you going to pay for all the fabric? I don't want you paying for my clothes."

Three shook her head. "Don't worry. You have an allowance. Your mother refuses to let you touch it, but I've been using it all along."

"An allowance? Are you kidding? Wow, how did that happen?"

She looked impatient. "You are some day going to be our Queen. You must be taken care of."

"But what if I end up not marrying Luc? I haven't even seen him in two weeks."

Her face became blank. "Of course you're going to marry Luc. I can't even imagine what might happen if you did not."

Okay, that was pretty scary. But an allowance?

I spent most of my money on shoes, purses and fun jewelry. So did Two and Three. They went through the mall like Sherman through

Georgia, armed with a gold American Express card and taking no prisoners.

We were meeting Carrie and Becca in the food court at ten. We got there a little early. Two ran off to Cinnabon—she had a real sweet tooth—and Three and I were looking for a table, when Garth appeared out of nowhere just as Three grabbed my arm and started steering me away from the Food Court.

"What," I asked.

Three shook her head and I saw Two walk past us, very quickly. She went up to a very good-looking guy, maybe my age, with blond hair and dark eyes. He was wearing skinny jeans and a tight-fitting button-down shirt with a thin, red tie. He did not look model-perfect. He was just handsome. When he saw Two, he kind of smiled. Two wasn't smiling at all.

"Who's that?" I asked.

Garth and Three ignored me. They were watching Two. They were both nervous and tense.

"What? What's going on?"

"It's Stefan Brunel," Garth said shortly.

I felt cold. "Isn't he your enemy?"

Three shrugged. Her eyes never left her sister. "Stefan has been, for several years now, the voice of reason in the Brunel Clan. We believe he sincerely wants peace. But it's disturbing that we should run into him."

Two turned from Stefan and came toward us, her face tight.

"We need to leave," she said shortly.

I looked back at Stefan. There was something in his face that I found very interesting. He felt me looking at him and turned, and when he met my eyes, I felt a jolt of something.

Two had her hand on my arm and was dragging me away. "What about Carrie?" I asked. I didn't feel afraid, just excited.

"I'm texting her now," Three said.

"I thought they were all supposed to be drop-dead gorgeous. Why does he look like just a normal good-looking guy?" I asked.

We were moving towards the nearest exit. The car, I knew, was parked all the way on the other side of the mall. "Why are we going outside? The car is way over—"

"We will be safer in the open," Three said. "It will be easier to get help if we need it."

"Why would we need help? What did he say?"

We practically ran through the glass doors, our arms still full of shopping bags. Garth stood completely still, then jerked his head to the left. We all followed him, walking quickly.

"What did he say," I asked again. They ignored me again, so I jerked my arm away and shouted "Fabienne, what did he say?"

Two stopped short and looked at me in surprise. Maybe because I yelled. Maybe because she didn't think I was smart enough to remember her real name.

"More are coming. You were followed from the house. He thinks there may be something going on."

We were all walking again, around the parking lot to the other side where the car was parked.

"Was he following me too? I mean, how did he even know I was here?"

Two and Three exchanged looks. You mean they didn't think of that? These were supposed to be my protectors? Yeesh.

The parking lot was almost empty. After ten on a weekday was not prime shopping time. I kept looking around for a bunch of beautiful people with fangs to appear from nowhere, but it was just the four of us, not speaking.

"Why wasn't he more gorgeous? He looked like a normal person," I asked again.

Three made a little smile. "He tries not to be so, I don't know, vampire-ish. He's trying to live his life like a mortal person. He has a job and an apartment in New York. He doesn't take Clan money. He doesn't use lots of Glamour."

"So he really looks like that?"

"What?" Three made a noise. "Sara, he's been dead for four hundred years, living off the blood of others. He's hideous. Vile. If you saw his real face, you'd probably throw up."

Two, who had grabbed my arm again, suddenly swerved down a row of cars, and started to run. Our shopping bags dropped to the ground and I heard Garth mutter under his breath. I was feeling scared now. But there were three of them. Surely, I'd be safe. And then I knew I wasn't safe at all. In the blink of an eye, we were surrounded. There were nine of them, all women, all heartbreakingly beautiful.

The parking lot seemed completely empty and silent. Except for us and them.

"What are you doing here?" Three asked.

One of them smiled. Her teeth were perfect. "We're shopping. Isn't that what you're doing here?"

It was suddenly very cold. Freezing. I could see my breath, and goose bumps rose on my arms and legs. Oh, my God. Where was the cavalry?

Three still seemed calm. "It's just odd, that's all, to see all of you together like this. You weren't following us, were you?"

I got the sense that we were all waiting. The women just stood around us, never making a move towards us. If I didn't know who they were I'd think they were a roving band of super-models out for a lark. Two still held my arm. What were we all waiting for?

A lime green Volkswagen bug, its convertible top down, pulled up beside us.

"You guys need a lift to your car?" the driver called out.

It was Stefan. He spoke perfect English, with a slight French accent. He looked friendly and relaxed behind the wheel, just like an old friend passing by.

One of the vampires kind of hissed. "Don't interfere," she said.

Stefan looked puzzled. "With what? I'm just trying to help out my friend Sara here."

I broke away and opened the car door. Three was right behind me, and jumped in the back seat. So did Garth. I sat next to Stefan and slammed the door shut.

He turned to me with an easy smile. "Where to?"

"We're by Macy's. Thanks."

He put the car in gear and slid past the group of vampires, who were now looking slightly frantic. I was suddenly warm again.

I turned and looked at Three. "Where's your sister?" I asked.

Three looked pale but relieved. "She went back for the shopping bags, of course."

I started to laugh. "Of course."

Three was laughing too, nervous, high-pitched laughter that told me exactly how close we had been to something awful happening.

I turned to Stefan. "Who were they?"

He shook his head. "No idea." He glanced at me, and grinned at my surprise. "Sara, there are millions of us. I'm not on a first-name basis with all of them."

"But you know who I am?"

He nodded, and we were close to the car. I pointed it out to him and he came to a stop. He looked over at me.

"We all know who you are."

Garth had climbed out of the back of the car and opened the door for me. I stared at Stefan a moment longer, and got out.

There was a sudden whooshing in the air. I glanced up, but could see nothing in the darkness. But as I turned around, there was Luc.

I'd forgotten how handsome he was. He put a protective arm around my shoulder, but I could see he was angry.

"If I see you around her again," he spat at Stefan," I will kill you myself."

I pulled away. "He helped us," I said, tugging on Luc's shirt. " He got us away from them."

He did not look at me, but was still glaring at Stefan. Stefan was sitting calmly, not reacting at all.

Garth stepped in front of Luc. "Sara is right. He put himself between us and the other vampires."

Luc looked hard at Garth, then back at Stefan. "How did he even know she was here?" he asked.

Stefan threw the car into neutral and sat for a moment before answering. "She is watched. By many. My people as well. I do not want any situation to arise that would damage the peace. You know that."

Luc took a long, deep breath, then said something in French. Stefan shrugged his shoulders and said something in French back. Luc nodded, and Stefan drove off.

Carrie and Becca came running up at the same time Two appeared, her arms filled with shopping bags.

"What happened?" Carrie asked.

"We got ambushed," I said. I looked around. "Why didn't you guys just Turn and kill them," I asked. My mouth felt dry as I said the words.

Luc shook his head. "Can you imagine what you happen if anyone saw us Turn? We only do that if we are outnumbered."

Three looked grim. "All that training we did with Toad? What did you think we were talking about? We don't need to be taught how to Turn. We need to be taught how to fight a being three times as strong and as fast as we are. If we would have had to fight the vampires we met tonight, it would have been simple hand-to-hand combat. That's what we are trained to do. Three of them against one of us is manageable. They travel in threes. We call it a Pod. So we would have taken them easily. But if there had been more of them, it would have been a very bad situation."

"Like the night Chris Turned." Carrie said. "There were six of them."

Luc smiled grimly. "Yes. It was a risky thing to do, but he had no choice." He put his arms around me and hugged me tightly. "Do you know how lucky you were just now?"

"No," I said. "But somebody is going to explain it all to me, right? 'Cause I'm tired of being the last one to know everything around here."

Luc brought me a necklace from London. It was a crystal the size of a dime, nestled in a thin, gold band, and attached to a gold chain. When I put it on, the stone rested just below my Adam's apple. I stared at myself in the mirror. It was beautiful.

"Thank you," I said, and reached over to give him a quick kiss on the cheek.

We were back at the house and it was very late. Mom had come home earlier to find us all gone, and had put on her rattiest sweats and was grading papers when we all came piling in, Carrie and I, Garth, Two and Three, then Luc, Abbott and Toad.

She immediately made coffee, because that's what Mom does in a crisis. She makes coffee.

Luc and Toad and Abbott were having this long discussion about who could have planned it, what the motives might have been, who they were waiting for—I was so seriously bored I wanted to scream, because none of the questions I thought were important were even being talked about. Like what made Stefan so different, why he would want to help me, and was he powerful enough to really make a difference? And when were Luc and I going to start going on real dates?

Finally, Luc took my hand. "I'm sorry, I do not mean to ignore you. What do you want to know?"

"Okay, first of all, how come your English is so much better?"

He threw back his head and laughed. Even Abbott smiled.

"Well," he said, "I told everyone to only speak to me only in English from now on. If I am to woo and win an American girl, I had better be able to dazzle her with my charm."

"Yeah, well about that. Are you going to be around here for a while? Or are you off again to London or wherever it is you go to do all your royal stuff."

He smiled but looked much more serious. "I am renting a condo just a few miles from here, and that it where I will be staying from now on. We have moved all our offices from Paris and London to New York, at least for now, and I should be able to stay in this country."

"Good. So I want to know who Stefan is and why he helped me."

Luc's face shut down. He looked over at Abbott, who shrugged, then at Toad, who was nodding his head.

Luc leaned in close to me. We were sitting side-by-side on the couch, and I could feel the heat from his body, and the tension in his hands as he held mine.

"Stefan in George Brunel's nephew. He is the brother of Renata who has been a worry to our Family for many years. She has always been unstable, unwilling to heed her uncle's word, and eager for war. Stefan was completely out of favor for a very long time, because he believes that the two races can and should co-exist. We feel that way too, which is why we have never broken a treaty. But Brunel had always been testing us. In the past fifty years or so, Stefan has been welcomed back into the Brunel inner circle. We hope it is because George is softening his position." He turned my hand over, running his fingertips across my palm. I felt a tingle of pleasure run down my back.

"It is politics. Plain and simple. So, we can claim Stefan as an ally. Not a friend. He knew what was coming, warned us, and helped to remove you from what could have been a very unpleasant situation." He lifted my palm to his lips and held it there for a moment. "We got there barely a minute after he picked you up in his car. The other vampires were gone. We do not know who they were, or who sent them. They were not recognizable to us as from the Brunel Clan , but there are hundreds of smaller clans. From what Amelie described, they were probably instructed to hold you until the arrival of someone else. Stefan interfering spoiled their plans, so they scattered. We will have to be extra cautious."

I took back my hand. "Well, we can start being cautious next week. I want to invite you to Varsity Night. It's a big deal at school, and my Dad and my brothers will be there, and I want you to meet them." I looked over at Abbott. "You too." I turned back to Luc. "And if you think you have any chance in the world of marrying me, you'd better start taking me a few places and letting me get to know you. Alone. I know all about this virgin stuff, but get over it. I'm tired of being chaperoned like a Victorian spinster. If you want to be my boyfriend, you better start acting like it."

Carrie burst out laughing and clapped her hands. Mom looked slightly mortified, but maybe that was because Abbott was seeing her looking like a real slob. Two and Three actually smiled at me, and Two gave me a thumbs up. Garth just sat there. He always just sat there.

Luc looked completely shocked. Then he laughed too.

Good thing. Having a sense of humor was going to be real important if he was going to get anywhere with me.

I never had a serious boyfriend before. To tell the truth, I've only been on about a half a dozen dates in my whole life, and every one of them ended up with the guy's hand on my boob or down my pants, and me feeling sick to my stomach and never wanting to see that particular guy again. But I know what dates in high school are supposed to be like. You hang around the mall before the movies, or you go out to eat and walk around town drinking coffee, or maybe, in the summer, have a picnic and go swimming out at the lake.

I'm pretty sure Luc never went to high school, because when he called me and asked if I was going to be busy Tuesday night, he suggested we go into New York City to see an Invitation Only performance of the opera, *The Marriage of Figaro*, followed by a late dinner at some French restaurant in the Trump Tower.

"Luc," I explained, "it's a school night. I need to be home by ten."

"Oh." He was silent. "Can you suggest something else?"

Seriously, it should not have to be up to me, but I had a feeling Luc was way out of his depth here.

"We could grab some dinner at Friday's, then go ice skating."

Ice skating was one of the few sports-related things that I enjoyed. I wasn't crazy about the cold rink part, but I was good at skating. Mom had taken both Carrie and me when we were little, and I always liked it.

"Can you skate?" I asked him.

"Yes."

"And it would be easy to have twenty or thirty bodyguards around the rink, right?"

"Yes." I could hear the laughter in his voice.

"But if anyone tries to sit at our table during dinner, I'm going to be a little pissed off."

He was laughing now. "Agreed. I'll pick you up at six."

I hung up and looked over at Three, sitting on the couch pretending she couldn't hear every word I said. "Luc and I are going out. On a date. Is it even possible for me not to see your face?"

She looked very serious, then her mouth twitched. "My sister and I will be invisible. I promise. Ice skating? You got him to go ice skating?"

"He wanted to take me to the opera. I would have loved that, but Mom would have a fit. Besides, I think it will be easier to talk if we don't have to listen to a bunch of arias." I shrugged. "I like ice skating, except for the cold part."

She sat up. "We have that wool and fake fur. We could make something?"

"One of those cool vests?"

"Yes, and a short, flared skirt. You can wear some black tights and your Uggs. Perfect."

"I'll need fuzzy gloves."

So Thursday I skipped my usual after-school practice so I could get my homework done and have plenty of time to get dressed before he picked me up.

He drove himself, a sleek gray Porsche, so it was hard to act like this was just a normal kind of date. I don't know where Garth was, or Two or Three, but I knew they were close. I was kind of glad. If a bunch of bloodthirsty supermodel types went after us tonight, I wanted lots of air and ground support.

He had never been to a Friday's before.

"Why do they deep fry the green beans?" he asked, reading the menu intently.

"Because they taste good that way."

"Are buffalo wings made of buffalo?"

"No. Chicken. They're fried, then tossed with buffalo sauce."

"Oh. So the sauce made of buffalo?"

I started to giggle. "No. It's just hot sauce."

"But fried? Everything is fried?"

"Not everything. Just the good stuff."

"And what is loaded?"

The waitress was hovering. "Hi. My name is Megan and I'll be serving you tonight. Can I start you off with something to eat?"

Luc was looking through the menu. "There is no wine list," he pointed out.

I was trying to keep a straight face. I grabbed the little plastic placard that listed the wines, and shoved it at him.

He frowned. "I have never heard of these," he said apologetically to Megan. "A nice, dry white?"

"Sure. ID?"

Luc pulled out his wallet and showed her something. I wanted to grab it and take a look for myself. How old did the rest of the world think he was?

I ordered water and we went back to the menu. I had never laughed so hard explaining food in my life. He needed to get out more.

When Megan came back we ordered, and Luc sipped his wine, shrugged, then took a bigger drink. He smiled at me and shrugged.

"In France, food is easier."

"Why? Don't you have restaurants like this over there?"

"I don't think so. Not that I've ever been to, anyway. Mostly, I eat bistro food—steaks and chops, salad, a little wine, and cheese for dessert. There seems to be very many choices here."

"That's the U.S. for you. Lots of choices."

"Yes. Are you applying to all those schools?"

"Of course."

"But why don't you pick just one that you really want?"

"But there's a chance they won't want me, and then where would I be?"

He made a careless gesture with his hand. "I can assure you, whichever school you want to get into, the Family will make sure it's done."

I felt a little heat in my cheeks. "I don't want special treatment. I don't want any favors. I want to get in on merit, just like anyone else."

"Yes, but—" He stopped. He was beginning to know me, because he quickly changed the subject. "What is this thing we will be going to next week? Varsity Night?"

"It's a big traditional football event. It's to get everyone pumped up for the game against Morristown. There are cheerleaders, and the marching band plays, and everyone screams and yells a lot."

"And this is fun?"

He was making me laugh again. "It's supposed to be. I'm not that into it myself, but I know lots of kids in the band, and Carrie will be there because she's playing soccer, and my Dad was a big football star when he went there. We've always gone, even when we were little kids."

"I played soccer a few years when I was at University in Berlin. 1971. That was my degree in Finance."

The Wasabi Green Beans appeared, so I kept my mouth shut for a minute. "You went to college in 1971?"

He put a green bean in his mouth and chewed carefully. He swallowed, and his whole face lit up. "This is delicious. What is the green stuff here?"

"Wasabi sauce. It's a dip. College?"

He was very good at following instructions. He took another green bean, dipped carefully, and ate. He grinned. "This is wonderful. I must get my chef to do this."

"Luc—college?"

"I have eight degrees, ranging from European History to Finance. I must know as much as possible about the world I will be involved in. I have gone to school all over Europe in the past one hundred years.

Now that my English is better, I am thinking about the Wharton School. Maybe in a couple of years. The Family is becoming more and more about business and commerce."

"And less about killing vampires?"

"No. That is always what we do first. We can never lose sight of them, and the threat they pose. That is why we need money, and property, and connections all over the world. If we ever go to war, we will need resources."

I didn't want to talk about war. Or vampires, for that matter. I was still pretty curious about Stefan, but I had a feeling Luc would not be happy talking about him.

We made it through dinner just fine, and got to the rink before eight. It was pretty empty. I did not look to closely at the people who were there, because I knew I'd recognize somebody and I didn't want to ruin the illusion that I was on a regular date with my boyfriend.

Luc had mentioned that he had spent lots of time as a kid in Switzerland, so I figured he was a good skier, but he must have put in a lot of time of the frozen ponds over there as well, because he was a beautiful skater. He made me feel like I was much better than I knew I was. We made circles and loops, and he put his arms around me and we waltzed. The other people on the ice were watching us. He grabbed me around the waist and raced across the ice, then spun me out and caught me before I could fall. It was like flying, and when they blinked the lights to signal the rink was closing, he turned me towards him and kissed me, very softly, and I kissed him back. Pretty hard.

It was wonderful.

Friday night we were supposed to go out again, but I suggested he just come to the house.

"And do what?"

"Hang out. Chris will be here, and Kevin and Becca, and I think they're going to watch 'American Horror Story'."

"What's that?"

"A television show."

"We'll sit around and watch TV?"

"And talk. And make popcorn. This is what people my age do, Luc. We hang out. And since I'm already surrounded by bodyguards, there should be no worries. "

He laughed. "I can do that. Hang out. What time?"

He ended up coming for dinner. Carrie and Becca were making pizza. Kevin and Chris were being annoying. Mom hovered for a bit, then decided that she and Abbott should go to the movies after all.

Carrie and Becca were very good at making pizza. They were also very good at making a huge mess all over the kitchen, which Chris offered to clean up. Then Luc said he would help. It was funny to watch, because it was obvious Luc had never had to clean up anything in his entire life, and Chris was going along like it was the most natural thing in the world for the next ruler of a vast magical empire to load a dishwasher.

Chris was being patient. "The glasses go on the top shelf."

"Okay," Luc said.

"But you have to put them in upside down."

"Why?"

"Because the water has to run down the glasses."

"What about the dishes?"

"On the bottom shelf. Have them all face the same direction."

"Why?"

"I don't know. It just works better that way. And the silver goes in upside down as well."

"Why?"

We were laughing.

"If you do marry him," Becca said, "I don't think he's going to be much help around the house."

"If I do marry him," I answered, "there had better be other people to load the dishwasher."

Luc looked up and said, very seriously, "I think I have someone who knows how to do this already. When I get up from the table at home, the dishes are always gone the next day.'

Carrie elbowed Chris. "Are there housekeeping fairies that you haven't told us about?" she joked.

Chris shook his head. "Not here. They are only found in Iceland these days."

I couldn't tell if he was joking or not, but Carrie started laughing all over again.

Then we went downstairs and started to watch TV, but it kinda creeped me out, so I spent the first hour practicing the flute in my head. Luc caught on, and suggested maybe he and I could just talk instead.

We went upstairs and sat on the couch, not next to each other exactly, but turned facing each other. He leaned over to kiss me, very softly. I thought he'd grab me and pull me down on the cushions, but instead, he leaned back and smiled.

"Tell me," he said, "about growing up."

I was surprised. "Really? You want to know about my childhood?"

He shrugged. "It defines who we are, yes? And I want to know who you are."

I smiled. "Okay. But then it's your turn."

He laughed. "Fair enough. But, you first."

"I remember when my dad was still living with us," I began. "And I remember him leaving. He'd just started his company, and he and Mom fought all the time about money. Now, I guess I understand more about what it takes to start your own business, and how hard it is, but then I was just really angry at him for leaving."

"Were you mad at your mother as well?"

I shook my head. "No. Because Carrie told me that it was Dad who wanted to leave, and that Mom had fought hard for us."

He frowned. "How would she know such a thing? She must have been very young."

I shrugged. "She was about three. But, she's always known stuff. I don't know if it's because she listens and understands so much better than I do, but she's always been the one to tell me what's going on. And I always have trusted everything she's ever said."

He nodded. "Go on."

"So, then I went to kindergarten, Carrie went to preschool, and Mom went back to work. And I just kind of floated along until I found the flute. It changed how I looked at my life. It gave me a focus. By then, Carrie had soccer and Mom was going back to school to get her Masters, and I really wanted something that was just mine. Playing the flute changed everything for me. It made me think about bigger things, you know?"

"What kind of bigger things?"

I laughed nervously. I wasn't used to talking about this kind of stuff. "Why we're here, and what our purpose in life is." I looked over at him. He was watching me intently, his eyes dark and beautiful. "I guess that was never a problem for you, huh?"

He shrugged his shoulders. "No. I have always known what was expected of me. I remember both of my brothers. We would play together. They were very gentle with me, because I was the baby, but they were fierce with each other. All their games turned into contests." He shrugged again. "Little boys, yes? I thought they were very wonderful. My grandmother was still alive, and she cared for us, because my mother was very busy." He smiled ruefully. "Being Queen is a very big job. We did not see her much."

"Wait," I said. "How could your mother become Queen if your grandmother was still alive?"

"As soon as the first heir is born, the crown is passed on. We live long lives, Sara, and ruling is a very difficult job. No one would want to do it forever, believe me. When we are married, and have our first child, then I will become King, and my mother will finally be able to step down and enjoy the rest of her life. That is why I must learn as much as I can now."

"What would I do? Once you become King, I mean."

"Whatever you want. Would you want perform in an orchestra? Fine. Would you want to stay at home and read all day and watch our children? That would be fine too.." He leaned forward. "You can do whatever you want, Sara. You will be a Queen."

"I don't think I'd be very good at reading all day."

"I don't think so either," he said with a smile.

I kicked off my sandals, brought my feet up on the couch, and wrapped my arms around my bended knees. "What happened to your brothers?"

His smile vanished. "Martin was killed while riding in the woods. He liked to ride alone. He thought he'd found a way to sneak out of the chateau, but he was always followed, at a distance, of course. He thought he was very clever, you see, and no one wanted to spoil his fantasy. So, when he was attacked, help was just a few seconds too far away. He did not die at once. We are very strong, we lions, and it takes a lot to kill us, but he had lost too much blood. There were no transfusions in 1838. And then Denys drowned. That's when my grandmother took me to Wales. As a child, I had not learned to Turn, or Sleep, so she had to do it for me. I stayed atop a very small church in the wild moors of Wales for almost fifteen years. Then, after my aunts had children of their own and the Family line was again safe, my mother came for me."

"Did you learn how to fight?"

"Yes. I am very good."

"Have you ever killed anyone?"

He shrugged.

"That's not an answer, Luc. Listen, here's the thing with me. If you don't want to tell me something, fine. Say, I'm not going to tell you, and I'll get it. But if I ask you a question, you need to answer me. And you can't ever lie. I would have a really hard time getting over a lie."

He looked at me steadily. "Yes, I've killed. Many Clan members. That is my purpose in life, remember? To protect."

"Chris said you didn't do stuff like that."

"Chris was probably trying to spare you the grim details of my life. I will not do that, Sara, if you don't want me to."

I rested my chin on the top of my knees. "I want to know everything."

"That could take a while."

I lifted my shoulders, then let them drop. "We have lots of time."

He nodded. "Yes. But that's enough for tonight. Perhaps I should go? It's getting late."

Then he kissed me again.

He left with Chris. Kevin and Becca left, then Mom and Abbott came home. Abbott left, and Mom and Carrie went to bed. I was still sitting on the couch, long into the night, going over his words in my head, and thinking about how his kiss felt against my lips.

Dad would have come to Varsity night even if Carrie weren't going to be involved. Dad graduated from Mansfield High back in the 80's. He was their wide receiver when the football team won the state championships two years in a row. Dad's team picture was still hanging on the wall in the main hallway, and the trophy he helped win was still on display in the gym. When we were little, we went with him to Varsity Night, even though we didn't understand what Varsity meant. This year, he was bringing the boys, and when I told him I wanted him to meet someone, he got quiet on the phone.

"Dad?"

"Is this guy your boyfriend?" he asked.

"Yes. He's... well, yes."

"How long have you known him?"

"We met over the summer. I wasn't sure where things were going, Daddy, that's why I didn't mention him before."

"Oh." He was quiet again. "I guess I should have seen this coming, right?"

I could feel my hand tighten up on the phone. "Well, yes. I mean, I'm going off to college next year. Weren't you kind of expecting something like this to happen eventually?"

He laughed. "Honey, no father wants to admit it, but I was hoping this would never happen."

"Oh." I was quiet. Dad and I didn't talk too much anymore. We still tried to see each other, but I had so many things going on in my life that I didn't even think about him too much. I felt bad about it, but there wasn't much I could do. I had school, and my music, and getting college stuff together, and now everything with Luc—I had to let go of something, and that something was time with my father.

"Listen, Dad, after everything, why don't you and the boys come over to the house? Carrie wants to make pizza, and Abbott made this beautiful pound cake, and you can get to know Luc a little bit."

"Who's Abbott?"

Good question. "He's been spending time with Mom," I said. Not at all far from the truth.

He was quiet again. Then he chuckled. "Is this guy *her* boyfriend?"

I laughed with him. "I don't know, Dad. You adult types have a different set of rules. But he's nice and a great cook, so we like having him around."

"Okay, Princess. I'll see you Friday."

I clicked off the phone. He had always called me princess. He had always told me I was special. He always made me believe in myself. I was moving away from him, and that felt a little scary. At the same time, I was moving towards Luc. And that felt right.

On Varsity Night, the night before our game with our greatest rival, Morristown High School, the cheerleaders drive all over town and pick up the football players at their homes, and then drive them over to school. While all that's happening, the athletic stadium fills with people, the marching band is in the middle of the football field playing their hearts out, and all the other Varsity athletes, girls as well as boys, mill around, waiting. Then the cheerleaders file in, leading the football team. The crowd, as they say, goes wild.

Football was a very big deal at Mansfield High.

Only the band was wearing uniforms, but every person in the stands knew the football players. Even in jeans and tee shirts, these guys were the stars. The athletic director introduced all the players from all the teams—soccer, track, wrestling - and the athletes waved and the crowd applauded, but when those football guys stepped up, the roar went up to the sky.

Luc bent down to shout in my ear. "I guess everyone likes the football team best?"

I nodded, clapping and shouting. When Carrie's name had been announced, we had all waved and screamed, Dante and Henry jumping up and down, Dad whistling through his teeth so loud I thought the bulbs in the stadium lights would shatter. But the football team—the din was amazing.

I didn't bother to try to introduce Luc to Dad when we first got there, because conversation was impossible. You didn't go to Varsity Night to talk. You went to scream and yell like a crazy person until your throat hurt.

Our little group was surrounded. Toad was right behind us. The new science teacher was three rows down. Two and Three were over a bit, closer to the field. And I saw Mrs. Grant sitting with the new janitor, just to our left, watching us. I wanted to ask Luc about her, but didn't have the nerve. She had caught my eye and actually waved, so I felt pretty good.

During a lull, while the Director was talking about last year's triumphs, I leaned over to Luc. "Is the Family worried something might happen here? Aren't there too many people for someone to try anything?"

Luc squeezed my hand. "They are always worried. After all, they have tried twice already." He made a gesture with his hand. "Look at all these people. They aren't paying attention to anything except what's happening on the field. Someone could drag you, kicking and screaming, from your seat, and no one would even notice." He squeezed my hand again and gave me a quick kiss. "I would never let that happen."

A few minutes later, the ceremony ended, and the bleachers became a loud, confused mess. Luc tightened his hand on mine and glanced around. Despite all the movement and confusion, Toad was still there, and Two and Three. Chris moved by Luc's side.

"I'd like to go down on the field," I told Luc. "What do you think?"

Luc glanced around again, then nodded. "Certainly. Let's go."

We moved cautiously down the bleachers. I kept my eye on Carrie. She was with Becca and Kevin, and a bunch of other kids. Carrie always seemed to be surrounded by friends.

Luc didn't let go of my hand as I made my way towards Carrie. I reached her, and pulled free from Luc to give her a hug. There was so much noise I could barely hear my own thoughts. Carrie was grinning, saying something to Becca. Chris was there, and he was hugging Carrie as well, and I watched them, trying to see if there was a bit a spark. I felt so happy and excited.

Jack Keller stepped in front of me. His eyes narrowed as he glanced at Luc, then he looked back to my face and he sneered. Jack grabbed me and hugged me. "No love for the team, Sara?" he said in my ear.

I tried to pull away, but couldn't. I put my fists between us, and twisted to get away. He tightened his grip on my waist, and stuck his tongue in my ear.

I didn't even see Luc move, but I was suddenly free and Luc was between us. Luc wasn't as tall as Jack, and looked slender next to him, but as he took a step towards Jack, Jack backed away. Something in Luc's face had frightened him. Chris stepped in front of Luc as Luc lunged. I couldn't believe it. Luc was going after Jack, and Jack was trying to get away.

It felt so good to see that. To see Jack afraid of something. Afraid of Luc.

I reached forward and grabbed Luc's shirt, pulling him back and around.

"He's not worth it," I said loudly. "He's nothing but a bully. Please, Luc, leave him alone."

I could feel Luc suddenly relax. He was so close, and his eyes were dark and serious.

"If he ever bothers you again, I will kill him."

I knew that he meant it. I knew that he would do that for me. I kissed him.

Hard.

And he kissed me back.

His hands were in my hair, and I could feel his body pressed hard against mine, and the noise faded away. This was different from his other kisses, which had been sweet and cool. This was more. We broke apart suddenly, both of us breathing hard. I had to close my eyes and clench my jaw before I felt the world stop spinning around me. When I opened my eyes, Luc was looking at me shyly, smiling just a little.

"Wow," I said.

Luc nodded. "Yes. Very wow."

Abbott's pound cake was the best thing I had ever tasted. Something in the coffee tasted better too. We were all in the kitchen, of course, and Dad and Luc were talking intently about something. Could it have really been the foreign stock market? Did Luc know about stuff like that?

Kevin and Becca were there, but there was something different going on with them. Kevin kept touching her, his hand on her shoulder or back, and she kept smiling at him.

I sat on the couch beside Carrie. "What's up with your two BFFs?"

She sighed. "Love is in the air. I guess I should have seen this coming. Ever since the night they were here together and we swore them to secrecy over Luc and the vampires and everything, they've become this, I don't know, unit. It's kind of cute, because they're obviously crazy about each other, but neither wants to admit it."

I looked at her. "You okay with that?"

Carrie shrugged. "Hey, why not? We're together all the time anyway. I'm just hoping they're going to be one of those couples who end up dying together of old age, because if they have a nasty break-up, I'm going to be pissed."

That's Carrie for you. Always thinking ahead.

"So, what happened between Luc and Jack? That looked interesting." Carrie raised one eyebrow. "Jack is such a jerk."

"I don't know. I couldn't see much. Luc must have said something, though, because Jack backed off really quick."

"Luc's face changed," Carrie said slowly. "I was watching, and Luc looked—" She chewed her lower lip. "Dangerous. Dark. I thought he was going to kill Jack."

"He offered. Luc did. To kill Jack."

Carrie raised an eyebrow again. "That's some boyfriend you got there."

I felt a kind of glow in my chest. "Yeah. I know."

"Dad and Luc seem to be getting along," Carrie said.

"Yes. Luc is good with that. Getting people to like him. It's a prince thing."

Luc slipped by my side and kissed my cheek. "Your father is very gracious," he said.

"Yeah, he's pretty good people. Were you dazzling him with international finance?"

Luc grinned. "I didn't want him to think I was just another pretty face."

Henry had wiggled his way to where we were sitting. He made a face at Luc.

"Are you going to marry Sara?" he asked.

I glanced at Luc and shook my head. Luc smiled at Henry. "Only with your permission."

Henry frowned, thinking. I loved Henry. He was such a sweet and serious little boy. His older brother was so brave and confident, and I did love him as well, but with Henry, there was an extra tug at my heart.

"Well," Henry said at last, "I guess it would be okay as long as she didn't move away."

Luc nodded his head slowly. "I can understand that. But she will be going away when she is playing her music. She will be traveling all over the world with a great orchestra ."

I felt something catch in my chest.

Henry thought some more. "Yes, but then she'll come home, back here, and be here for Christmas and my birthday."

Luc leaned towards Henry and took his hand. "I promise you, if I marry Sara, she will always be here for your birthday. Okay?"

Henry grinned. "Okay. Then you can marry her."

Luc beamed. "Why, thank you very much, Henry." The two of them shook hands, and Henry scurried off. In that moment, something in the back of my throat tightened, and I couldn't have spoken for all the money in the world.

Luc looked at me. He was so handsome. His eyes were shining bright blue, and his smile flashed. "He is a wonderful little boy," he said.

I could only nod. I glanced over at Carrie. She was smiling broadly.

"That's some boyfriend you got there," she said again.

I felt so happy I could have burst.

Chapter Three

IT DIDN'T TAKE LONG FOR THE story of Jack and Luc to get all over the school. Someone had actually taken a video of what happened. It was so blurry that no one could see Luc's face, but Jack was there, in all his glory, backing away and looking scared. I was afraid that Jack would somehow try to get even with Luc for making him look the fool in front of the whole school, but when I saw him the next Monday in the hall, he didn't even look at me. He completely ignored me. Then it occurred to me that the only person who had any control over Jack's behavior was the football coach. The football coach had a new assistant. And the new assistant spent a lot of time talking to Mrs. Grant.

I had chosen a Bach Partita for my audition piece. Well, one of the pieces. I had to memorize over a dozen pieces of music. I had to send in pre-screening recordings with my applications, and then had to prepare for the live auditions. And every different school had different requirements. So I was practicing Mozart one day, Bach the next, then Debussy—there were so many notes in my head, sometimes I had to just sit and try to empty my head of everything so I could hear myself breathe.

But the Partita was my favorite, and it was what I was counting on the most. I had been practicing since summer. Carole, my private instructor, thought it was perfect for me. I ran through it every night before I went to bed, no matter how many times I had played it during the day. Carrie was probably sick to death of hearing it, but she was usually good about not making cracks about my music all the time.

But one morning I found Fabienne stretched out on the couch, watching television, obviously waiting for me. "I've been listening," she said.

I frowned. "To what?"

"Bach. Last night, you nailed it. I don't know what was different, exactly, but it was perfect."

I sat down on the chair across from her. "Thanks. I mean, I didn't even think you all noticed."

She made a face. "How could we not notice? Let's face it, that's all you do."

I felt heat rise to my face. "If it bothers you so much—" I started.

She cut me off. "It doesn't. Even if it did, we are not here on vacation. We have a job to do. But we are all from France, remember, and we listened to Bach as children. We were brought up listening to musicians playing in our salon. The Partitas were always my favorites. It's been a pleasure listening to you play every night."

I stared at her. I kept forgetting that they were all much older than they looked. Possibly hundreds of years old. "Did you ever hear Bach himself play?"

She laughed. "No. I'm not quite that old, Sara. But we had a quartet that played for us once a month. My father fancied himself a composer."

"What did he write?"

She shook her head. "Nothing that was ever published. He knew he wasn't good enough. But it gave him a great deal of pleasure to hear his pieces performed once in a while."

"Is he still alive?" I asked. This was uncharted territory for me. Isabeau, Fabienne and Amelie had been living in the house for over a month now, but I knew very little about any of them.

"No. He died in 1856."

Oh.

She smiled as she got off the couch. "I want you to make sure no one tries to change your mind about your music," she said. "Someone as talented as you deserves the chance to go all the way."

"Thanks. But why would anyone try to change my mind?"

She took a deep breath. "We may be going to war, Sara. Things happen in wartime. But stay strong. Luc will always support you. This, I know. But he is not the only one who will try to influence your life."

Then she went upstairs. I smelled smoke, and when I went to the kitchen a few minutes later, there she was, a tiny, delicate lioness, half-hidden under my mother's palm tree.

Mrs. Grant wanted to see my college essay, so I made an appointment with her one afternoon after school. I usually practiced after my last class. I stayed in one of the practice rooms, usually for an hour or so. Sometimes I played with other students, sometimes not. Luc had started picking me up after school, and he would sneak in and sit and watch me practice. I'm used to people watching me play, but with him in the small room, I felt different. There was an electricity in the air, and my playing seemed more intense. The people I played with noticed it, and started teasing me about it. I laughed and shrugged it off, like it was no big deal, but it was. As long as I can remember, people always thought I had all sorts of boyfriends, and there were always comments made about me and some guy because he called me or asked me out or followed me around at school. I never paid any attention to the boys, or what was said about them.

But this was different. Luc was my boyfriend. No one had ever teased me about a real boyfriend before. It felt wonderful.

Mrs. Grant waved me into a seat and took the essay from my hand. She read slowly, and made several notations with a red pen. Then she read the whole thing over. Twice.

"This is good, Sara," she said at last. "A few things to tweak, but very well done. And your audition pieces?"

"They're coming along fine. I've got them all memorized. Carole, my private teacher, has been working with me. She says I'm doing well. We have an appointment at a small studio to do the recordings that are due in December, then I can concentrate on the live audition work. My main piece is Bach. I should be more than ready."

She smiled serenely. "I love Bach. He was a lovely man. Anything else?"

I looked at her carefully. She still didn't know that I knew she was

Luc's mother. We had been meeting once a week over one thing or another, and I had a real respect for her. She was a Queen, and the fate of an entire race had rested on her shoulders. That, I realized, was her number one priority. In all the conversations we had, and through all the questions she had asked me, I knew that she liked me, and might even grow to love me, but her responsibility to her Family would always come first.

"It's going fine. Once I get all these applications and prescreening recordings sent out, I'll be able to relax, but I feel like it's all under control."

"Good." She smiled and tilted her head to one side. "And your personal life?" she asked lightly.

"Ah." What was I supposed to say? I mean, he was her son. Was I supposed to tell her about the last time we kissed, and I felt a tingle in all sorts of inappropriate places? "It's good."

"I'm very happy," she said quietly. "For both of you. I think that's all I need for today. We'll talk again next week, okay?"

I nodded and gathered up my books. I was having dinner with Dad tonight. It was the first time we were going to have a chance to talk since he had met Luc. I was a little nervous and excited to hear what he had to say.

Garth picked up Carrie, along with Fabienne and Amelie from the house, and drove us all to the restaurant. The sisters sat at the bar while Carrie and I went to meet Dad. Dante and Henry were with him, and I was happy to see them, but had been hoping for a little quiet time with Dad.

Carrie must have felt the same way.

"Heather not home tonight?" she asked right away.

Dad shrugged his shoulders. "She's got a new client. Some hotshot in finance has a kid who got busted on a minor drug charge. She's a little pissed off about the whole thing, because it should be an easy fix, but the father is always calling her and asking to see her. She's calling him Ball-buster Brunel."

I had been looking at the menu. I suddenly felt cold. Had I just heard right?

"Brunel?" Carrie asked. She had heard the same thing. This could not be a coincidence.

"Yeah. Some foreign guy, Heather says. Apparently he's very

handsome, because all the women in her office are going crazy whenever he comes by, but Heather thinks there's something strange about him."

I lowered the menu and looked at Carrie. She seemed completely calm. She smiled at me.

"Sara—I forgot to tell you—Mom said she needed to talk to you. Have you got your cell?"

Thank God for Carrie. My brain was so rattled that I was starting to shake. "Yeah. I'll call her now, thanks. But I think I'll take it in the restroom." Henry and Dante were both staring at me. Was I doing something wrong? So I made a face at them. "This way, if she starts yelling at me about something, you guys won't have to hear it too," I said, and Henry grinned.

I walked to the Ladies room and speed-dialed Luc. "Luc, listen. Something's happened. My Dad's wife, Heather? She's a lawyer, and she has a new client named Brunel."

Luc was silent for a moment, then I heard him say something very quickly in French, muffled, like he was speaking over his shoulder. "Where are you now?" he asked.

"We're eating with Dad and the boys. Your cousins are at the bar. Garth is outside in the car."

"Okay. This is very interesting information. We'll look into this. Enjoy your dinner. I love you, Sara."

"Thank you, Luc," I said, and closed the phone. I made my way back to the table, glancing at the girls at the bar. Fabienne had her phone to her ear. I sat back down.

"Okay?" Dad asked.

I nodded, and we ordered. The boys were full of news, as only little boys can be, and Dad let them ramble until the food came. Then he looked at them seriously.

"Okay, you two, I want you to eat very slowly and not say a word until every bite is gone. I need to talk to your sisters, and I do not want to be interrupted. Got it?"

They both nodded and started to eat. Dad smiled down at them, then turned to us.

"Alone at last," he joked. "How have you both been?"

"Did you like Luc?" I asked.

Dad smiled. "He's quite the interesting young man. Very smart. He seems, I don't know, old-fashioned? More than that, really. Almost like from another century. We were talking about the international economy, of all things, and he was amazing. He had this grasp of international politics, but from a very interesting perspective. Like some old Roman prince. Where on earth did you find him?"

I almost choked on an onion ring. I had an elaborate story all worked out, but I was afraid I'd get caught on the details, so I just kept chewing.

"He's actually with Abbott," Carrie said at last. "Abbott is kind of an, um, friend to Luc's family. And since Abbott met Mom, he introduced Luc to us. And bingo—Luc was smitten. That's my word, by the way."

Dad smiled. "Wow, that's a great word. And a great story. So Abbott is, what, seeing your mother? How did they meet?"

I swallowed. I could answer this one. "Mom kind of ran into him. Not hard, of course, but he took notice." There. I didn't even have to lie.

Dad nodded a couple of times. "I'm glad for your mother. He seems very nice too. The accent is very cool." He was trying to be nonchalant. "Is he smitten too?"

Carrie had her mouth full, but she managed, "Big time."

Dad shrugged. "Well, then Carrie, that leaves you. How's your love life?"

Carrie swallowed, and frowned. "Well, I've kind of got my eye on somebody, but I'm not sure if he's noticed or not. I think I've got a pretty good shot, though."

I glanced over at her in surprise. Did she mean Chris?

Then we started talking about college stuff, and Carrie's soccer playing, and it was almost like old times, when the three of us would sit together at the table while Mom was making dinner, and we'd talk about our day. It had been a long time since we'd done that. But the boys were getting restless, and Henry started whining about dessert, so Carrie and I got up from the table and gave hugs and kisses all around.

We were walking out of the restaurant, and had stopped in the glass-enclosed vestibule, when a very beautiful girl suddenly came in from outside. It was like she appeared out of nowhere. She was tall and thin, with impossibly golden hair and dark eyes. She smiled, showing brilliant white teeth.

"Have you the time?" she asked.

Carrie pulled out her cell phone to check the time, and as I glanced outside, I saw Garth running towards us, his face white. Suddenly, Fabienne and Amelie burst thru the door behind us. Fabienne immediately put herself between the girl and me. Carrie took it all in in a heartbeat, and pulled me back into the corner. The beautiful girl never stopped smiling.

"A long time," she said to Fabienne. Her voice was low and soothing. "You're looking well. And how is Marc?"

Fabienne lunged for the girl. Garth was through the door, and he picked Fabienne up in a smooth motion and pushed her back against the wall where Carrie and I stood, watching. Amelie was there, looking very tough and completely in control.

"Go away, Renata. Find another place to eat tonight."

The girl, Renata, shrugged. "As far as I know, we are still allowed to dine in whatever public place we choose. Has something changed?"

Amelie shook her head. "You're not fooling anyone, Renata. Go back to your sick uncle and tell him he's being more of an idiot that usual. Leave us all alone."

Renata shrugged, turned and walked out of the restaurant. Carrie and I stared at each other for a minute, then Carrie said to Fabienne, "Are you okay? "

Garth was pushing us all out the front door. "Let's get home," he said quietly. "Now."

Fabienne was on her cell phone again, and we practically ran to the car. Garth drove quickly, and kept glancing in the rearview mirror.

"Who was she?" I asked.

"That girl," Amelie said, "is George Brunel's niece, Renata. She's ruthless and completely evil."

Carrie frowned. "Who's Marc?"

Fabienne made a sound. Her sister answered quickly. "Someone Fabienne used to know. Renata destroyed him."

We drove the rest of the way in silence. I was tempted to ask them more about Marc, but didn't have the nerve. I had lots of questions, especially now that my Dad was involved through Heather.

But I wouldn't have long to wait for answers. The minute we got into the house, Mom told us that Luc would be coming for dinner

Friday night.

And his mother was going to be with him.

They arrived right on time. Luc was in a dark suit and looked so handsome I could hardly catch my breath. Abbott and Toad came through the door next. And then came Luc's mother.

She did not look at all like Mrs. Grant. Instead of a sensible suit, she was wearing something obviously designer. Her hair was swept up, and her eyes were glittering with pride and power. She had a stunning diamond necklace on, with diamond earrings the size of hazelnuts.

She looked at me coolly, then winked.

Abbott was making introductions, very formal, but she waved them aside.

"Abbott, I know it's your job, but really." She came forward and kissed Mom on the cheek.

"Maggie, it's a pleasure to meet you at last. I know I'm a queen and all, but please, don't let this impossible man intimidate you. I'm Violetta. I want to apologize for everything that my over-zealous Family has put you through the past few months. You and your daughters are obviously made of much sterner stuff than we thought. Good for all of you."

She looked Carrie up and down, and Carrie stared back. A smile crossed Violetta's lips.

"Carrie, I've been watching your soccer playing. If you live your life the way you play that game, you'll leave us all in the dust."

Carrie grinned.

She turned to me, and gave me a sudden hug.

"I was so worried," she said at last. She was looking me right in the eye. "It's not that I don't trust my son, because I do. In all things. But love is a tricky one. But I shouldn't have worried. You're a lovely woman and you'll be a perfect fit."

She turned to Abbott. "Be a love, and make Maggie and I drink. I'm told you know your way around quite well. Go on, be useful. I'll have some wine, and I'm sure you know what Maggie likes. We have some serious business to discuss, and it's best to get it out of the way first, so we can all enjoy dinner."

Abbott nodded briefly and went off into the kitchen. Mom, smiling now, led the way into the living room.

It felt like a play. I was center stage with Luc. Amelie had made me a beautiful cocktail dress, pale lavender silk that reached nearly to my knees so when I sat down I didn't have to tug at the skirt. Luc was glowing, radiating a kind of power. Toad and Abbott were staying in the background. Mom and Violetta were all smiles, but you could feel the steel undercurrent. Carrie hung back, but you knew that she saw and heard everything.

"To begin with," Violetta said, sipping her wine, "Sara needs to narrow her focus for school. Michigan, California and Chicago are no longer options. We're going to have to keep her close to New York. Hartford is good, and of course Juilliard and Eastman. But we can't scatter our resources."

My heart fell. I had been excited about Chicago. Three girls from All-State Band had gone there this year, and they had all raved about it.

"We are also concerned about Heather Fleming," Violetta said. "Her law firm has taken on not only George Brunel as a personal client, but it seems there has been some corporate work being thrown their way as well. The original contact was about defending Brunel's son against a drug charge. George Brunel does not have a son, so the entire thing was a set-up. Obviously, Brunel is trying to find another way to get close to Sara, and working through her father is a very smart, if obvious move."

"I don't want my brothers put in danger," I said.

Abbott spoke up. "They are not in danger. Our concern is that if you tell your father about any plans you may have, then it may very well get back to Brunel. So we need you to cancel the concerts in St. Louis. And Philadelphia."

I turned to Luc. "I can't back out of those," I said hotly. "These performances are by invitation only. I won't turn those down now. I've got music schools to think about, and I can't start pissing people off."

Luc smiled gently. "It will be difficult to protect you," he said.

"That's not my problem," I said. "You knew about these concerts before, and you never said I couldn't go. I need to be in St. Louis right after Thanksgiving. And in Philadelphia the week after that."

Luc looked over at Abbott and Toad and shrugged. "Make the necessary arrangements," he said.

There was an awkward pause. Carrie rolled her eyes at me. I knew what she was thinking, that I was being a real brat, but I didn't care.

Violetta took a deep breath. "And we also want the wedding to take place this spring."

I looked at Luc again. Spring?

Mom cleared her throat. I could tell she was thinking very carefully before she spoke. "I don't think there's a problem with Sara applying to fewer schools. I know that Juilliard was at the top of her list, as was Hartford. The application process for these schools is exhausting, and flying out to Chicago and the rest for auditions would have been a big expense. So I'm on your side there." She looked at me and took a deep breath. "But I'm not going to allow my daughter to marry a man she doesn't know. I have been trying very hard to be patient about all this, because you and your Family are obviously serious about this entire thing. But this is the United States in the twenty-first century. That so-called vow may have power in your world, but not in mine. Sara will marry who she wants, when she wants. She's an eighteen-year-old student. Legally, she can do what she wants, and if that's her choice, fine. But if it's not, nothing you can say or do can force her to marry Luc."

Violetta narrowed her eyes. "Your daughter is in a very dangerous position."

"Which your son put her in. Without her knowledge. My understanding is that she's a target because Luc chose her. If your Family cannot keep her safe, then I strongly suggest that Luc 'choose' another person to marry, and then you can go and bully her."

Luc looked at me, his eyes going wide. Violetta made a noise.

"That cannot be done," she said.

Mom looked cold. "Why not?"

Abbott cleared his throat gently. "It's not that it can't be done, exactly. We really don't know if it can or not. This has never been an issue in the past."

"You people had better figure this out. Sara's not marrying anyone until she feels it's right."

There was a huge, gaping silence. I could feel the blood thrumming in my ears. I looked at Mom. Her face was set. I knew that expression. Violetta had as much a chance of changing Mom's mind as she did of going to the moon. Carrie's eyes were blazing. She was loving this.

"Well," Abbott said at last, "this is interesting. Maggie, I think you need to know that our ability to protect Sara is dependent on her marrying. If Sara marries, then she becomes a member of the Family and is protected by our treaties. The Brunel Clan cannot harm her for fear of starting a war that no one wants. We have been very successful so far, and I'm sure that we can maintain the safety of all of you for as long as need be. In fact, once Sara moves out of the house and goes off to school, the threat to you and Carrie disappears. But keeping Sara safe is going to become more difficult."

"What do they want?" Carrie asked. She suddenly moved forward, and was looking down at Violetta. "What would they go to war to get?"

Violetta sighed and shrugged her shoulders. "They want to come out of the shadows. They want to stop being the creatures of legend. They want to walk among the peoples of the world as a recognized race. Can you imagine a world like that? Do you think we could survive a world like that? A world where the stuff of deepest nightmares is suddenly real?"

We all sat in silence. Smokey appeared out of nowhere and jumped up on Violetta's lap. She stroked his back gently.

"The Brunels," she said softly, "are the oldest and most powerful of the vampire Clans. They have been kept in check for centuries. Not just by us. All the dark beings left in the world understand that once they are acknowledged, once all the bogeymen are found to be living, breathing creatures, there will be panic. There will be much bloodshed. Which is why the Brunel will not break the treaty themselves. If they do, none of the other Clans will support them. But if we break the treaty, then all those living in the dark will rise up behind them. We cannot allow that to happen." She gently ran her finger along Smokey's throat, and she smiled as he purred. "We might not survive a thing like that."

"So that night, back in August, when those vampires came here," Carrie said, looking at Toad, "they were not Brunels. So the treaty remained intact even though you ate one of them?" She stopped and made a face. "I shouldn't have said that, right?"

There seemed to be an awkward silence. What was Carrie talking about? I knew that a vampire came to the door, but what else had happened?

Mom was confused too. "Honey, what do you mean?" she asked.

Abbott looked uncomfortable. "On the night in question, there was a bit more, ah, activity then I may have told you," he said to my mother. "Toad intervened in the situation, and a vampire was, ah, decapitated."

Mom went white. She glared at Abbott, and was about to say something, but Violetta interrupted.

"That particular night is something of a puzzle to us. The vampires involved were apparently not from the Brunel Clan. If they were, Brunel would have undoubtedly made a huge stink, even though, technically speaking, Toad was acting in the defense of three innocent people, which makes his actions in compliance with the current treaty. They have remained silent, which leads us to think that there may be other, smaller Clans acting outside the sphere of the Brunel's influence. What happened at the playground was something else we can't explain, and Stefan Brunel's involvement in the mall incident is worrisome. He must think danger is imminent if he's willing to interfere in such a manner. That is not a good thing." Violetta shrugged.

"The one at the restaurant," Carrie said suddenly. "Renata. She's the crazy one, right? What if she is acting on her own? If she doesn't care about the treaty anyway, it wouldn't matter to her if Sara was married or not."

Nobody said anything. Abbott and Toad looked at each other.

Violetta stared at Carrie. "That's true. But if we reacted against Renata, it would still be considered breaking the treaty."

Abbott cleared his throat. "If Sara were taken, even if it was an action independent of the Brunel Clan, and outside the treaty, someone might do something rash to get her back."

I glanced at Luc. He was staring down at our clasped hands.

"Luc," I said, "you must promise me. You cannot start a war. Your mother is right. It would be too terrible. Please."

Luc looked up at me, and his beautiful eyes were full of such anger I drew back. This is how he must have looked at Jack, I thought. That look would frighten any living thing.

"Please," I whispered.

Luc squeezed my hand. "Then we will have to work extra hard to protect you."

I looked at him. Only at him. "Can you do what Mom said? Choose someone else?"

He shook his head. "I do not think that is possible."

"I'm just beginning to know who you are, Luc." I said. It was hard to look into his eyes and say things that hurt him, but I had no choice. "And I know that you're a good man. But I don't love you. I can't marry you if I don't love you. I just can't."

He squeezed my hand again, gentler this time. "I know that. I am so sorry to have done this to you. But know that I do love you. This is a true feeling in my soul. Even if I said the words to someone else, it would not change a thing, because they would be just words. I cannot change my heart. I can only hope you can change yours."

There was another huge silence. Toad cleared his throat. "We'll have to take extra precautions. We may have to be a little more intrusive. Maggie, we've tried to keep things as normal for you and your family as we could, but that may have to change. Any travel Sara does will be via the Family jet. We have safe places around the country for her to stay. Hotels are out of the question. Luc, if you and Sara want to spend time together, it will be here or at the condo. Understood?"

Luc nodded.

My mother let out a long, deep breath. "Well then. If we're finished here, let's have dinner."

Chapter Four

ERIN CARSON WAS THE CLOSEST thing I had to a best friend. We'd sat next to each other in concert band since the fifth grade. She didn't mind that I was a music freak. In fact, I think she was actually proud of me. We didn't hang out together a lot outside of school, but she was the person I sat with at lunch and we always managed to have classes together. Because of her, I had a group of girls to be around when I needed to step outside of myself. She also loved clothes, just like me. We spent lots of time texting about where we were shopping.

She nudged me at lunch. "Where did you get that jacket?" she asked. "It looks amazing. And I did not see it in Forever 21."

"It's vintage," I said. That was almost the truth. I had seen a maxi-skirt from the 70's on eBay, sage green with dusty roses on it. I bought the skirt and Amelie made a tight-fitting jacket out of the fabric, with a ruffle below the waist and slightly puffed sleeves. It fit like a glove and looked amazing with a lace cami and straight-leg jeans.

"Where are you shopping vintage?" she asked. "Or is that going to be another one of your big secrets?"

I looked at her in surprise. "What do you mean?"

"Well, you never tell me anything anymore. You've got this hot boyfriend that you never talk about, but he shows up and blows away Jack Keller like some kind of superhero. Your sister is an uber-jock with the girls' soccer team, but you never show up for her games. Ethan Sullivan, cutest junior ever, is making a big play for Carrie, and you won't even give me the inside scoop. What the hell is wrong with you these days?"

"Ethan and Carrie? Really?"

Erin snorted and shook her head. "Please don't tell me you don't know. Ethan is a huge catch, and he's been panting after your sister, who, by the way, has been polite and friendly and nothing more. I thought it was because of the new kid, Chris, but she doesn't seem to be hooking up with him either. I'm usually not concerned with the romantic goings-on of underclassmen, but Ethan is a big deal. And Carrie is your sister. So I'm keeping an eye on the situation."

I stared down at my half-finished lunch. "I've been busy getting ready for my auditions," I said, feeling suddenly miserable.

Erin nudged me until I looked up into her eyes. "You have always been busy with your music," she said. "Ever since the fifth grade. But you've always had a life, too, with me and a few other friends who care about you. But lately you've blown everyone off. I can see where a guy like Luc would be a major distraction, but I miss you, you know? And Carrie is your sister, for God's sake. You should at least be paying attention."

It suddenly felt like too much. My eyes filled with tears that came out of nowhere, and my throat started to close. "I'm so sorry," I choked out. "I've been a crappy friend lately, haven't I?"

Erin made a noise. "God, Sara, stop. You don't have to feel that badly about it, honest." She put her arm around my shoulder and gave me a shake. "Stop crying, sweetie. Please?"

But I couldn't. Everything suddenly felt like it was pouring out of me. My shoulders started to shake and I could hear myself sobbing. I put my hands over my face and tried to stop, but I couldn't. After a minute of two, I heard a calm, quiet voice in my ear. Violetta. She raised me up and walked me out of the cafeteria.

I don't even remember walking down to her office, but when I finally stopped crying, I was sitting in her office, crumpled tissues in my hand, my face almost dry. She was sitting quietly, watching me.

I took a final sniff. "Thank you."

"You're welcome. Should we talk?"

I nodded. "What happened to Carrie that night? "

Violetta told me. How a vampire tried to get into the house. How Carrie and her friends had been driven out of the house, into the street and chased. How Chris tried to save them. How Toad killed one of them. I listened in amazement. I knew nothing about what was really happening. People were in danger, and I kept thinking it was all a real-life fairy tale.

"I think," I said slowly, "that people have to stop trying to protect me from what's going on."

Violetta looked at me. "Your life is complicated. We're just trying to make things as easy as possible."

"Yes. And while you're making sure I have plenty of time to practice playing my flute, my baby sister is getting chased down a street by strangers who want to kidnap me."

She sighed. "I know you think we are being cold-hearted," she said, "but this is how I have kept the Family intact for generations. Luc had chosen you, and you are the most important thing right now. You alone. Your sister is in no real danger. That incident was a mistake, and the Brunel Family never makes the same mistake twice."

"But if this is Renata, and she's not playing by the rules, then maybe Carrie is in danger."

"We've thought of that," she said softly.

I stared at her. "Carrie's playoff game is Thursday. I haven't watched her play all fall. I want to see her."

She nodded. "Fine. We know what precautions to take. Maybe I will see you there."

I got up and left her office in a bit of a daze. I had to lean against the wall for a moment just to steady myself. How did everything get so complicated? I had thought that the toughest thing about this year was going to be my audition.

I started down the hallway and saw a familiar figure. I called out, and Ethan Sullivan stopped and waited for me to catch up.

"How's it going?" he asked. "Applied to any schools yet?"

I shook my head. "Nothing 'till after Thanksgiving. I need all my prescreening materials in by December first. Then I have to schedule an audition. It's complicated."

"Yeah, I bet." He glanced quickly at me, and then away. "Is your sister dating Chris?"

I tried to hide a grin. "No. They're just friends. She's big on baby birds and lost puppies, and he is the new kid on the block."

He nodded to himself. "She's got a big game this week."

"Yep. I'm going. Will I see you there?"

He grinned. God, he was cute. "Yeah. Probably. Here's my class. See you."

I ran to the cafeteria and gathered my stuff, and just made class by the sound of the bell.

I had a concert band rehearsal right after school, and Carrie was playing soccer at seven. I knew I'd have to blow off homework, but I didn't care. Luc brought sub sandwiches for dinner, and after we ate them he walked me from the music rooms outside to the soccer field. It was almost Halloween, and starting to get cold.

I could see there was quite a crowd and I felt a little pop of pride. Carrie had proven herself to be a real star on the team, and they had been winning all season. I scanned the bleachers and quickly found Chris, saving our seats, and, of course, Toad a few rows behind. Fabienne and Amelie were huddled together right by the entrance to the field, and they had their heads down, phones out, texting. I scrambled up next to Luc who dragged my backpack behind him. My legs were chilled under my tights, and as I sat down on the cold metal, I shivered. Luc put his arm around me, pulling me close. He felt warm and solid, and he gave me a lingering kiss on the lips. That warmed me right up.

"Are we winning?" I asked Chris.

He nodded. "Your sister's really quick. She has scored once and the center forward, you know, the blond one, also scored. The other team doesn't have a chance. I watch a lot of soccer. I can always spot the winner."

I grinned happily and watched Carrie race up the field. She was all speed and grace and determination out there. I glanced around. Kevin and Becca were in the first row, standing up and shouting. I turned back to say something to Luc, but the look on his face stopped me cold.

"What's wrong?" I asked loudly.

Then, both Luc and Chris stood up, as though they were listening for something above the noise of the crowd. Luc turned, grabbed my wrist, and started pulling me down the bleachers.

"What?" I yelled. I pulled on my arm and Luc turned to face me. His eyes, his beautiful blue eyes were very dark and had a dangerous glint to them. His jaw was set. "What?" I asked again. I couldn't hear him. But I could read his lips.

"They're here."

We were running. Toad materialized next to me, and Fabienne and Amelie were in front of us, leading the way off the field. I focused on the back of Luc's head. He was here with me. Toad was here. I was safe.

We ran out toward the parking lot. I knew that Garth usually parked the Volvo on the other side, by the entrance to the school. But when we got into the parking lot, Toad thrust a set of keys into Luc's hand, and we ran to Luc's Porsche, parked facing outwards, right by the street entrance. Luc opened the door and I scrambled in the back seat. Fabienne came in from the other side and sat beside me. Amelie slid into the front seat beside Luc. Luc slammed the car door and started the engine. We were creeping along with the line of traffic going out to the road. No one spoke. Luc was breathing heavily, and the sisters were staring out the windows.

Once onto the street, Luc gunned the engine, and we passed several cars. He turned quickly down a side street.

Fabienne was staring into her cell phone. I could see a tiny map on the screen.

"Next left," she said shortly.

Luc turned.

"Three blocks, then left again."

We drove. I tried to look around Luc to see the speedometer, then decided I didn't want to know how fast we were going.

"Merde," said Amelie, looking out the window.

Someone was running next to the car. A beautiful blonde girl in a gray tee shirt was alongside the car, her arms moving effortlessly as she kept pace with the car. I knew her. It was Renata Brunel. I turned my head. There was another person, a very handsome man, on the other side of the car. He was also running, gracefully and impossibly fast.

"Where did Chris go?" I asked.

Fabienne shrugged. "I think he stayed behind."

I breathed a sigh of relief. He stayed behind. With Carrie. He stayed to protect her. Thank you, Chris.

"Where's Toad?" I asked.

Amelie twisted around to look behind us. "He and Garth are right behind," she said. "Others are watching if we need help."

"Why isn't Toad with us?" I asked her. Luc was driving very fast, making sharp turns as Fabienne gave him directions. Renata was still outside of the car, smiling at us as she ran.

Amelie nodded to the vampires outside. "They will try and wreck the car. If that happens, Toad will need to be able to get to us." She looked at me. "If Luc crashes into a tree, no treaties have been broken. If any of us are hurt, we cannot keep them from taking you from the car. But Toad would still be able to protect you." She flashed me a smile. "But don't worry. Luc is a very good driver, even at this speed. He loves this. The excitement. We need to get you to a safe house. They are probably watching your home. We can't go there."

I felt my chest tighten. "Mom is home. She didn't come to the game."

"Don't worry about your Mother. Isabeau is there."

I nodded. Isabeau was always at the house. She never came with us anywhere. She was always watching. And waiting.

Amelie's phone chirped as she received a text message. "The road is blocked ahead,' she said calmly. "We need to turn around."

I closed my eyes and heard a squeal of brakes. I felt the car spin, and my stomach lurched. When I opened my eyes, we were heading in the opposite direction. We sped past the Volvo.

"How did you know the road was blocked?" I asked.

Amelie shrugged. "I told you. Others are watching everything that happens. Remember, we can fly."

I glanced out of the window, upwards into the dark sky. They were watching us. I took a deep breath.

There was a sudden noise, loud and hard, as though something had fallen on the roof of the car. I shrank back against the seat.

Someone was crawling down the front of the windshield from the roof of the car. I could see two arms come down, fingers splayed out against the glass. Luc sped up the car. We were in a residential neighborhood, with no traffic, and he was going very fast. I realized that whatever was coming down the roof would block Luc's vision.

Luc knew that too, because he slammed on the brakes. We all were thrown forward, and so was whatever was on the roof.

The vampire shot off forward and onto the hood of the car, but somehow managed to grab hold of something, because instead of being flung into the street, it clung to the hood and turned. The vampire was the same one who had been running with us, with a handsome face that pressed against the glass and grinned at all of us. Luc slammed the car in reverse and, looking over his shoulder, hit the gas again. I stared at the vampire's face. I could see it clearly by the dashboard lights. It was a beautiful face, perfectly formed, with white teeth that gleamed.

Amelie opened the car window and pulled herself up and out of the opening until she could grab the vampire by the arm. Fabienne reached forward to grab the back of her sister's jeans, keeping her from falling out of the window. The vampire snarled and tried to shake her off, but could not.

"Now," Amelie said. Luc slammed on the brakes again, and this time Amelie pulled against the vampire and it shot off the hood, vanishing in the darkness beside the road. I could hear a thump, and a sickening crack. She slipped back in the open window, and refastened her seatbelt.

"Good," she said.

There was a whooshing sound, and a huge figure dropped down next to the car. It was a dragon, shining silver in the streetlights, wings folding against its body. A dragon meant a warrior. A warrior had been circling above us. But he hadn't been needed.

Luc opened the window and said something in French, and the dragon spread its wings and lifted off into the night. Luc put the car in gear and shot forward again. It all happened in seconds.

My jaw dropped. I felt dazed. They were operating like a well-oiled machine, each knowing their role. "How do you know what to do?" I asked. "Have you been practicing this?"

Fabienne shook her head. "We have been fighting vampires for thousands of years," she said. "We know how they think. We have always known what to do."

"Where are Toad and Garth?" I asked.

Amelie shrugged. "They must have been stopped," she said shortly. "Luc, head for the highway."

In another minute we were on the ramp to Route 80. There were no longer vampires running alongside of us. There was no sign of Renata Brunel. I started to feel better. It would be hard for anyone to catch us here on the Interstate. There was too much traffic, for one thing, too many cars for even the fastest vampire to run without being in danger.

"Fabienne?"

She jerked her head around, her eyes wide

"How can they run so fast?" I asked. "And the way he clung to the hood, like a spider or something..."

She smiled grimly. "It's part of what they are. Luc, get off again."

Luc nodded and darted back into the right lane.

"Wouldn't it be safer to stay with all these other cars?"

Fabienne shook her head grimly. "They will create a situation. They will make the other drivers think that something has happened—an accident, a fallen tree, something. Traffic will slow down to a crawl and we will be trapped."

I stared at her, horrified. "They'll make a tree fall on the highway?"

She shook her head again. "No. They will just make all these drivers think so. A vampire cannot make something happen. But it can make a person think that it has happened. And that is just as dangerous."

We were off the highway. Fabienne was giving Luc directions again. Amelie got another text.

"Toad and Garth are fine, but the car is wrecked. We have to get to Montclair."

"What's in Montclair?" I asked.

"A safe house," she said.

Fabienne reached over to hold my hand. "Understand, this is what we were born to do," she said. "We have been protecting the Family for generations. We are very good at it. Don't worry."

Montclair was a beautiful town filled with older, gracious homes. In less than ten minutes, we were pulling into the driveway of a huge Tudor house. Lights blazed out of every window. Luc turned off the car and we all sat in silence. Then, Toad came out of the shadows, and Garth reached down to open the car door.

Toad put out a hand and helped me out of the car. I fell against him gratefully. "I'm so glad you're okay," I sputtered. "Thank God you're here. But I thought the car was wrecked."

Toad gave me a crooked smile. "It was." He glanced upward. "I took a short-cut."

I turned to Luc. He put his arms around me and I felt myself starting to shake. All the terror of the past half hour suddenly hit me. I felt cold and sick. He scooped me up in his arms and carried me inside. I had buried my face in his shoulder, trying to calm my ragged breath and racing heart. He held me quietly until the trembling stopped and my breathing became normal. When I finally looked up at him, his eyes were serious.

"I told you, I would keep you safe," he said simply. "I love you."

I felt my eyes fill with tears. "I know."

And I suddenly thought, I love you, too.

PART THREE

WINTER

CHAPTER ONE

ETHAN SULLIVAN WAS PROBABLY THE main reason I stayed on the Girls Varsity Soccer Team.During the first week of school, after a practice, on a day I was thinking very seriously about quitting, he did a story on me for the school paper. Well, not me, exactly. The story was on the whole team, but his leading question to each and every girl was asking them how they felt about me, a mere sophomore who had not played Junior Varsity the year before, playing on the team.

He's a good actor, by the way, because he managed to ask all his questions with a very straight face. Like he hadn't been watching for the past two hours how those girls treated me. Never a word of encouragement. Completely ignoring me if I signaled I was open for the ball. Pretending I didn't score four times during our twenty minute scrimmage. I mean, it was obvious how they felt about me.

But they couldn't say how they felt, could they? So, they all lied. Talked about what a nice kid I was, and how I was a real team asset. After about six or seven of them had to say the same things, I think they started believing in them. Because the next week, the day the article appeared, they were nice to me. And they'd been nice ever since.

So I stayed on the team and we'd been kicking serious butt all season, and we were finally heading for District playoffs, and I was kind of the star. It was so cool.

Kevin and Becca had decided to fall in love, seriously threatening our very long-standing and successful and totally non-sexual threesome. I watched as it happened in the first weeks of school. They started showing up to watch my practices, and we would walk home together. Becca told me right away when she started liking him because, she told me, she would back away if I "had my eyes on him."

I stared at her. "Me? And Kevin? No, Becca, don't worry about that. Ever. I mean he's like my brother. We used to play naked in the sprinkler when we were two. It's too creepy to even think about."

Maybe I shouldn't have mentioned the naked thing, because she looked a little freaked out, but we were two, okay? And it was our mothers' idea.

I kept an eye on them, and it took a couple of weeks, but when it happened, it happened with a bang. All of a sudden, they were joined at the hip. Lucky for me, Kevin meant it when he said he was going to be Chris' best friend, because Chris started hanging around with us all the time, so I didn't feel like a third wheel. And Chris was definitely cool. Very smart, seriously cute and he had a very wicked sense of humor. He would start making fun of someone at lunch, usually a teacher, and the whole table would be cracking up. He was also a pretty good soccer player himself, and we would talk a lot about the game. But—as great as he was, I knew the truth about him. He was a couple of hundred years old. And he could eat vampires. Every time I looked at that smiling mouth, I could imagine huge teeth snapping off someone's head.

It looked like Sara was falling for Luc. Not that I blame her. The guy was wonderful. Smart, handsome, charming and he adored her. You could tell by the look in his eyes when he watched her. She was his forever. I know—they didn't even know each other, she was just eighteen—the whole thing looked like a complete and epic fail on paper. But when you saw them together, you thought that maybe, just maybe, they were going to live happily ever after in spite of it all. I hoped so. I didn't think un-happily ever after was going to be an option for her.

I developed a major crush on Ethan Sullivan, and not just because he saved me from leaving soccer and fading into the typical underclassman obscurity. He was adorable, very nice, a good writer, and he could have a conversation with my sister without falling all over himself trying to impress her. He obviously had a great deal of self-esteem.

Ethan's a junior. He not only had a license, he had a car, a part-time job with the local throwaway paper, and about half a dozen girls hanging all over him pretty much all the time.

But I think he liked me. He's always finding me in the hallway. He'd send me short, funny texts about nothing, sometimes at seven in the morning, usually on the weekends, and I'd always be happy to read them. And he made a point of telling me that he would be watching me play right before the first of the play-off games, even though it would be cold and dark.

Kevin and Becca would be there too. And—surprise—Sara. She told me that she and Luc would be watching the game. Sara hasn't sat through any of my games. Did they put something in the water?

Dad texted me good luck, and so did Mom. Dad was working, but I think Mom and Abbott had a date. I tried not to think about the two of them too much.

I played well through the whole game. We'd faced The Knoll before, and we knew how tough they were, and we were blowing them away. I found Chris in the bleachers, and when he caught my eye he waved and pumped his fist in the air. He was such a cute guy, but my feelings about him were shaded by the fact that I knew he could sprout wings and turn to stone. I wasn't sure he was realistic boyfriend material.

During halftime I looked for Chris again, and saw that Sara and Luc were with him. Sara looked so pretty, and Luc had his arm around her. They waved and smiled, and looked so happy together. Luc was so in love with her. And Sara was starting to soften around the edges. I could tell. She was becoming warmer, less self-absorbed. She was not only nice to Isabeau and Fabienne and Amelie, she had actually started calling them by their real names.

We won the game, and we did the usual jumping up and down, then shaking hands with the other team, then headed for the locker room. I planned on getting a lift from Luc and Sara, so I didn't shower, just pulled my sweats over my uniform and started out. But then I saw Ethan by the gym door, obviously waiting for someone, maybe me, and I wished I had not only showered but also curled my hair, put on some make-up, and worn a padded bra.

He grinned when he saw me. "Great job," he said, and fell in beside me. He had been waiting for me after all. How cool was that?

"We'd beaten them before," I told him. "But they're tough."

He nodded as we walked down the hallway. "Yeah, I remember. But you only scored once in that game, no?"

"That's right. How do you remember stuff like that?"

He shrugged. "I'm a font of obscure and useless information," he said, and we laughed. "So listen," he said. "How about some coffee or something? I've got my car outside. What do you think?"

Perfect. He was asking me out on a date and I looked like crap. Why was this happening to me? Could I run back into the gym, shower, blow-dry my hair, change and be back out fast enough for him not to either fall asleep from boredom or completely lose interest?

"Me? You're asking me?" I was stalling for time. "I'm just a boring sophomore."

"Yeah, I know, but I keep hoping you'll do something interesting."

Crap, what was I going to do? Go for coffee covered in dried sweat with grass stains on my knees?

I didn't have the chance to find out.

We turned the corner and I saw Becca running towards me. I could tell right away something was wrong.

She glanced at Ethan, her face tight. "Chris said that they came for Sara," she said quietly. "Luc got her away."

My breath caught and I felt cold. "Where is Chris?"

"Outside. We're trying to get a ride home."

I broke into a run and started down the hallway. There was no cell phone service in the school building itself. If you wanted to call or text, you had to be outside.

I burst through the exit and found Kevin and Chris on the steps, both on their phones. Chris shook his head at me.

"I can't get in touch with anyone right now," he said.

Kevin also shook his head. "My mom's down in Princeton. I'm trying to get my sister to pick us up, but it's going right to voice mail."

I looked around frantically. I had to get home. There were still a few people milling around after the game, but no one I recognized.

I stood, trying to think. Who could I call to get me back to the house? I quickly looked up to the top of the school. Could I possibly signal to one of the gargoyles that were usually up there to swoop down and help?

The rooftop of the school was empty. The gargoyles were no longer there. That could not be good.

"Carrie, what's wrong?" Ethan asked quietly.

I had forgotten he was even there. I turned to look at him, my mind still racing. "I have to get home," I blurted. "Something may have happened to Sara."

He put his hand on my arm. "Okay. Don't worry. I'll take you home. My car is right here."

I blinked. "You'd do that?"

He nodded. "Of course. But what's going on? What's with Sara?"

Oh God, how can I possibly explain? "Ethan, it's complicated. Can you just give me a ride?"

He nodded again, then turned to Kevin and Becca. "You guys all coming?" he asked.

"Can we? I mean, we don't want to get you in trouble," Kevin said. In New Jersey, you only got a provisional license at seventeen. Driving with more than one passenger was not allowed, but Ethan just shrugged.

"It's just a mile or so from here, right?" he said. "Duck down. We'll be fine." He looked at Chris. "You too?"

Chris nodded.

"What are you guys," he joked as we started for the parking lot. "The Scooby Gang?"

I shot him a look. He lifted his head and our eyes met. Something in mine made him stop.

"What?" he asked.

"Nothing."

Ethan's car was a fairly new RAV4. I got in beside him, and the others piled in the back, slouched down so they wouldn't be seen.

"Where to?" Ethan asked. I gave him the address, and he turned out of the lot, heading in the right direction. My heart was pounding. They had come for Sara. But she had to be all right, I thought. Luc was with her. And Toad. Fabienne and Amelie were always with her. Of course she'd be safe. I turned around.

"Chris, why are you here? Shouldn't you have gone with them?" I asked.

His voice came out of the darkness. "I wanted to stay with you. You're probably not in danger, but I wanted to be sure."

Did that make me feel better? Yes. Absolutely.

"Ah, Carrie," Ethan asked, "why would you be in danger?"

I took a deep breath. "Ethan, you're just going to have to trust me on this. It's just a kind of family thing."

"Family thing? "What are you, in the Mafia?"

I had to laugh. "Not quite."

He made a face as he came to a stop sign. He looked over at me. "Are you trying to create an air of mystery in a feeble attempt to make me find you interesting?"

I looked at him. Was he flirting? I was trying to think of a comeback. Then there was a thump. I looked out and there, in front of the car, was a woman. A beautiful woman.

Ethan jumped. "Shit. Where did she come from?" he muttered.

Chris was opening the back door but I reached out and grabbed his arm.

"Wait," I said. "You can't start anything."

He closed the door and we sat in silence. The woman did not move. She stood, mere inches from the front of the RAV4. Ethan honked the horn gently. She still didn't move. He looked back at me.

"Seriously, is there something I should know?" he said.

"Back up," Chris ordered. Ethan frowned, put the car in reverse, and we started to back away from the woman. He turned to look over his shoulder and slammed on the brakes.

"Shit," he said again.

We looked. It was a man this time. So handsome he could have been an Abercrombie model.

I could hear Becca starting to hyperventilate.

"We're trapped," she whimpered.

Ethan threw the RAV4 in gear and turned sharply into a driveway. He turned again across the lawn, avoiding a clump of pine trees, and bounced back onto the street behind the man. He hit the gas.

"I just ruined that guy's yard," Ethan muttered. "I could get into so much trouble. And who the hell are these people?" He was yelling now. "Why are beautiful people chasing us?"

I turned to look at Chris. He was shaking his head.

"They are not Brunel," he said.

Kevin grinned. "You can tell? Just by the smell? God, that is so cool."

Becca punched him in the arm. "Nothing about this," she said between clenched teeth, "is cool."

I was trying to think. "Is it Renata?" I asked Chris.

He was frowning. I could almost hear his brain working. "I don't know. Must be."

"Who's Brunel?" Ethan shouted. He was driving very fast, away from my house, his eyes moving between the road and the rearview mirror.

"You're going in the wrong direction." I said to Ethan.

"I know," he yelled. Then he took a breath. "I know," he said again, in a normal voice. "Tell me where I should turn. And tell me who this Renata is."

"Turn right." I told him. He turned and slammed on the brakes again. A huge tree had fallen, completely blocking the road.

"Drive through it," Chris said.

Ethan turned around to stare at him. "What?"

"Ethan, he means it. There isn't a tree in the road. You just think there is," I said.

Ethan stared at me like I was a crazy person.

"Ethan, we're not trying to trick you," said Becca from the back seat. "Just close your eyes and step on the gas."

He turned to stare at Becca, then his face went white. I turned as well and saw the woman running up to us, so fast that she would be on us in seconds. Ethan whipped around to face forward, closed his eyes and stepped on the gas.

The RAV4 shot forward. There was not even a ripple as it passed through the fallen tree.

Ethan's eyes were open again and he made a sharp left. He was trying to get back to the direction of my house. I didn't blame him. If I were him, I'd want to get rid of us as soon as possible.

He was breathing fast and his knuckles were white on the steering wheel. "Who are they? If you don't tell me, I'll have to crash into a tree and kill us all," he said.

"Turn right again," I said. "They're vampires. Happy?"

As he was turning, he cut too sharply and hopped over the curb. As he did, I heard a loud crack, almost like a gunshot, and could feel the RAV4 skid to a halt.

Ethan looked around wildly. "Did they do that?" he yelled.

Chris opened the door. "No, you just blew out your tire. Come on, we're just two blocks away. We can make it."

I heard Kevin and Becca scramble out of the back, but Ethan remained where he was, hands gripping the steering wheel for dear life. I shook him gently until he turned to me.

"Ethan, if you don't come with us, the vampires might find you and suck out all your blood. So, what do you think? Coming?"

He nodded, and got out of the car.

Kevin and Becca were already halfway across the yard. They were hand in hand, moving quickly and quietly. We were less than two minutes from my house. I grabbed Ethan's hand and pulled him after me. Chris was behind us.

The air turned cold. A thick mist, almost like smoke, swirled around us. I started to run. Ethan was right behind me. Thunder rolled and lightning cracked so loudly that Becca screamed. I was freezing cold. I could see my house, just barely, through the haze. I couldn't see Chris, but knew Ethan was next to me, with Kevin and Becca just a bit ahead. Lightning flashed again, striking the ground right in front of us. Kevin and Becca never even flinched. They ran straight through the flash. I grabbed Ethan's hand again and pulled him with me.

We were at the driveway. We were safe. The house was dark, except for the porch light. There were no cars in the driveway, so I knew the house was empty, but I also knew that Isabeau was always on guard, and the front door would be open. Instinctively, I glanced up at the roof. Isabeau was not there. The small lion-like gargoyle that had been perched on the rooftop every night for the past three months was gone.

"Stop," I yelled as Kevin reached for the door. He froze and looked back at me. Chris came up behind me.

"What's wrong?" he asked.

I pointed to the empty space next to the chimney. "Where's Isabeau?"

He turned white. "Oh, no," he whispered.

The air was growing colder. My teeth started to chatter. "Is the house safe?" I asked. He shook his head and looked, for the first time since I met him, as though he did not know what to do next.

Then we heard a scream.

It was a man's voice, but it was definitely a scream. Of pain. Chris started around the side of the house, and we all followed.

The motion-sensitive spotlight Mom had installed on the back deck after the vampires attacked last August flooded the whole yard with a blue-white halogen glow. There were five beautiful people circling Isabeau. At least I assumed it was Isabeau. She had Turned, and was at least eight feet tall, a beautiful, tawny lioness with wings that flashed gold. At her feet, lying broken beneath her terrible front claws, was a body. The body screamed again.

She turned toward us and growled deep in her throat. Chris stood still, hunched his shoulders, and I smelled smoke. Ethan, standing beside me, made a harsh, gasping sound. I heard a chuckle. I looked at Kevin.

Kevin was grinning. He dug into the pocket of his jeans and pulled out a handful of small glass vials. He held out his open hand to us. "Holy Water," he said simply. "If they get close, snap off the top and throw it at them."

I pushed the vial into Ethan's hand, but I'm not sure he was paying attention. He was too busy staring as Chris dropped to all fours and sprang forward, taking down one of the vampires with a single swipe of his paw.

The remaining vampires ran. They melted away, and with them the mist and cold. The one that Chris had struck had turned to a heap of ash. Isabeau's captive, however, was still twisting, trying to get away from beneath her paw. She bent down and snapped off his head. He turned to ash. She stepped back and shook her paw delicately, as though trying to flick off the last bits of blood and ash.

There was a hissing sound behind us. I whirled around, and the woman who had chased us through the streets was standing behind us. Isabeau roared as the vampire took a step forward. I was frozen. Becca gasped. The vampire's eyes were on me, beautiful, amber eyes, and they were filled with fury and hate. I thought in that moment that she could reach out and kill me with a single touch of her fingertip, when she suddenly screamed and the side of her body began to smoke, and she backed off, screaming again, and was gone.

I realized I hadn't been breathing, and took a sudden, ragged breath. I looked at Ethan. His eyes were practically falling out of his head. In his hand was one of Kevin's vials of Holy Water. The top was broken off. He had thrown the contents at her and driven her off. He swallowed hard and looked at me in disbelief.

I started to shake. Then I started to laugh. "So Ethan," I said at last. "Am I interesting enough for you yet?"

CHAPTER TWO

ETHAN WAS SITTING AT THE dining room table, his hands folded together in front of him, not saying a word. He had been sitting like that for almost ten minutes, and I was starting to get a little worried. But there was too much else going on.

Isabeau and Chris finally both got texts at the same time saying that Sara was safe and that they should sit tight and wait for Abbott. Abbott and my mother were together and on their way. So was Toad.

Isabeau told us that the six of them simply appeared on the front steps just minutes before we arrived. She would have been happy to let them stand there, but one of them jumped on the roof and tried to snatch her, so she Turned, grabbed him, and flew into the back yard with him dangling from her claws.

"You mean he just jumped from the ground to the roof?" Kevin asked. When she nodded, he whooped with delight. Becca punched him in the arm again.

They were not Brunels, which I could see worried both Chris and Isabeau. Someone was trying to break the fragile treaty that existed between the Gargouille Family and the rest of the supernatural world. Isabeau got a lengthy text from her cousin Fabienne, and she told us what happened to Sara and Luc, and how Toad and Garth had been deliberately sidetracked, and how Renata Brunel had been seen.

"She's it, then," I said. "She's the one who's starting all the trouble. Could she be doing all this without her uncle knowing?"

Chris and Isabeau exchanged glances, and Isabeau spoke. "If that's the case, then we could be in trouble. Renata Brunel is crazy. Legitimately crazy. For centuries, her Clan has been cleaning up her small messes. If they can't control her any longer, God help us." Isabeau shook her head slowly. "They attacked Sara again with Luc right beside her. That is bad. They know who Luc is. They went after her anyway. That is so bad."

"If they were chasing Sara and Luc, why were they here too?" I asked.

Isabeau shrugged. "They were covering all their bases. If Sara came here, they would have taken her. They would have waited for her."

Becca had boiled a kettle full of water and made us all tea. I carried a cup over to Ethan, sat down across from him, and slid the cup over to where he could reach it.

"Tea?"

He looked at the steaming cup for a bit, then nodded slowly. He grasped the mug with both hands, as if to savor its warmth. He took a few small sips, and nodded his head again.

"So, Ethan, is there anything you'd like to ask me?"

He stared down into the mug.

"They were really vampires?"

I cleared my throat. "Yes."

"So vampires exist. They're not just for television anymore?"

"They were never just for television. They have always existed."

"Ah." He nodded again and drank more tea. "So. That Holy Water stuff isn't just make-believe?"

"No. It's real. You may have saved my life. Thank you."

"You're welcome. And Chris? He's not just some junior transfer?"

"Not exactly. He's a gargoyle."

"Gargoyle? Those things that are used as drain spouts on churches?"

Chris sat down beside me. "That's what we do most of the time," he said. "But once in a while we're called on for more strenuous tasks."

Ethan finally lifted his head and looked at me. "So, what are you, Carrie? A witch? Werewolf? The Good Fairy?"

"Oh, Ethan. I'm nobody. Honest. I'm just a person like you. It was

Sara, you see, who started it. Well, no, that's not right either. Luc saw Sara and fell in love. That's what started it. The rest was just being in the wrong place at the wrong time."

Ethan looked over at Kevin and Becca. "And the lovebirds? They seem very accepting of vampires and winged lions."

"Yeah, well, they were also in the wrong place at the wrong time. They're just people too. Remember what you said, earlier, about the Scooby Gang? It's kind of true. We don't have any power or magic or anything. We just sort of know people who do."

Ethan kept nodding his head. "I'm still trying to get a handle on all this. Chris is a gargoyle. So he can turn from a regular person into a winged lion? Just like that?"

I sighed. "Yes. He can also Turn into stone if he wants. And he can Turn other gargoyles into stone."

"I see. And that hot looking girl over there is also a gargoyle?"

Isabeau flashed him a smile. "That's right. Did you like the way I broke that vampire's neck?"

Ethan stopped nodding his head and turned a little pale.

"Your mother is almost here," Isabeau said, staring at her cell phone.

"Where was she?" I asked.

"With Abbott at the hotel," Isabeau answered.

Oh. I'm not sure I wanted to know that.

"Awkward," Becca muttered.

"What?" asked Kevin. Becca punched him again.

Mom came through the door and ran to me, looking frantic and disheveled. I stood up to meet her and she threw her arms around me, hugging tight.

"Mom," I said finally, "I'm fine. Honest. We're all fine."

She stepped back and tears were running down her cheeks. She glanced over at Kevin and Becca, giving them a thin smile. Then she saw Ethan and stared.

"Who are you?" she asked.

Ethan smiled and waved his hand. "Hi. Ethan. Gave Carrie a ride."

Abbott had been hanging back, speaking to Isabeau and Chris, but he stepped forward, put a protective arm around Mom's shoulders and steered her towards the couch in the living room. She sat down, her eyes never leaving his face.

"You told me they were safe," she said, her voice hoarse and breaking. "You told me I didn't have to worry."

He brushed away the tears from her cheek. It was a very tender gesture, and I felt like I was looking through a peephole at something I wasn't supposed to be seeing.

"I'm sorry, Maggie," he said at last. "No one could have seen this coming. We don't know yet what is going on, and until we get some more intelligence, we can only sit and wait. Sara is safe. Carrie is here with us now. We have to wait and see."

He stood up and motioned to Isabeau. She and Chris followed him downstairs.

Mom put her head down into her hands for a moment, then shook herself and stood up.

"Anyone hungry? I'm going to make some coffee, and I think there's pie."

"Becca made us all tea, Mom," I told her. "We're good."

She hung up her coat and disappeared down the hallway into her room. I exchanged looks with Kevin and Becca. What were we supposed to do now?

Ethan got up and walked across the kitchen and put his empty mug into the sink. He took a deep breath and leaned back against the counter.

"Okay," he said. "So, now, can you tell me anything?"

Oh, what the hell.

So I told him. Kevin and Becca had little to say, except for adding their own observations on the whole unusual cast of characters. Ethan stood silent, arms folded across his chest, listening. When I was done he ran his hands through his hair.

"Wow. Okay, so I guess this isn't something I can write up and send to the Times?"

"No," said Abbott. He was standing at the top of the stairs. I didn't know how long he had been there, but he hadn't thought to interrupt.

"No. Ethan, is it? You cannot write this up and send it anywhere. We are closer to war than we have been in three centuries." He looked at me. "George Brunel has called for a meeting. He would like you and Kevin and Becca to be there, since you are all witness to some of the events we'll be discussing. I did not mention Ethan here, because if I did, his presence would have been requested as well. Ethan, be a smart young man and chalk this entire experience up to bad sushi, and try to forget it."

Ethan suddenly grinned, and for the first time in hours looked like his old adorable self. "Are you kidding? Forget that. And tell that George guy I'm coming too. I've got plenty to say about what I've witnessed." He turned to me. "So, Carrie, I'm going out on a limb here and guessing that going out with me and getting some coffee is off the table right now, but how about after the meeting with old George? What do you think?" I could hear Kevin snort. Then I heard Becca punch him in the arm.

"That would be great, Ethan. I mean it."

"Good. So now I'm going to walk back to my car and see if I can change the tire, and then I'm going home and throwing out all my 'True Blood' DVD's."

He leaned forward and gave me a quick kiss on the cheek. "Let me know about this meeting," he said to Abbott on the way out. Seconds later, the front door slammed. I stood in the middle of my kitchen, and if it hadn't been for the fact that Chris and Isabeau were staring at me, along with Abbott, I would have squealed and done the Happy Dance all over the house.

I turned to Becca with a huge grin on my face. "Can you believe it?" I whispered.

She was grinning back at me. Kevin rolled his eyes.

"Jeez, Carrie, why so surprised? You're cute and funny, you're a jock with a hot body, and you pal around with vampire killers. You're pretty much every fan boy's dream."

Becca punched him in the arm. Again. Tough night for Kevin.

When Mom came back, her eyes were red and swollen. She made coffee. Of course. We all just kind of watched her. Abbott hung back in the living room with Chris and Isabeau, not saying a word. Finally, Kevin broke the silence.

"Auntie M, did you say something about pie?" he asked.

Mom grabbed him, threw her arms around him, and hugged him tightly. He patted her back awkwardly. When she let him go, she brought the pie out of the refrigerator. Coconut cream. She had made it the night before. We all sat down and each of us had a piece. It was delicious. We were all on our last mouthful when the doorbell rang. Fred went crazy as Toad let himself in. He scooped Fred up in his arms and sat down with us at the dining room table.

"Sara is fine. They are all safe," he said. "The house is secure and well protected. Isabeau, please spend the night here, just in case, but then go with your cousins. Your place is with Sara."

Mom threw the fork down with such force we all jumped. She didn't look scared and weepy any more. She looked pissed off.

"Those people were here, at my house. Again," she said through gritted teeth. "And they chased Sara across two counties. I talked to her, you know. She said a vampire crawled across the roof of the car while they were going about sixty miles an hour."

Toad shrugged, picked up Chris' fork, and took a forkful of pie from the pie plate. "Yes. That's true. And I know that sounds as though we weren't doing our job. But that particular vampire ended up with a broken neck, so he is out of the picture. So, apparently, are two of the six who were here tonight. And no harm was done to anyone. All in all, I'd say we had a good night." He took another bite, and glanced up at Chris. "What happened here?"

Isabeau and Chris told him. Mom's mouth became a tight, hard line, but Toad actually smiled.

"Kevin, you had Holy Water?" Toad asked. "Outstanding." Fred, sitting happily on Toad's lap, put a paw on the table. Toad clucked and dropped him to the floor.

"I hardly think," Mom said in a very small voice, "that you should be encouraging these children to participate."

Toad put down his fork, folded his hands together, and leaned across the table towards my mother.

"Maggie," he said "I'm not a parent, so I can't imagine the fear you have for your daughters. But I have watched hundreds of members of this Family fall, and each and every time I felt a piece of my soul die with them. The best thing 'these children' can do is to learn everything they can about how to protect themselves. Because if a war happens, it won't matter who you are or who you know. Everyone will be a target. Every human being on the planet will become prey. Whoever is doing this does not appear to be bothered by consequences. Even Brunel is frightened, because as much as they have fought against us for generations, they have always known the cost of war. Whoever is responsible for what happened tonight doesn't care about that. That is very bad. I hope you never have to know how bad." He sat back, picked up the fork again, and had another mouthful of pie.

Abbott cleared his throat. "Brunel wants to meet?"

Toad nodded, his eyes sweeping across all our faces. "Yes. You are all invited. This should be very interesting. We have not sat face-to-face across a table with them in almost a hundred years. Tomorrow evening. He has a house in Far Hills."

Kevin looked interested. "So, this guy is rich?" he asked.

Abbott nodded. "Beyond measure. He has acknowledged that Renata has been out of favor for some time, and has distanced herself from the rest of the Clan. Considering how she has always wanted control, this can only mean she has formed her own army. He's nervous. He made it very clear that anything she has done has been without his knowledge or approval. It could be that he's just as worried as we are."

Toad sighed, and looked very tired. "Yes, well, even if that's true, Brunel cannot be trusted." He stood up. "We're meeting at eight tomorrow night. I'll have cars sent."

Kevin and Becca stood up and started making going-home noises. Abbott stood up as well, and looked at me.

"You'll have this Ethan person here tomorrow night?" he asked.

Toad looked at me as well. "Ethan?"

"Yes," Abbott said. "It seems that Carrie has managed to involve yet another perfectly innocent young man in this mess."

"I did not," I said. I could feel my face getting red. "We just needed a ride home. It's not my fault we were chased down by vampires and then forced to witness Isabeau beheading somebody."

"Not somebody. A vampire." Isabeau said gently.

"Whatever," I said. "Not. My. Fault."

Toad threw up his hands. "Just don't be late."

The house emptied quickly after that. Isabeau found a spot by the front door and Turned. Mom and I cleaned up the kitchen in silence.

When we were done we stood and looked at each other.

"Are you afraid, Mom?" I blurted.

Her eyes filled with tears. "All the time."

"Maybe they should get married right away," I said. "Then we'd all be safe."

Mom shook her head. "I don't think so, honey. There's more to all of this than we know. I'm not sure what will keep us safe."

I crossed to her and gave her a hug. We held on to each other for a long time. When I stepped away I had a sudden, terrible thought. "What about Henry and Dante?"

She frowned. "Why would they be involved at all?"

"Because Brunel knows about Heather," I said slowly. "And maybe Renata knows about Heather too. If she's not playing according to the rules…"

Mom swallowed hard. "We'll have to ask about that tomorrow night," she said. "Among other things."

I let the dogs out the back. The yard looked peaceful, except for two small piles of ash. The wind had picked up, and most of the ash had been blown away, but I could still see the soft, gray mounds. The dogs sniffed them without interest, and came back into the house. Mom hugged me long and hard, then we both went to bed.

Chapter Three

THE NEXT MORNING, BECCA SAT next to me on the bus, as usual. Even though she and Kevin could have sat together, she chose to continue a ten-year-old tradition by sitting with me. Kevin had recently started his own tradition. He sat behind us, hunched forward, arms resting on the back of our seat, his head directly between ours. Which made it very hard to share confidences, especially about Kevin, but Becca was in love, so I didn't complain.

"So, tell me," Becca said in a low voice, leaning towards me and glancing around.

"Tell you what?" I asked, dropping the tone of my voice as well.

"What exactly do you wear to a meeting with the Number One Worst Vampire In The World?"

I thought for a minute, frowning. "A turtleneck?"

Behind us, Kevin laughed. "That's good. Turtleneck. I like it. So, does this mean we can double date with you and Ethan? I mean he has a car and everything. This could be very cool."

Becca didn't bother to turn around. "He can't have all of us in the car, number one, and number two, they're just having coffee. Don't get carried away, okay?"

"Sure," Kevin said. "Maybe I could get Chris to show him a few tricks. In case, you know, you guys are out making out somewhere and—bam—vampire attack. He was pretty good with the Holy Water, but he could use some training in evasive maneuvers."

"You're doing it again," Becca said, sounding very patient. "This is not a real-life version of your sword and sorcery on-line game. This is real. Stop having so much fun."

"Are you kidding?" Kevin made a noise. "This is so much cooler than any game. And I know Ethan, he's kind of a geek. I bet he can't wait to meet this Brunel guy."

I looked at Becca. "I love him too, but he really is a jerk about this whole thing, isn't he?"

She nodded. "Yes, I know. I'm scared to death and he's thinking up code names for each of us in case we're sent on a secret mission to kill Brunel ourselves."

I shook my head. "Does he spend a lot of time talking about that?"

She was squinting at her phone and texting, but still managed to make a noise. "Yes. He's ridiculous."

"Hey," said Kevin, "Right here, you know?"

"I guess it's a good thing he's such a good kisser," I said casually.

Becca never missed a beat. "That's the only thing that's keeping me going."

"Hey, what do you mean?" Kevin asked.

Becca and I looked at each other and tried not to laugh.

"Is Sara coming today?" Becca asked, trying to keep her voice steady.

"No, I mean it," Kevin said. He lowered his voice. "Becca, what do you mean? The only thing? And do you tell Carrie about, well, that stuff?"

"She tells me everything," I lied over my shoulder. "I called Sara this morning. She's staying in. I don't even know where she is."

"Becca, come on," Kevin's voice was a fierce whisper now. "Becca?"

She was still playing it straight. "I wonder if being chased by vampires will count as an excused absence." And then we couldn't hold it in any longer, and we both started to laugh.

Kevin finally got it and made a very rude noise.

As I got off the bus, there was Ethan, leaning against the side of the building, waiting for me. I flashed him as smile as he fell in step beside me.

"So?"

"How's your car?" I asked.

"I need a new tire, but it's okay. They were shot anyway. So what about this meeting?"

"Can you be at my house tonight by seven-thirty?"

"You bet. Listen, are you okay?"

I glanced at him. "What do you mean?"

"Well, things were pretty intense last night. No, I take that back. Things were really intense last night. I was in shock through most of it. Weren't you freaked out?"

"No. Chris was there. And Isabeau. It's their job to kill vampires. If they're around, I feel pretty safe. And I guess now I can count Kevin in with them, sort of. The Holy Water thing saved my butt. Don't tell him that, by the way. He's too full of himself right now as it is. You couldn't have been in too much shock. You thought enough to save me."

He turned slightly pink, not a good look with the red hair. "I don't even remember what I did. When I saw that woman, I just, I don't know, reacted. It was weird. I didn't even think about it." We were inside the main hallway now and he stopped by the stairs. "She was beautiful."

I shifted my backpack. "They're all beautiful, Chris says."

He looked at me then looked away. "You and Chris are pretty tight?"

"Yeah. That's what happens when you're surrounded by vampires and somebody saves your life. You get pretty tight."

He suddenly grinned. "So, I guess I have something to look forward too." Then he turned up the stairs, leaving me feeling way too happy.

The day crawled by. I ducked into the Guidance Office, but Mrs. Grant had called out for the day. No surprise there. When I finally left school, I glanced up and smiled at the gargoyles that had been perched there since September. Was I the only one who noticed that?

Apparently not.

"Were they always there?" a voice said behind me. It was some guy, a friend of Sara's, I think, and he was looking up at the roof as well. "I noticed them when school started this year. I had never seen them before. I least I don't remember them being there. Do you?"

I nodded. "Sure. They've always been there."

"Your sister said the same thing. But nobody else seems to remember them. Why is that, do you think?"

I shrugged. "No clue. See ya." And I hurried to the bus.

The house was very quiet when I got home. I had automatically checked when I came up the front walk, but Isabeau was not there on the roof where she had been sitting for what now seemed like forever. I went first into the kitchen. Fred scurried in, his nails making clicking noises on the tile floor. I grabbed a pear out of the fridge and went downstairs.

Chris was sitting on the couch, Moon curled up in his lap.

He looked asleep, his head back against the cushions. He also looked very tired and, well, old. His face seemed lined and kind of gray. He opened his eyes when I came down and smiled.

"How was your day?" he asked.

I let my backpack slide to the floor. He had not been in school. The whole day had been such a jumble, I hadn't noticed, but now I realized I had not seen him at all.

"Fine. Where were you?"

He shrugged and stared down at the floor. "I may no longer be enrolled at Mansfield. It is still under discussion. I was sitting in for some of it, but I was sent here to meet you and make sure you stay safe."

I had taken a bite of my pear, and chewed it slowly before swallowing. "Not enrolled? What does that mean, exactly?"

"I don't know. I'm not important enough to be told why. My guess is that your sister is also no longer enrolled."

I stared at him. "But she has to graduate."

"My understanding is that she has enough credits to graduate this January. Something will be worked out for her final weeks of school."

I took another bite, thinking. Sara had taken extra music and literature classes in the summers her first two years of high school, even though she had been working. I guess those were the extra credits she needed to get out early. "Does Mom know?"

He shrugged. "She's probably being told today. Abbott was a wreck this morning. He's in love with your mother, you know. I've never seen him like this. He may be replaced."

I stared at him. I didn't know what stunned me the most, the fact that Abbot might be replaced, or that he was in love with Mom. "Who would replace him?" seemed the safest question.

Chris stood up and stretched. "Somebody is flying in from London today. The same office has represented our interests for generations. Luckily, there are firms is England that have been around almost as long as we have." He flashed me a smile. "Ready for tonight? This is a big deal, by the way. It's not every day mere mortals get called into a meeting with the A-Number-One Vampire in the world."

I grinned. "Is that what his license plate says? A#1Vamp?"

His smile faded. "Carrie, we are on the brink of war, closer than we've been in centuries. Brunel is in an impossible situation. If Renata is doing all this on her own, he has to admit he can no longer control his own Clan. If she's acting on his orders, he has to admit he's been provoking us. Either way, it's bad. Having you there makes me think he's desperate."

That didn't sound good. I didn't want to think about the A-Number-One Vampire in the world being desperate.

The front door slammed open a few minutes later and I heard Sara call my name. I flew upstairs and she was standing in the living room with Abbott and a man I didn't recognize. She turned to look at me, and we ran into each others' arms.

"Are you okay?" I whispered to her.

She nodded. "Are you?"

I nodded back.

We stood apart. She looked very tired, with dark circles under her eyes, which were red-rimmed as though she had been crying. She took a deep breath and turned to the strange man who had stood there very quietly, watching us.

"Carrie, this is Monroe. Sir David Monroe. He's going to be advising us from now on."

Monroe was older than Abbott by at least ten years, and looked exactly the way a "Sir" should look—handsome, dignified and stoic. I shook his hand, then walked over and gave Abbott a hug. I think I surprised him, because it took him a few seconds to hug me back, but when he did, it was for a long time.

"What are you going to do?" I asked him when we finally stepped apart.

He cleared his throat. "Luckily for me, there is still a financial empire that needs watching. I'll be moving here from London to take care of all that. I just, well, I'd become too attached to make impartial decisions about the Family. That's why I asked a replacement to take over."

I breathed a tiny sigh of relief. At least Abbott wasn't in trouble, and his replacement was his own idea. But Sir David Monroe did not look like he'd be hanging out in our kitchen, chopping mushrooms.

"So, welcome aboard, Sir David," I said.

He cracked a smile. "Monroe, please Carrie. We are always called by our surnames."

Ah. Well then. I nodded. "Okay, Monroe. Can you give me some advice then, about what's going to happen tonight?"

Chris had come upstairs and sat down on the couch. Monroe also sat. He was short and slim, with very dark eyes and snow-white hair. He looked like he belonged on a painting by some old Dutch master.

"George Brunel is going to ask you to describe what has been happening to you over the past few months. We're fairly certain that Renata is behind everything, and that she is acting on her own. Brunel is probably thinking the same thing, but in order for him to do something as drastic as act against his own niece, he's going to need lots of proof. Just tell him the truth. Describe what you saw. Who you saw. He has no children of his own, and Renata and Stefan had always been considered his heirs. If Renata is stripped of his support, it's possible she will give up and retreat gracefully, so we're trying to present as compelling a case as possible against her."

Sara and I were sitting side-by-side on the sofa. Abbott was standing by the stairs, watching.

Chris cleared his throat. "What about going forward?" he asked. "What is going to change?"

Monroe spread his hands in front of him. "We're still working out the logistics. Sara can no longer stay here. She must be placed in a safer location. She will also not be going back to school." He looked at her with, I thought, a bit of sadness in his eyes. "I'm sorry, my dear girl, that you have been such a target. We are hoping that once Renata is, well, neutralized, your life can go back to normal. I understand you have a life that you want to get on with. The problem is that your concerts and auditions make you vulnerable and may have to be put on a back burner for now, although we will do everything to accommodate you until the situation is stabilized. Luc and Her Royal Highness are having this same discussion with your mother right now, but we thought it might be, ah, less emotional if we spoke to you girls separately."

Sara tilted her head. "Because you knew that Mom would be screaming bloody murder right about now, and you figured without her around Carrie and I would just sit here and nod our heads like two good little girls, right?" She made a noise and looked at me. "Can you believe this guy?"

I took a deep breath. "Abbott should have been a little more direct when he briefed you, Monroe."

Sara was pissed. "First of all, this is my senior year in high school. Maybe that's not a big deal where you come from, but it's pretty huge here. And for the first time, I've got a hot boyfriend, my sister is practically a star, and Jack Keller is being polite to me, all of which makes me almost popular. Plus, I've got some great clothes. If you think I'm giving all that up, you're crazy."

I stared at her in amazement. Where did this person come from?

She wasn't finished. "All those concerts and auditions you're going to try to accommodate? You damn well better. I've spent my whole life waiting for these opportunities, and I'm not going to put them 'on the back burner' now because you people can't do your jobs. When we talk to Brunel tonight, I hope you're going to show a bigger set of balls than you showed right here, because if you can't, Carrie will have to take over." She shot me a look, her eyes dancing. "Right, little sister?"

I grinned. "Right."

Monroe raised his eyebrows and looked at Abbott.

Abbott shrugged. "I tried to warn you," he muttered.

Monroe cleared his throat. "I'm not sure you appreciate the position you are in, Sara," he said.

Sara shook her head. "No, Monroe, I think you're the one who doesn't have a clue. Luc is a great guy. So far, he's been a terrific boyfriend. In fact, he's the best boyfriend I've ever had. Of course, I don't have a lot of old boyfriends to compare him to, and I'm pretty sure none of the guys I ever dated before would know how to evade a gang of vampires who were stalking me, but then, vampires were never an issue until Luc. We're not getting married anytime soon. Even if I was madly in love with him, I certainly wouldn't want to be married at eighteen." She took a deep breath " You people have got to pull your heads out of the nineteenth century and get a grip. So let me tell you a few things. You have to keep me safe. You have to keep my family safe. And my dogs and the cat. I do have a life I'm supposed to be living, and you are not to interfere with that any more than you already have. And when I see that Brunel guy tonight, I will make sure he understands that all of this is mess belongs to the Gargouille Family, not me. So, since you're in charge of the advising end of things now, maybe you should go to Her Highness and tell her exactly what HER position is."

I looked at Sara in complete awe. "Amen, sister."

She shook her head. "I am SO done with this crap," she muttered. "Imagine me having to do this when I should be getting ready for St. Louis."

"Yeah, but—seriously? Private jet?"

She grinned. "I know. Way cool." She gave Monroe a hard stare. "St. Louis is a month away. After tonight, I expect everything to start to fall back into place. If I still need the jet to get there, fine. But I am going. Luc knows I'm going, and supports my decision. So start getting a plan together. And as far as me leaving school? Try again. If I need to leave in January, fine, but I certainly am going back next week and will attend all my classes just like I've been doing all along."

Monroe's mouth turned into a hard, thin line. "Sara—"

"And another thing," she said. "This is my home. I am not going to be hiding out in Montclair or anywhere else. Make this house a safe house." She stood up. "I'm going downstairs to take a nap. I got no sleep last night, and if I'm supposed to be meeting some hot-shot vampire, I need some rest. Where's Amelie?"

Abbott was trying not to smile. "She's close."

"Well, she's supposed to be here. Protecting me. Besides, I need her. I've got to put together a serious outfit for tonight."

Sara marched downstairs. I glanced at Chris. He was staring straight ahead, looking very serious, but I could see his shoulders shaking as he tried not to laugh.

I kind of felt sorry for Monroe, so when I got up, I gave him a gentle pat on the arm. "Look on the bright side," I told him. "She's going to make one hell of a queen."

By seven that evening, there were three black limos parked around the house.

It had been a very entertaining afternoon. Abbott and Monroe left, just as Isabeau and her cousins arrived. They were looking a bit confused, but after ten minutes with Sara, all three of them were laughing. Then the three of them came upstairs, told Chris and me that Sara was napping, and demanded a word-for-word recap of the conversation with Sir David Monroe. My feeling was that they did not like him all that much. Fabienne referred to him as a pompous ass. I was so glad Sara had turned super-bitch on him.

Chris went to lie down in the guest room. Kevin and Becca came over, way early, but I was glad for the company. Amelie told us what had happened last night with Sara and Luc. It sounded terrifying. Kevin was impressed, and gave them his version what had happened to us. If we hadn't been talking about real life-and-death situations, we could have been at a Demon Hunters fan-fiction convention.

Food arrived a little after five. Garth came in, followed by two men bearing sandwich-laden trays. Mom and Abbott came in. Then Toad arrived, woke up Chris, and started peeling off the plastic wrap and eating off the trays. That's all Kevin needed. So when the heavy-hitters arrived, Violetta, Luc and Monroe, we were all sitting around the dining room table, laughing and carrying on like it was somebody's birthday.

Amelie ran down to wake up Sara. When my sister came upstairs, everyone stopped talking.

She was dressed in black. Not her usual color. In fact, she usually looked like one of those flirty girls in lacy skirts that you see on the cover of fashion magazines. But not tonight. Tonight, she wore black leather pants and high black boots. She had on a silky, silver-gray blouse that clung, and over that a black military-style jacket. Her hair was down, in long, loose curls. She looked beautiful. She looked powerful. She had put together a very serious outfit.

Luc stood up so abruptly that his chair almost fell over. He was in a suit, by the way. All the men were, except Chris and, of course, Kevin. After all, this was serious business.

Apparently, Sara had also gotten the memo and had taken it to heart. If I were a Brunel, I would not want to mess with her.

"Wow." Luc said. "You look amazing."

She was very cool. She walked over, kissed him on the lips, then reached for a sandwich.

Mom cleared her throat. "I've never seen that outfit, honey."

Sara shrugged. "I didn't want old George to think he was dealing with a lightweight," she said.

Kevin made a noise. "He may try to recruit you," he said.

Everyone laughed, including Sara.

"Exactly," she said. "It was Amelie's idea. She brought everything over this afternoon. She wanted to make sure I sent the right message. No victim here."

The doorbell rang. Fred started yapping. It could only be Ethan. I suddenly wished I were dressed in tight black leather too, although I doubt I could have carried it off quite the same.

I ran down to let him in. " Come on up. Are you hungry? We've got great sandwiches. And beware of my sister—she looks like a Goth-warrior queen."

He grinned. "Cool."

He came up, introductions were made, and I was very impressed that his eyeballs did not drop out of his head when he saw Sara.

As much as I wanted to hang with Ethan, not only because he was kind of the outsider and I wanted to make him feel comfortable, but also because he looked so cute, I wanted to talk to Mom. About Abbott. And everything else, of course. I kept glancing at the clock. It was getting closer to seven, and I knew we'd be leaving soon. But Mom had it all worked out. I should have known.

She'd been in the living room, sitting next to Abbott, when she stood up and called out, 'I need to speak to my girls before we leave. I know you'll all understand if we leave you for a few minutes."

Sara and I followed her into her bedroom, and she shut the door. She reached out and grabbed both of us. Group hug. Then she stepped back and took a deep breath.

"Well, here we go. Sara, you look perfect. I keep imagining you with a whip and a chair, which is a little disturbing, but I'm glad you're going into this fighting. Carrie, honey, just tell the truth. If this goes well, we will be left alone. And that's what we want."

"Mom," I asked, "is Abbott in love with you?"

She didn't even blink. "Yes."

"Are you in love with him?" Sara asked.

Mom nodded. "Yes. It's very strange, to find another someone at my age. But he's a wonderful man. I hope we are together for a long time."

Sara was nodding. "Good. It looks like the women in this family are all doing pretty well in the true love department. It's about time."

Mom looked at Sara carefully. "True love?"

Sara looked straight back. "I'm not going to marry him," she said. "Not this week anyway. But something happened, I don't know when, but it's all different now."

Mom's face went all soft. "Oh, baby, I'm so happy for you." She reached out and took Sara in her arms, and they stood together, arms around each other tight.

When they broke apart, Mom looked at me. "And you?"

I shook my head. "Mom, I'm still trying to get the guy to have coffee with me."

She laughed. "Well, I don't think you'll have much longer to wait. Come on, girls, we need to kick some vampire ass."

I did not want to drive in one of the limos, so Chris said he'd take the blue van. Isabeau came with us. Ethan and I sat in the middle seats, and Becca and Kevin sat in back. It felt like a road trip to the mall, not to a major sit-down with the forces of evil. And of course, Kevin was bursting.

"So, how do we believe them?" Kevin asked.

Chris frowned. "What do you mean?"

Kevin shrugged. "We know that they can make us believe things that aren't true. How can we trust that there isn't an army of vampires waiting for us? That they aren't all carrying guns to shoot us down."

Ethan nudged me. "What?" he asked in a low voice.

I turned to face him. Our faces were very close. "Remember when we told you to drive through the fallen tree? Vampires can get in your head and change your perception of reality. They can make you think things are real that aren't. So, even though we'd walk in and see one old guy sitting in a chair, the reality might be that there are two hundred vampires waiting to take us down." I raised my voice and turned back to Chris. "Right? So, how do we trust them?

Chris was grinning. "You guys are pretty smart. You're right. We can't know what's real and what isn't, so we asked for help. Witches will be there."

Isabeau suddenly sat up. "Do we know who?"

Chris looked over at her, still grinning. "One of them is Deanne."

Isabeau clapped her hands. "Oh, I am so happy. I love Deanne."

"Wait," Becca said. "Witches? There are real witches?"

Isabeau made a little noise. "Of course. There have been witches for thousands of years. Where have you been?"

"But, I mean…" Becca exhaled loudly. "I know about Wiccans and all that, but are you talking about, like, supernatural witches? Who can do, like, magical stuff?"

Isabeau turned around in the seat to look at us. "It's complicated. Magic is the manipulation of energy. Every single thing in the world has energy, and in that energy are certain properties. There are properties for healing, killing, telling the future—all sorts of things. People can learn how to combine those properties for desired results. That is how people make potions and spells." She waved her hands around. "Anyone can learn how to do that. That's why there are so many people who say they practice witchcraft, and rightfully so."

"But witchcraft is different than being born a witch. If you are born with the Power, you do not need a book or Grimoire to tell you what to do. Real witches can touch an object and know what Power it holds, and can take from it without effort. A real witch can wave her hand and draw upon the energy of a hundred different objects and use it as she wishes. Some of the great ones don't even need the objects to be on hand. They can concentrate on the Power they need and draw from it, even though it may be miles away."

"Wow." Becca said. "That's pretty cool."

Isabeau smiled. "It is very cool. Deanne is incredible—very talented, but also a good friend to our Family. Witches have always had a place in the world. They have managed themselves very well. They have relationships with us as well as the Clans. Because they are so intuitive, they see only what is real. They cannot be fooled by Glamour. So they are always invited to any of our meetings with the Clans, and they are always welcome." She frowned. "Understand that, for the most part, the Brunels have as much at stake as we do. They understand that if the world knew of them, they very well might be hunted out of existence. It is as much to their benefit as ours that this meeting goes well."

"Back to witches," Becca said, leaning forward. "Can I become one?"

"Hey, wait a minute," Kevin muttered. "A witch?"

She glared at him. "If you can be a macho vampire killer, I can be a witch," she said.

Isabeau laughed. "You can study witchcraft if you like, Becca. It takes many years to master its nuances. Some humans become very proficient. But you must be born a true witch."

Kevin wasn't happy. "Are there only women witches?" he asked.

Isabeau shrugged. "Women are naturally more intuitive than men. I have never met a man who was born a witch. But men have studied witchcraft and become good at it." She shrugged again. "Men are a very strange sex. They cannot stand for women to be better than them at anything. That is why witches have been persecuted throughout the ages. The men in power knew they could never be as good, so they killed them off rather than admit their inferiority." She flashed a grin. "There's a lesson, there, Kevin. If you'd like to take it."

Becca laughed as Kevin settled back, frowning.

Ethan nudged me again. I turned and once again our faces were very close. "Would you want to become a witch?" he whispered.

I shook my head. "Nope. I'm pretty happy with who I am right now."

He nodded. "Good. Because I'm pretty happy with who you are right now, too."

There was a small explosion of something in my chest.

"Okay," Kevin said. "I have another question. When you guys Turn, and become gargoyles, then go back to being people, how come you're not naked?"

We all turned to stare at him, even Chris, who then had to look around quickly to get the van back on the road.

Becca got right into his face. "What are you talking about?"

"Well, like when the Hulk and the Wolfman change, then change back, all their clothes are shredded and stuff, or they're naked. So what about you guys?"

Ethan looked over at Kevin. "That's an excellent question."

Isabeau was laughing quietly. "I guess it is. Did you just hear me explain about magic? How its properties are in all different things around us? When we Turn, we draw from that Power. The ability comes from within, but the change comes to us, it surrounds us, and transforms us. So when the Power is released, it leaves us just as we were before."

"What about vampires?" Ethan asked. "How do they change?"

"They don't. They have no magic at all, just strength and speed. They get inside your head and manipulate your perception, but they cannot alter reality."

Becca was grinning. "And the Wolfman?" she joked.

Isabeau made a face. "Werewolves do change from within. It is part of their genetic makeup. It is not magic at all."

Becca's face fell. "Wait. You mean there are werewolves?"

Chris and Isabeau exchanged looks. She shrugged. "Not so much anymore. They have been hunted for centuries, and are very reclusive. But they can be found, if you know where to look."

We were all very quiet for a while.

"Are they on our side?" I asked at last.

Chris looked in the rearview mirror and caught my eye. "They used to be," he said. "We can only hope they would still be if we needed them."

Becca said, in a very small voice, "…and the Hulk?"

We all laughed.

We pulled off the highway and followed a dark two-lane for a while, then pulled over behind a line of black cars idling on the side of the road. We sat for a few minutes, then we all moved forward. As we passed through a pair of massive stone pillars, I could see there had been a huge iron gate that had to be opened.

I cleared my throat. "I hope they leave the gate open," I said, to no one in particular.

The drive wound through some tall trees, still full despite the leaves mounded on the ground. Then, a mansion came into view. It looked like the set of a PBS series, light pouring out of a hundred windows, with a fountain in the middle of a circular drive surrounded by spotlights.

"Wow." Becca breathed. All the cars sat, headlights on, until a man came out of the front door. Then, all the headlights went off, the doors of the limos opened, and everyone got out.

We followed the crowd into a two-story foyer, with the obligatory winding staircase and massive crystal chandelier. The man who had shown us in was kind of a letdown. He was very handsome, of course, but he wasn't tall and lean, in white tie and tails. What kind of a butler wears khaki pants and a button-down shirt?

Monroe came over to our little crowd. "You will be shown to the library until you are needed," he told us.

Shown to the library? Perfect.

Chris cleared his throat. "Can we have Deanne?"

Monroe nodded. "I'll get someone."

I elbowed Chris. "What?"

He explained. "We want a witch with us. At all times. If you need to pee or take a walk, make sure there's a witch with you. Do not let yourself be alone."

Isabeau suddenly ran forward, and hugged a tall, very young girl dressed in a bright lime-green tunic that flowed down over her jeans to her knees. I looked closely. Deanne? She didn't look like a witch. She was neither beautiful nor grotesque. In fact, she looked like any high school student, with short, curly hair held back in a barrette and a few piercings—lip, nose, and several tiny studs that ran up her left ear. Then, you saw her eyes. They were orange.

The library looked the way it was supposed to—all windows flanked by taller bookshelves and lots of leather chairs. When the door was closed behind us, Kevin exploded.

"Holy crap, what a place! Did you see that staircase? I was waiting for Scarlett O'Hara to come swooping down. And did you check out the room they were going into? I swear, there was gold on the door handles."

Isabeau coughed. "Kevin? Everyone, this is Deanne. She will be our eyes and ears tonight."

Deanne smiled at us all, then went over to give Chris a kiss on the cheek. "Good to see you," she said. Chris turned very bright red. Becca elbowed me and raised her eyebrows.

Isabeau made introductions, and Deanne shook all our hands. Her own hand was small and very warm. It was hard not to stare at her. The orange eyes were hard to get past.

Kevin barely skipped a beat. "There must be, like, a million books in this room. And that fireplace? I bet you could roast an ox in that thing, it's so huge."

Deanne suddenly laughed. "Why would you want to roast an ox? They are disgusting. Stringy and tough."

Kevin grinned. "You've eaten ox? That is so cool. This may be the best Friday night ever."

Becca made a noise. Kevin caught her eye and ducked his head.

Deanne laughed again. "It is good to meet you all. Abbott gave me a brief rundown of what's been happening. It seems that you all have had a very interesting time these past few months."

We'd sat down in front of the fireplace. Kevin had been right—I could have stood in the middle of it and done jumping jacks.

"Ah, Deanne? Do you have any idea what's been going on?" I asked her.

She stopped smiling. "George Brunel has a big problem. Renata has amassed an army. Small, to be sure, but slavishly devoted. The fact that it happened without his knowing makes him look weak. He has called for this meeting because he needs proof before he can denounce her. She has always had, well, a certain appeal to those who chafe under the current treaty. If he declares her an outlaw, he needs to justify his actions, or she will look like a victim and may gain even more followers."

Isabeau leaned in. "Stefan?"

Deanne shook her head. "He's been trying for years to get her to pull back. She no longer listens to him. In fact, I think they have become completely estranged. He has openly acted against her. He has placed himself in danger. We all know what she is capable of."

"No, we all don't," Ethan said. Until now, he had just been looking around, taking in everything with wide eyes. But his reporter's instinct

170

must have kicked in.

Deanne looked at Isabeau, who shrugged. "Renata is different," Deanne said. "She is sadistic and brutal. All vampires feed on the blood of the living. They can nest for long periods of time, a kind of hibernation, when they don't have to feed at all. And the blood of animals is enough to keep them going for months. But, eventually, they need human blood. It is what they must do to survive. There are no longer bands of starving vampires roaming around, attacking people and leaving their bloodless bodies in the street. There are places where people are kept, barely alive, so that vampires may feed off of them. But Renata will hunt. And she chooses her prey carefully. She does not kill. She makes them one of hers."

I suddenly remembered Renata in the lobby of the restaurant, taunting Fabienne. I turned to Isabeau. "Marc?"

Isabeau turned white, and her jaw clenched. "Marc Armantige was a student. He and Fabienne were lovers. Renata saw them together, and she watched them for a long time, waiting until she saw a crack in their relationship. She went after Marc. First, she seduced him away from Fabienne. That broke her heart. Then she made him. He is still out in the world, somewhere. A monster. Like all of them."

Deanna put her arm around Isabeau and hugged her quickly. "Lately, Renata has been gathering around her the lowest and most mindless of her kind. They are very dangerous. George knows that. He wants peace. Stefan has convinced him. But Renata," she shrugged. "It has become a fragile and volatile situation."

We all looked at each other. Becca grabbed Kevin's hand. I wanted to do the same to Ethan, but he was sitting across from me, leaning forward, his forearms on his knees, hands dangling.

"What about this treaty?" Ethan asked.

Chris answered. "It has been in place since 1919. Vampires felt the need to take advantage of, well, the consequences of modern warfare. We're talking about almost one hundred years of little or no disruption of the peace. But about ten years ago, there were ripples. Small infractions." He smiled. "It is very difficult, with today's technology, to live for hundreds of years without someone taking notice. You have no idea what we have to go through, finding false identities, moving records, property and money, from one place to another. It's exhausting. That's what Luc spends most of his time doing, trying to make us look like ordinary people, living ordinary lives."

"What," Ethan asked, "are the consequences of modern warfare?"

Chris looked away for a moment, then turned back. "Bodies. Thousands of dying bodies, lying on open battlefields." He looked very grim. "Major warfare is very good if you're dependent on fresh human blood. Small, guerilla wars in remote locations, not so much."

Ethan sat back. "Whoa," he said.

Isabeau nodded. "Exactly."

We sat in silence. I was trying not to think about what Chris had said. Kevin, of course, came to the rescue.

"So, Deanna, I don't know if this a rude request or not, and if it is, I'm sorry. But could you do something?"

Deanna tilted her head in surprise. "Do something?"

Kevin grinned. "You know. A witch thing."

Deanne looked delighted. "Oh course. I love doing witch things. Like what?"

Kevin looked around. "I don't know. Can you make a book fly?"

She giggled. It was a high, happy sound that cut through the tension in the room and made us all smile. She sniffed a few times, and pointed her index finger. We all looked. A book came flying off a shelf, circled the room once, then nestled back into its place.

"Cool," Kevin breathed. "That was way cool."

Chris shook his head. "Come on, Deanne. Is that all you've got?"

She stood up and crossed over to where Chris was sitting, leaned forward and gave him a kiss on the mouth. "As a favor to you, love," she said softly.

She stood straight and closed her eyes. Her hair began moving gently, as though a breeze had lifted it. The air became warm, and I could feel something, like the static before a thunderstorm. She drew in a long, slow breath, and I could actually feel the air around me moving towards her, as though she was drawing it all in. She lifted her hand, and the books began to move.

All the books. Hundreds of them. They floated off the bookshelves, and hung in the air. Then, they went to the left, slowly at first, and then they gathered a bit of speed, and then more, and in seconds, we were surrounded by books. We ducked our heads as they flew past us, so fast they became a blur of brown and black, completely silent except for a faint crackle of electricity in the air.

Suddenly, they all stopped moving, hung again perfectly still, then backed slowly into their original places.

Deanna sighed. "Better?" she asked Chris.

I burst out laughing, and started to clap my hands. Kevin let out a whoop and stood up, shaking both fists in the air.

"That was amazing," Kevin shouted. "Seriously amazing."

We were all laughing and clapping, and Deanna bowed playfully, so no one noticed a tall, very beautiful woman who appeared suddenly and cleared her throat.

"Mr. Brunel would like to see you now," she said.

We followed her across the foyer into another room, the one with the gold door handles. It was huge and high-ceilinged, with three fireplaces and groupings of furniture scattered around. Mom and Abbott stood with Monroe and Violetta. Luc and Sara were sitting together on one of the couches. Fabienne and Amelie also sat together, across from two women I did not recognize. Toad, Garth, and a man I recognized as one of the janitors at school stood in a corner. I looked around for George Brunel.

There were four vampires in the room, all terribly good-looking, three men and the gorgeous woman who showed us in. But I could tell which of the three men was George.

He was very tall and perfectly proportioned, with a classically handsome face, dressed in a beautifully made gray suit. He was drinking something from a crystal wine glass, and I saw glimpses of gold at his wrist and on his fingers. He turned to look at me, and that's when I knew who he was. He was a powerful person. It radiated from him, and when he saw me, there was something in his face that made me think that he could crush me with a twitch of his hand, but he chose not to. He looked at me as an emperor would look at a slave. I was completely insignificant. For a second, his mouth softened. Then he turned away.

Isabeau whispered in my ear. "That's George," she said. "The young man talking with him is his nephew, Stefan. The other, older man is Constantine De Carreau, Brunel's advisor. The woman I've never seen before. The women with Isabeau and Fabienne are witches. Sitting with Amelie and Fabienne is Deanne's mother, Allegra. The other witch I've seen before, but I don't know her name."

"Thanks," I whispered back. "But more importantly, what's with Chris and Deanne?"

Isabeau grinned. "Chris is a man and a fool. Deanne fell in love with him last year when he Turned and became involved with the Family again. He keeps saying he just wants to be friends, but he turns into a marshmallow every time they're together, solid looking on the outside but totally without resistance. She could have him with a flick of the wrist, of course, but she wants him the old-fashioned way. And she'll get him, I think."

Becca, who had been standing right beside me, elbowed me. "That explains everything," she said.

"What kind of everything?" I asked.

"Why Chris never made a play for you. He was wrapped up in Deanne."

I stared. "Me and Chris?" I whispered. "You really thought we could be a couple? He's well, you know."

"Not human?" Becca shrugged. "Obviously, not a problem for your sister."

Ethan, who had been hovering, grabbed my hand. "I won't hold your gargoyle prejudice against you," he said. "I'm glad you prefer mere mortals."

I fought down a smile.

Stefan Brunel crossed the room and stood in front of me. He held out his hand.

"It's a pleasure to meet you at last, Carrie," he said. "I'm Stefan."

His hand was cold, but not icy like I was expecting. And he wasn't as good-looking up close. He was just normal good-looking, not in the male model range.

I wasn't sure what to say, so I may have said the wrong thing. "Are you the one who's on our side?"

An odd look crossed his face. "I am hoping that, after tonight, there will be no more sides," he said. He nodded briefly, then went back to his uncle.

The woman asked us if we would like a refreshment. We all shook our heads. Isabeau crossed over to her cousins. Chris went to Toad and Garth. Deanne wandered over to the windows.

"What now?" Kevin asked softly.

I shrugged. "Not a clue."

Constantine De Carreau and Monroe got in a small huddle in the center of the room, and when they broke apart, De Carreau went back to whisper in Brunel's ear. Brunel nodded, and De Carreau cleared his throat.

"If our young guests could be seated, please?" he called. That was our cue. We went over to a long, narrow, backless couch in front of the center fireplace and sat down together. Brunel came and stood in front of us. De Carreau brought over a chair, and Brunel sat down and nodded.

"I know who you all are," he said. His voice was like honey, slow and golden. He sounded perfectly reasonable and friendly.

Deanne had come over and stood behind us. I glanced up at her. The orange of her eyes burned in the firelight.

"Tell me, " Brunel said, "about the night that you were chased through the streets of your neighborhood."

"Pizza night?" Kevin asked.

A smile played around Brunel's mouth. "Yes, pizza night."

We told him. Monroe had coached us before we left the house—just stick to the facts, no drama, nothing about what we were feeling or thinking, just what actually happened. And Monroe told us not to bother telling Brunel what our attackers looked like, because the Glamour that was used made a physical description useless.

He listened without moving, his eyes half closed. When we were done, he raised his finger and De Carreau who was standing behind him leaned down. Brunel whispered something in De Carreau's ear then, turned back to us.

"What happened at the playground?" he asked, sounding concerned and interested. We told him.

"And now, the night that they came after Sara at, what, a soccer game? I understand that was another very eventful night for all of you."

We talked again, this time with Ethan adding his part. It seemed like we talked for a very long time. Brunel just listened.

When we were done, he nodded. "Thank you."

I was bursting at that point—why hadn't he asked us any questions? But I got the feeling that Brunel was a don't-speak-until-spoken-to kind of guy, so I sat with my mouth twisted shut. Even Ethan, who I figured would have a hundred questions, didn't say anything else.

Brunel stood up and moved to the other end of the room. Monroe and Abbott hurried over to us.

"Excellent job," Abbott said. "You stuck to the facts, didn't get emotional, and sounded very reasonable."

"Sure," I said. "As reasonable as you can, when you're talking about vampires."

Monroe smiled gently. "Yes. Exactly."

"How did things go with Sara?" I asked.

"I believe that your sister," Monroe said, "made her point. And for some reason, she had Stefan in her corner. He was something of a champion for her."

I looked over at Stefan. He was staring at Sara. I felt a chill across the back of my neck.

It appeared that the meeting was over. Violetta was talking to Brunel, and Luc stood respectfully beside her. Sara was next to Mom, and Mom had her arm around Sara's shoulder, making Sara's whole bad-ass look a little less intimidating.

There was a definite vibe in the air, and I realized it was coming from Brunel. He was happy. Or maybe not happy, but positive, and the feeling was everywhere. I found Deanne, sitting with Chris, making him smile.

"Ah, Deanne? Is Brunel glad about something?"

She looked at me with a surprised expression. "You can tell? You can feel that? How interesting. Yes. I think this was a very successful meeting all around. And Brunel is feeling good about something. I hope it is because he has finally made up his mind about what to do next. There was a great deal of uncertainty in the air earlier, and that is all gone."

"What about Stefan? And my sister?"

Her eyes widened. "My goodness, little girl, where did this come from? I think that Stefan has an attraction to Sara. I can see it very clearly. And your sister is very confused about it. It could become dangerous. Stefan needs to stay away from her."

I swallowed and looked at Sara again. She was talking to Luc now, and their heads were very close. Luc was so in love with her, I could see it from across the room. I wanted the two of them to work it all out. I wanted Sara to love him. I looked at Stefan again.

He was watching Luc and Sara together, and his face was perfectly expressionless. But there was something in his eyes. It wasn't hunger. It was yearning. I knew that Deanne was right.

Stefan Brunel wanted Sara.

We all got into the van and drove slowly down the drive. My heart was in my mouth until I saw that the iron gate was still open. They were letting us leave. I was never so grateful for anything in my life.

As soon as we were on the open road, everyone started talking, so I knew it wasn't just me who was worried about ever getting out of there alive.

Isabeau was riding shotgun with Chris again. She was smiling and speaking to Chris so quickly that, with Becca and Kevin talking behind me, I didn't understand what they were saying.

"Not fair, you guys," I told them loudly. "What's going on up there?"

Isabeau turned and grinned at me. "I was just telling Chris that I thought Deanne looked very pretty tonight, and that Monroe had mentioned having a witch stay with Sara."

I could barely see Chris' expression in the darkness, but he stared resolutely ahead, his face carefully blank.

"I think she'd be a great addition to our little entourage," I said. "She could tutor Becca."

Becca stuck her head forward. "I would love to be able to do that stuff," she said.

"Deanne said that Carrie was the gifted one." Chris said. "She called you deeply intuitive."

"Me? Are you kidding?"

Becca nudged me. "Well, yeah, Carrie. You always know what's going on. I always figured it was because you kept your eyes open, but maybe there's more. Maybe you're one of those 'born' witches."

"I am not," I said, " a 'born' anything."

Isabeau looked her head at me, a serious expression on her face. Then she shrugged. "We'll know once Deanne comes on board. She'll know one of her own."

"I'm not a witch," I said again, loudly this time.

"No, " Kevin said. "But you can be a bitch."

We all cracked up at that. I looked at Ethan. "Not very often, " I explained to him.

"Oh, I'm sure," he said, and we all laughed again.

"Seriously, Isabeau, what happened between Brunel and Sara? Did your sisters say?"

Isabeau turned around in the seat. "Sara made quite an impression. First of all, she told Brunel that she wasn't going to marry Luc or anyone else for quite a while. Then she gave him a detailed outline of her schedule for the next few months, and told him that she could not afford to be worried about being chased around by Renata or anyone else, and would he please do something about it? Amelie said that Brunel's jaw dropped. He's probably not used to being spoken to that way, at least not by American teenaged girls in black leather." Isabeau shook her head. "Sara is a real piece of work. And Amelie also said that Stefan Brunel not only agreed with Sara, he kind of encouraged her. Luc and Her Highness were shocked of course, and Monroe was mortified, but then your Mom pitched in about the holidays coming up, and how she'd appreciate nice, quiet family time. Brunel actually agreed with Maggie, and said he would try to assure that her holiday would not be spoiled."

"Man, I wish I could have been there," I said. "Deanne said that Brunel was happy with how things turned out."

Isabeau nodded. "My cousins feel the same way. Her Highness was very glad about the feeling in the room. Now that Brunel has a clear picture of what is happening, he can try to get a handle on the situation. But that will mean dealing with Renata, and her army. That is out of our control."

"Would he kill her?" Ethan asked. "She's his niece, right? Would he go that far with his own Clan?

Isabeau shrugged. "It may be the only way. It would be hard to contain her. There are places, of course, but she is powerful."

"Places?" Kevin asked. "Vampire prisons?"

Isabeau nodded. "You could call them that, yes."

"Wow," Kevin said.

Ethan turned to grin at him. "Way cool."

"Right?" Kevin said. "Imagine the guards."

Becca made a rude noise. "Isabeau, tell me more about Deanne."

Isabeau threw a look at Chris. "Well, she's barely a hundred years old, just a baby."

"Wait," Becca said. "I didn't realize that witches were, ah, immortal."

"They're not," Isabeau said. " But because of their abilities, they can, of course, make adjustments to their bodies as they see fit. Some do nothing to halt the aging process, and have a normal life span. Most born witches have a longer life, usually about two hundred years."

"And how long have you known her, Chris?" I asked.

Ethan nudged me. "Give the guy a break," he muttered.

"What?" I asked.

"Some guys don't like to talk about this kind of stuff."

"Do you?"

"No. Not to other people, at least."

"Yeah," Chris said loudly. "What he said."

I decided to be brave, so I reached over and grabbed Ethan's hand. "You mean you didn't tell fifty of your closest friends that you wanted to take me out for coffee?"

"No. And it's a good thing I didn't. Can you imagine me trying to explain why we had to cancel our date?"

"You're right. But think of all the 'likes' you could have gotten on Facebook. I mean, being chased by a vampire has to be the best excuse for ducking out on a date ever," I said.

"Much better than having to do homework," he said.

"Or getting grounded."

"Or jail."

We both laughed.

"And it looks like tonight is a bust," he said, squeezing my hand. "It's after eleven now, and my curfew is midnight."

"Mine too."

"I could pick you up tomorrow afternoon, we could hang out at the mall for a while, then catch a movie."

I nodded, trying to look cool. "Sounds good."

He leaned in to whisper in my ear. "Should we ask Kevin and Becca?"

I turned around. "You guys wanna come?"

"Where?" Becca asked, like she hadn't been straining to hear every word Ethan and I said.

I played along. "Mall and a movie?"

She nodded. "Sounds good."

"Hey," Ethan said loudly, "Chris, you and Deanne want to join us?"

Isabeau started to giggle. Chris cleared his throat.

"I'll let you know," he said. Then he turned up the radio pretty loud, so I sat back and closed my eyes and held Ethan's hand for the rest of the ride home.

CHAPTER FOUR

IT WAS TURNING OUT TO BE the best winter of my life.

Ethan and I were a couple. There was no drama, no anxiety. We slipped into something exciting and comforting at the same time. We were not one of those cloying couples that huddled in corners sucking face between classes. We spent most of our free time together. He stayed for dinner a few nights a week.

Poor Mom—she was feeding more and more people. Abbott was still always around. So was Chris. Deanne showed up at Mansfield high as a transfer student right after Thanksgiving. She and Chris pretended not to know each other in school, but she started hanging out at the house as well. Sara was getting the entourage I know she always wanted.

She had gone to St. Louis and Philadelphia. Each trip had been a production—driving to Teaneck Airport and getting in the private jet, the safe houses, everyone tense and miserable until she was back home, safe and sound. And home had never felt so safe. There were so many people around all the time, I felt claustrophobic.

I really liked Deanne. It was obvious that she was totally into Chris. I could tell right away. That first night, when we all got together at the mall, was a blast. We had so much fun. Deanne had an easy-going personality, and fit right in with the rest of us. And I could tell every time she looked at Chris that she was completely gone. Chris, on the other hand, acted like having her around was no big deal. He walked with her, his arm casually around her shoulders, as though it meant nothing that this amazing woman had fallen for him.

Guys are so stupid.

Right after Thanksgiving, I came home one night from Ethan's to find a full house. Luc was there with Toad, and Monroe, and they were drinking champagne. Even Sara, with Mom right there in the room.

"What?" I asked.

Mom looked happy. Her eyes were kind of sparkly and Abbott had his arm around her shoulder. "Our Renata problem is solved, " she said.

I looked at Luc. "Really?"

He nodded. "Yes. Brunel found her, and she has been ah, restrained."

Monroe nodded, beaming. "I spoke to Brunel this afternoon. He instructed her army to be disbanded, and he has placed her under what can best be described as 'house arrest'."

I grinned. "So, does this mean everything goes back to the way it was?"

Monroe's smile disappeared. "No. Just because Renata has been neutralized, that doesn't mean Sara is completely safe. That will not happen until she is married."

I glanced at Sara, who caught my look and rolled her eyes.

Luc missed it, and came up behind her, kissing her gently on the neck. "Everything will remain just as it is," he said. "After all, we can take no chances."

Toad cleared his throat. "I think we can do away with the private jet for Sara's concerts."

"Hey, that's the only part I liked," she blurted.

Luc threw his head back and laughed. "Then, you shall still use the jet whenever you travel. But not, perhaps for the audition at Juilliard? I don't think there's an airport in Lincoln Center."

Everyone laughed, but I felt a little chill on my neck.

As they were leaving, Luc pulled me aside. "Can you come with me tomorrow?" he asked.

I shrugged. "Sure. Where?"

"I need to buy your sister a Christmas present. It must be very special."

I nodded, and watched him go.

Sara, I knew, was knitting him a scarf. She was the most un-domestic person I knew, but she asked Fabienne to teach her, and had bought beautiful, fine wool in a brilliant red. She was almost done, and then she planned to embroider a lion on each end, in gold thread.

He picked me up from school the next day in his gray Porsche, and I told him to head to Short Hills Mall. That wasn't the mall we usually went to.

"Why this mall?" He asked. "What is there?"

"Tiffany's," I told him.

He laughed. He had a great laugh, deep and rolling. "Excellent. There is something about that little blue box, yes?"

I nodded. "Yes." He turned quickly onto the highway. He drove very fast.

"Is someone following us?" I asked. I assumed he'd have a couple of bodyguards.

He flashed me a smile. "Always. They have had to learn to drive on these highways. Driving is very different here. I like the Autobahn best. There is no speed limit there."

"Aren't you afraid of getting a ticket?"

He shook his head. "No. We can take care of things like that."

"Luc, your family sounds like another well-known family around here. The Mafia."

He laughed again. "No! We are the good guys, right?"

"Right." He was a very good driver. "Hey, Luc, can I ask you a question?"

"Anything."

"How could you fall in love with my sister without ever even speaking to her?"

"Ah. Well, I must tell you, that when I listen to music, I like to keep my eyes shut, especially if there is a solo artist. I don't want to see the person, because the music is so beautiful, and what if that person is not so beautiful, yes? So, when your sister was going to perform, I closed my eyes." He glanced in the rearview mirror, and moved into the far right lane, going a little faster.

"But she played so beautifully, with such fire, that I wanted to see who was capable of such amazing passion. I knew that it was a girl, I saw the name on the program, which is why I almost didn't open my eyes. If it had been a boy, it would not have mattered, do you understand? An ugly young man is not such a blow." He shrugged, and moved back into the right lane. He whipped the car onto the exit ramp, his eyes going to the rearview mirror again. He let out a whoop.

"What?" I asked.

"It is like a game, almost. But they are very good. They do not lose me too often anymore."

I twisted around. There was a black limo two cars behind us.

"So, you almost didn't open your eyes. Why did you?"

"Because my mother was sitting next to me, with my Aunt Chantal, Isabeau's mother. And she said, 'my, how lovely she is'. So I opened my eyes." He smiled. "And she was. So lovely. She glowed in the spotlight. She was as graceful as a swan upon the water. And you could see, in every line of her body, that she was burning with love for her music. That was a very beautiful thing to see. And when she was done, she looked out at the audience, and her eyes met mine for a moment, and I felt a jolt. Electricity, yes? And I had to have her."

"But what if she had been a real bitch?"

He laughed again, and pulled into the mall parking lot. He found a space quickly, turned off the engine, and sat very still.

"But she is not. She is fierce and stubborn. And spoiled. She is used to getting what she wants. But she is also kind and helpful, like a child, with a child's open heart. She is eager to learn, and to believe. She is eager for love."

When he turned to me, there were tears in his eyes. "I will live a long time, Carrie. It is possible that I will find other women to share my life with, but perhaps not. So I am grateful that I found Sara first, because, if there are no other women, I will at least have had her love. And that will be enough to carry me through the long, lonely years of my life."

He took a deep breath. "Come, little sister. We must shop for my future queen."

I had spent Christmas Eve with Ethan and his family. Someone had followed me, I knew, because as I left, I saw a flicker of wings lifting off from Ethan's rooftop. We were still all being carefully guarded. That was Luc's doing.

The opening of presents lasted all day. Mom and Sara and I got up early and sat around the tree, just the three of us with Fred and Moon. Then, Sara and I went over to Dad's, and helped the boys. Henry and Dante had been up since dawn, of course, but they always saved a few gifts to open with us, in addition to what we got them. Heather made us all a great breakfast, waffles with strawberries and whipped cream.

Then, we went back home, and Luc and the Family were there, and the packages were piled everywhere. He opened the scarf from Sara and jumped up, laughing with delight, and wrapped it around his neck, where it stayed all day. For Sara, there was a rope of diamonds, slender and tied in a love knot, that Luc placed around her neck with a tender kiss.

He was so in love with Sara. Completely. Anyone with two eyes and a brain could see it. And watching her, I thought that maybe she was starting to fall for him. She was allowing him time, something she had never given to anyone or anything if it meant being away from her music.

Isabeau and Amelie cooked us all Christmas dinner. It was the best food I had ever eaten. It was more like a banquet than a dinner, with more than twenty of us sitting around long, rented tables crowded into our dining room. It was a wonderful Christmas.

Luc threw a big New Year's Eve party at his place. When I first heard he had a condo, I imagined a typical three-bedroom townhouse. But I don't think Luc did 'typical'. He was living in a three-story palace — twice as big as our house, with a three—car garage and a finished basement with a pool table, full bar and extra bedrooms for his staff. It occurred to me that being his wife would certainly have some amazing advantages. When I mentioned it to Sara, she just shrugged. She was too busy thinking about her upcoming auditions.

Kevin, Becca and Ethan came with me to Luc's party. There were lots of adults there, some familiar faces, but I knew that these people were part of Luc's world. Not the world he shared with us, joking around the dinner table or teasing Sara. These were people paying respects to the future king. They all were gracious and courteous to

Violetta, but the attention was all on Luc. And on Sara.

Luc was introducing his bride to his world. Sara had to have known. She dazzled. She was beautifully dressed and had switched on her charm. The two of them stood by the fireplace and held court. Ethan and I watched for a while, and I was stunned by my sister and her poise and grace. If anyone really was born to the role, it was Sara.

We finally went downstairs. Kevin and Chris were playing pool. Becca and Deanne were huddled together. I sat down next to them.

"Are you teaching her how to turn water into wine?"

Deanne laughed. "I try not to step on God's toes. Or his son's. No, I was just telling Becca about concentration. It's the first and most important thing to know."

"Well, good, because she's starting to drive, and I think concentration is a big issue."

Becca scowled. She had taken Driver's Ed the previous semester, so she had her learner's permit. Kevin and I weren't taking the class until spring. Becca had done pretty well with her instructor, or so she said, but didn't like driving with her Mom. Not that I blamed her. Becca's mom stressed out about little stuff, so I imagined her driving with Becca was not a pleasant experience. Especially since Becca admitted to not paying much attention to the road because she kept looking at the dashboard to make sure she wasn't speeding.

Deanne laughed again. "She had better not use any of my advice when she's driving. This kind of concentration involves closing your eyes, shutting out the world, and looking inward."

"I can drive just fine," Becca muttered. "Mostly."

I hugged her. "I know you'll be just great. So, Deanne, who are all the hot-shots upstairs?"

She pursed her lips. "It's kind of a gathering of VIP's. Many of the Royal Family are here, uncles and cousins and the like. They all want to see Sara. They're curious as to what all the fuss has been about. I felt a little hostility, but mostly curiosity."

"Why would anyone be hostile?" Ethan asked.

Deanna frowned, thinking. "They are a Family on the brink of war. You can't even imagine what is at stake. The situation is much better now than it was a few months ago, but they are still in a perilous position. And Sara has become something of a sore point. It is Luc's fault for pursuing her, and making her say the words which has bound them together in the eyes of the Family. But Luc will be King. Nobody wants to suggest that anything is his fault. So, the blame is falling on Sara. If she married him tomorrow, everyone would feel much safer. But she has made it clear that's not going to happen." She shrugged. "People need someone to blame when things go wrong."

"If anyone is to blame for anything," I said, "it's Renata. She's the one that went after Sara. She wanted to start something. Sara did nothing wrong."

Deanna reached over and grabbed my hand. "Carrie, you don't have to tell me. I know exactly what happened. I agree with you. But I'm not a member of the Family. I don't have their loyalty. Even Chris, who thinks the world of all of you, will stand behind Luc if there's any kind of division."

"But Chris is our friend," I blurted.

Deanne looked at me steadily. "Chris is a Gargouille," she said quietly. "Never forget that."

Chris came over, holding a pool stick. "Game?" he asked Ethan. Ethan nodded, and got up. I turned back to Deanne.

"Do you really feel things are better now?"

She nodded. "I see Stefan quite a bit. He had become very interested in seeking out my company. It's because of Sara, of course. He knows I have access. And he is much more relaxed. He did not tell me much about what happened to his sister, but wherever she is, he feels she can no longer hurt Sara."

Becca's jaw dropped. "Where do you see Stefan?"

Deanne smiled. "He works at Saks, right in Midtown. He sells men's clothes. He goes to work five days a week, and I drop by there to say hello when he asks to see me."

"Just like that? In daylight and everything?" Becca asked.

She threw back her head and laughed. "As long as their skin is protected from direct exposure, yes, in daylight and everything." She sobered. "Theirs is a hard and unhappy life. They cannot help what they are. They have not been my enemy for thousands of years, so I don't see them as monsters. There are worse beings in the world, believe me. They are hidden, and may never again see the light of day, but they are there. Vampires are not the only creatures to go bump in the night."

I heard a noise on the stairs, and Isabeau was coming down, carefully holding a tray of champagne glasses and a bottle of Moët. "I don't want to encourage underage drinking," she said, "but Maggie didn't think there was any harm in you guys having a taste."

She poured a few inches in each glass. I watched the bubbles rise and then fall. I drank a sip. It was slightly sweet and tickled the back of my throat.

Isabeau was grinning. "Good? Good. This is my favorite." She took a much longer drink than I did, and closed her eyes with pleasure. "Perfect."

Chris and Deanne clicked their glasses softly together. Chris leaned forward and said something in Deanne's ear. She smiled and blushed.

Kevin finished his in one gulp. "Better than beer," he said. "I wish it had the kick of vodka."

Isabeau looked at him sternly. "Kevin, you are not supposed to know anything about what kind of kick vodka has."

He grinned. "Ethan told me," he said, pointing. Ethan grabbed the offending finger and twisted it. Becca rolled her eyes. I just shook my head.

"Isabeau," I asked. "How's she doing up there?"

Isabeau shook her head from side to side. "Sara can be a real charmer when she chooses," she said. "Tonight, she has won over most of them, I think. It's a tough room. But she's used to performing in front of a demanding audience. And she has a gift of pleasing the crowd. I wouldn't worry too much about Sara. She can handle herself just fine."

Later, she brought down more champagne, and we all went upstairs in search of food, and I drank even more and felt a little tipsy when Ethan and I kissed at midnight. It had been a wonderful party.

We were back at school on Wednesday. I felt happy and, for the first time in months, relaxed. I stopped worrying about Sara.

That was a mistake.

Sara had fulfilled the requirements for graduation that January. She could have stayed in school, but she decided she'd use all her time practicing for her auditions. Mom wasn't real happy, but Sara was pretty stubborn about the whole thing. And the Family was happy because it was easier to keep an eye on dedicated, practice-all-day-in-the-basement Sara than lets-run-all-over-New-Jersey Sara.

By the end of February, Sara had completed her auditions at Hartford and Eastman. All that was left was Juilliard. That had become her first choice. The Family owned several places in Manhattan, and if she attended Juilliard, she could move into a co-op right by Lincoln Center.

Luc had moved all the Family's business offices into the several floors of a building down on Wall Street. The Family was in it for the long haul. Isabeau told me that Violetta was looking for a house in Mendham. Toad was also looking for a house. A major relocation was underway. All around Sara.

Because her two other auditions had gone so well, Sara was feeling great about Juilliard. She was no longer talking if, but rather, when. So the morning of the actual audition, she wasn't even nervous. In fact, she joked around with everyone at breakfast, and when I wished her luck, she waved her hand.

"It's not about luck anymore," she said, laughing. "I've got this."

When I got back to the house after school, things were pretty quiet. Isabeau was downstairs, watching television. When I asked her if she'd heard anything, she shook her head.

"Nothing. I'm sure it will go well. You know how good she is."

I nodded, and went upstairs to find something to eat. Chris and Deanne came through the door a few minutes later. Chris was laughing about something. He was so much happier now that Deanne was around.

I got a text from Sara. She got a callback. That meant she was being seriously considered for admission. It also meant she was not coming home till much later. Mom called. She was having dinner with Abbott, so we ordered pizza and ate in front of the TV.

After dinner, we decided to bake cookies. I was calling them Bach-late chip cookies, in honor of Sara's audition piece. We were pulling the third batch out of the oven when Isabeau appeared, her face white.

"They took Sara," she said.

I stopped, spatula in hand, and stared at her. "What?"

"Right off the street. She was leaving the audition."

Deanne came over and put an arm around my shoulder. There was a rushing noise in my ears and I was having trouble breathing. I was aware of Chris pulling out his cell phone. Deanne took the spatula out of my hand and pushed me gently to a dining room chair. I sat. My eyes never left Isabeau's face.

"How?"

She shook her head. "I don't know. They're coming here. Abbott is bringing your mother. Luc was not with them."

Chris crouched down in front of me. "They will not harm her," he said softly. "Please know that. Sara will stay safe, at least for a while. I don't know how Renata got her, but something must have happened in the Brunel camp. Someone must have turned, and that's how Renata escaped. And it must have just happened. Today."

"You know it was Renata?"

He nodded. "Yes."

"Somebody helped her escape?"

He nodded again. His cell phone rang. So did Isabeau's. They both went down the hall to talk.

I stared at the floor. Deanne put her hand on my shoulder. It felt tiny and warm and strong.

By the time Mom and Abbott came, the house was full. Amelie and Fabienne were back, as were Toad and Mr. Jenkins. Mr. Jenkins was a janitor. He was also, I found out, a dragon.

Luc and his mother arrived separately. The look on Luc's face was frightening. Violetta appeared pale but calm, and hugged her son for a long time. She was whispering to him, her mouth to his ear as she held him, and he nodded.

Monroe came in with Mom and Abbott. Mom's face was tight, her eyes were red, and the line of her mouth told me just how angry she was.

Mom threw her coat on a chair and glared at everyone. Violetta started to speak, but my mother held up her hand. She took a deep breath.

"Tell me exactly what happened."

Toad cleared his throat and started talking. They had been on the way home. The audition was over, everyone had been dismissed, and Sara had been coming out of the building. There was a swarm, Toad said. He thought there had to be at least a hundred vampires, all over the steps and street. They were hopelessly outnumbered. It would have been impossible to turn in the middle of New York City during rush hour, with hundreds of people around. So they did what they had always planned to do if that situation ever arose. Get Sara to the safety of the car as quickly as possible, and try to keep the enemy at bay while the car drove away. Everything worked perfectly. They got Sara through the crowd. They got the back door open, and she rushed inside. But before Amelie could follow her into the car, it sped off.

Garth, they discovered later, had been overpowered. He was not hurt in any way. He had been standing outside the car and they surrounded him, making it impossible for him to do anything but stand there and wait until he was suddenly released. In that time, a vampire had taken his place at the wheel, and used Glamour to look like him.

Allegra, the witch who had been with them, would have known at once that it was a vampire at the wheel, but she had also been surrounded and was too far behind Sara to give warning. Another vampire had been crouched in the back seat, and had literally pulled Sara in. They found themselves surrounded, unable to give chase. It was all perfectly executed. Perfectly planned.

When Toad stopped talking, he seemed exhausted. He looked gray and old. "I'm so sorry, Maggie," he said. Even his voice sounded beaten.

Mom unclenched her jaw. "For months now," she said quietly, "you people have been telling me how safe she was. How you had everything under control." She looked at Abbott, and my heart broke for him. She needed someone to to be mad at. "You all promised," she said, and her voice cracked.

Luc went over and took her in his arms. She tried to stay stiff, but after a few seconds, she slumped against him and started to cry. He rocked her gently.

"We'll get her back," he said.

Mom nodded her head against his shoulder.

Monroe cleared his throat. "Brunel," he said, "has already spoken to me. He does not know how she got away. It happened early this morning. He says it was Jelenak."

Violetta made a noise. I looked at Isabeau. She and her cousins looked worried.

"Who's that?" I asked.

Violetta let out a long breath. "Brunel, for several hundred years, has been the largest and most powerful of the Vampire Clans. But he is not the only one. There are hundreds of small Clans all over the world. We knew that Renata was getting help from someone outside her Family, but we did not know who. Now, it looks like we do."

"Can Brunel tell them to give her back?" I asked.

Mom pushed herself away from Luc. "Can he?"

Luc walked over to the window and looked out. "All the vampire Clans signed the same treaty. They all have agreed to live by the same rules. But just because Brunel is the largest and most powerful Clan, that doesn't mean that he can tell those outside of his Clan what to do. They're all like little kingdoms, with their own loyalties. Jelenak and his Clan are in Poland. They have always considered themselves a breed apart. It makes sense that Renata would go to them for help in defying her uncle."

"But can't Brunel tell them Sara needs to come home? Surely, they don't want a war either," I said.

Monroe shook his head. "They would welcome war," he said.

Mom wiped her cheeks with her fingers. "So, how do you propose to get her back," she said. She was speaking to the room, but her eyes were on Abbott. "Can you find out where she is and go and rescue her?"

Violetta shook her head. "That would be considered an act of aggression. It would be the excuse they need."

"But couldn't Brunel explain to the rest of them what's going on?" I asked.

"He's lost power," Luc said slowly. "His niece broke away from him, put together an army, and defied his wishes. That made him look weak. When he found her and imprisoned her, he gained back some ground, but he does not have that kind of influence. Not anymore."

Mom sniffed. "So, what is your plan, then?"

Violetta and Luc exchanged glances. Violetta spoke.

"We can do nothing until we hear from them. I'm sure we will get a list of demands. That's why they took her in the first place, to try to compromise the treaty. Once we hear what they have to say, we'll figure out what is next. The most important thing to remember is that we cannot act against them."

"The most important thing to remember," Abbott said, "is that they will not hurt her in any way. It would not be in their best interest to lose their only bargaining chip."

Mom looked at him gratefully and nodded. She looked at me and I went over to her and hugged her tight. She started to cry again.

"Mom," I said quietly, "I bet Abbott could use some coffee."

That was all she needed. She pulled herself together right in front of my eyes and headed to the kitchen. I looked at Toad. He was talking to Chris and Amelia. I went over to them.

"So, listen, if you guys can't go against them," I said, "can we find somebody who can?"

Toad frowned. "Like who?"

"The witches?"

Amelia shook her head. "They will not act against the Clans. They have a very controlled and strong peace with them, and have had for centuries. They will not break it."

"How about somebody—or something—else? Don't you guys have allies?"

Toad exhaled loudly. "Yes, we do. But they are all bound by the same treaty."

"So, what about hiring people, you know, mercenaries? You have lots of money, right?"

Chris made a noise. "Carrie, first of all, for a mortal to go against a vampire is suicide. They are just too strong. And where would we get these mercenaries? Put an advertisement in *Soldier of Fortune Magazine*? And what would we tell them? That they need to become vampire-slayers?"

Toad was nodding. "We never could have imagined what the twenty-first century would be like. We cannot use out greatest strengths, because if too many people see us, we would be discovered. And then vampires would be discovered, then everything else in the world that has remained hidden, and for good reason. We must negotiate."

"Can we ask Brunel to get her? By force, I mean."

Toad laughed. It was an ugly sound. "If he went against other Clans, it would start a civil war. And because he is seen as weakened, there would be many who would not follow him at all. He might even lose. We cannot count on him for help."

Luc came up to us. He hugged me and gave me a cool kiss on my forehead. "You know how much I love your sister," he said. "You know I will do anything to get her back."

I nodded. He did love her. He must have been feeling just as angry and afraid as I was. "Luc, would you break the treaty?"

He looked into my eyes. "I don't want to think about that," he said at last. "We have to find a way of getting her home."

I glanced at Toad. He was looking worried. Next to me, Luc's body was tense and stiff. I could feel the rage in him, the pent-up energy waiting to burst free.

I knew we could be in a lot of trouble.

I went to school the next day because I had to. Mom was home. Abbott had stayed with her. I finally slept, and when I got up in the morning, Abbott was in the kitchen, making my tea, his eyes bleary and tense.

"What are we going to do?" I asked.

He shook his head slowly. "I don't know. We don't even know where she is. My gut says they would not have taken her far."

"Do they live around here? I mean, is that just a coincidence?"

"No. It's only been in the past six months that they've nested here. Because of Sara. You know that saying about keeping your friends close but your enemies closer? They're here because Luc is here. When he moved, the Clans followed."

"Perfect," I muttered.

"Actually, it's a good thing. Otherwise, they would have taken her to some remote Italian mountaintop by now."

"That's where Brunel is from?"

"No. Jelenak."

"I thought he was in Poland."

Abbott cracked a smile. "Yes, he is. At least, that's where most of the Clan is. But Jelenak is something of a pleasure seeker, and the Italian Alps are much more beautiful."

"Can't we ask Brunel where Jelenak is staying? Around here, I mean?"

"Carrie, understand something. Brunel will not go against his own kind. Even if he disapproves of what another Clan is doing. Going after Renata was all in the family. But going against another Clan would be political suicide."

"Politics? This is about politics now?"

"It's about power, Carrie. It has always been about power."

I finished my tea. "What are we going to tell my dad?"

"Luckily, Sara spoke to him right after the audition. If we can find her in the next few days, it won't even be an issue."

"He has a right to know what is happening."

Abbott sighed. "I know that, Carrie. How would you suggest we explain it to him?"

I put my mug in the dishwasher and left for the bus.

Becca and Kevin knew right away something was wrong. I asked them to meet me after school in the parking lot. I told Ethan the same. I needed them around me.

Chris and Deanne were in school, and after the last bell, they both appeared at my locker.

"Where are you going?" Chris asked.

I shrugged. "I'm meeting Kev and Becca. And Ethan. I need to tell them what happened. I'm going crazy."

Deanne looked like she had gotten no sleep either. She took out her cell phone and sent a text. "Somebody wants to talk to you," she muttered."

"Who?"

She turned and went down the hall. I looked at Chris, who shrugged.

"No idea," he said. "Can I come with?"

"Sure."

Early March weather can be a crapshoot, but that afternoon was sunny and not too cold. We met by Ethan's RAV4.

"They took Sara," I told them.

Becca started to cry. Kevin put his arm her. Ethan hugged me. I tried not to melt into his arms, because I wanted to stay strong and angry, but he just felt too good, and I wanted somebody to make me feel like it was going to be all right.

I heard Chris mutter, "What's he doing here?"

I looked up, and a lime green Volkswagen bug pulled up next to us. Stefan Brunel got out of the car.

"I know where your sister is," he said to me.

Deanne came running up to us. I had stepped away from Ethan and glared at her. "Is this who wanted to talk to me?" I asked her. "Did you tell him where I'd be?"

She nodded. "Listen to him, Carrie."

"Why should I?" I tried to keep my voice down. "He's a monster. His family took my sister."

Stefan's face remained calm. "You have every right to hate me," he said. "But I want your sister to get home safe. You must believe me."

"Why should I?"

"Because Renata will not send Luc the list of demands he is expecting. She does not wish to negotiate. She wants him to come for Sara. Sara is unharmed, and she will stay that way forever. But Renata will never let her go. Someone will have to go for her, and bring her home."

"Why?"

"She wants war. And she has found other Clans who also want war." Stefan spread his hands. "I am sorry. She is my sister, but she is mad. And I will do whatever I can to stop her."

Hope leaped into my chest. "Then you can go and get Sara, right? If you know where she is."

He shook his head. "No. I can't fight them all. Besides, Renata knows I am not with her. The people around her do not trust me. I might get close, but I would never have the chance to be alone with her."

"I thought you had people. You said they were watching her. I remember Sara telling me you said that."

He nodded. "Watching your sister is one thing. Acting against her and a small army of fanatics is another. I don't have that kind of help."

"Then why are you here?" I asked,

"To help you. You can get her out."

I stared at him. "What?"

"If you get her, no treaty will be broken. Luc will get his bride back. Renata will look weak and foolish to her army. My uncle will have saved face."

"And how the hell am I supposed to rescue my sister? Just go in there, take her hand and walk out with her? Like magic?"

Stefan nodded. "Yes. I can help you. So can Deanne. They will be watching Luc and his Family. No one is watching you. No one will expect you."

I took a deep breath. "Where is she?"

Stefan stepped closer. "Do you know anything about an shopping center called White County Mall?"

I almost laughed. I'd practically grown up there. Mom would take Sara and me there every Friday night when we were little, to have dinner at McDonald's, which had been a huge deal. Then we'd walk around and look at the shops. It hadn't been a very big mall, and it was all one level. It had been built behind a knoll, tucked down and away from sight, so that not many people even knew it was there. It was never crowded, and when the leases all expired a few years ago, everything closed down at once. Now it was a big, empty building with a 'Retail Space Available' sign in front.

"Wait. Are you telling me that Sara is being held hostage at the mall?" I asked.

Stefan nodded.

I looked at Becca. "Oh, my God."

Becca was fighting back a giggle, I could tell.

I looked at Chris. "Will you help us?"

He shook his head. "I can't. You know I can't."

I shrugged and turned to Deanne. "I thought you guys wouldn't do anything against vampires."

She made a face. "I wouldn't. I will do nothing to harm a vampire. But that doesn't mean I can't use whatever Power I have to help you."

"Help me how?"

"Help you go in there, take her hand, and walk out with her. I *have* magic. Remember?"

I could feel that hope again. Just a spark, deep inside. I looked at Stefan. "How do you know where she is?"

"I took an educated guess. My uncle bought the property a year ago, as an investment. Renata went with him on the walk-through, so she's familiar with the layout. She knew it would be empty, and that there was no chance of anyone interrupting her. I was there this morning. There are two of her army guarding the perimeter. I don't know how many are inside, but I don't think there are a lot of them. Maybe just a few pods. We need blueprints or something to can learn the layout. And then we need to find where they're keeping her."

"You don't need blueprints," I told him. "I know every inch of that mall. So does Becca. We practically grew up there."

"Excellent," Stefan said. "Now, we have to figure out how we can find where she is."

"What we need is a pair of those heat-sensitive goggles," Kevin said. "We could find her easily that way."

Becca rolled her eyes. "And how are those going to tell where Sara is? She's being guarded, remember? How will we know which one of those little lights is hers?"

Stefan smiled gently. "Sara will be the only one who shows up," he said. "She's the only one who's going to be generating any heat."

Becca swallowed. "Oh," she said, in a very small voice.

"But where do you get something like that?" Ethan asked. "They probably cost a fortune."

Stefan nodded. "Probably. I'll get it."

"We'll need a plan," Chris said. "I mean, you will need a plan."

Stefan nodded again. "I would go in front, distract them. You could get in a back door and find her."

"Go on." I was trying to think, trying to imagine myself doing this. Trying to get the courage.

"Deanne will go with you. If any of them see you and try to follow, she can create obstacles."

"Do you think they would leave her alone? If she's guarded, or locked up some way, how could I get her out? I don't think I could kill anyone, not even a vampire."

Stefan was frowning. "Yes. I can't imagine they would leave her unguarded. Whoever is with her would have to be killed."

I swallowed. "Could you do that? Kill one of your own?"

Stefan took a deep breath. "They are not of my Clan, so, yes, I would gladly kill. But I couldn't be in two places at once."

"We could do that," Kevin said. "Create a distraction."

I stared at him. "What?"

Ethan was nodding. "Yeah. We could break in one of the doors, maybe throw some fire crackers, make some noise."

"What are you talking about?" My voice was getting loud again.

"Kevin and I can help you," Ethan said. His eyes were bright.

"This is not," I said, almost shouting, "A damn TV show. This is real. This is my sister."

Kevin grabbed me by the shoulders and shook me. "I know, Carrie. Listen to me. You need help. If Stefan goes with you to get Sara, he can do all the heavy lifting, and all you have to do is run."

"What happens," I said, "if they go after you? You can't outrun them. You'd never make it to the car in time."

Kevin shrugged. "Then we'll just have to take down a few vampires."

Stefan was shaking his head. "You don't know what you are up against."

Ethan cocked his head at him. "Listen, I know you guys are strong, but seriously, you don't think Kevin and I couldn't handle a few of you?"

Stefan reached out very slowly and encircled Ethan's wrist with his thumb and middle finger. Ethan made a face and pulled away. At least he tried to. He could not move his wrist from the circle of Stefan's fingers. I could see him straining back, and the flesh around his wrist dug into Stefan's hand, turning white with the effort. Stefan suddenly let go, and Ethan staggered back. He rubbed his wrist slowly, his eyes on Stefan's face.

"Holy shit," he said softly.

Stefan smiled grimly. "Yes. Can you imagine five or six of us?"

Ethan turned to Kevin. "We gotta figure something else out," he said.

"I will go with you two," Deanne said. "Stefan can keep Sara and Carrie safe. You two will be in less danger, and I will be able to protect you."

"Deanne," Chris began.

"It's the only way," she said softly.

I was shaking my head. "No. You guys can't do this."

Ethan kissed me on the cheek, and I turned towards him.

"Carrie, who else is there? You need help. We're all you've got."

I swallowed, then looked at Becca.

"I suppose you want in too?"

She shuddered. "Carrie, I love you, but I can't. If I had to go in and maybe be chased by a bunch of vampires, I'd curl up in a ball and cry like a baby. But, I could probably drive the getaway car."

"What getaway car?"

"You're going to have to get away before they figure out what's going on. Ethan and Stefan can't be driving, they'll be doing other stuff. But I can have the car ready to go. I've never driven at night, though. Can we do this during the daytime?"

Stefan actually smiled. I didn't see fangs. "Night would be best," he said.

I took a deep breath. "This is crazy."

"Yes, it is," Chris said. "But it might work. I cannot help you get in and take Sara. But once you're out, I can protect you against anyone who might try to stop you from getting away."

"Then it would definitely have to be at night. You could not risk being seen if you Turned," Stefan said.

Ethan nudged Kevin. "We'll need more Holy Water," he said.

Kevin nodded. "Sure. I just took it out of the basin in church. I can get more."

Becca punched him in the arm. "You stole from church?"

"Well, I didn't know where else to get it. I looked for a website."

Ethan turned to Stefan. "What else kills you guys?"

Stefan was still smiling. "Silver bullets are good. And wooden stakes. But hopefully, Holy Water is all you'll need. After all, you'll have Deanne with you. She can put a stone wall between you and whoever might be chasing you. You'll be safe with her."

Chris reached over and grabbed Deanne's hand. "Are you sure?" he asked her.

She nodded. "This needs to happen. I will help. But we need to plan every detail. Where can we meet?"

"My house, I guess," I said.

Chris coughed. Stefan looked at the ground.

"What?" I asked.

"You would have to invite me into your home," Stefan said. "Would you be comfortable with that?"

"Oh." I hadn't thought of that. "And that might be hard to explain."

"My place," Deanne said. "Chris can get you there. "

Stefan nodded. "Tonight?"

I shook my head. "Mom will freak. It's a school night. Friday?"

He nodded. "The sooner the better. As soon as Luc figures out that Renara is not going to reach out to him, things are going to get dangerous." He nodded again and got into his car.

I watched him as he drove away, then I turned to Deanne.

"Is it even possible." I asked her, "for a vampire to fall in love?"

Her eyes were very sad. "Yes," she said. "It is."

Mom did not want me leaving the house Friday night. I was expecting a fight but she was so exhausted, she caved after three minutes. I almost felt guilty. Chris had already picked up Kevin and Becca, and was waiting for me in the blue van. I climbed in, and Garth was sitting in the front seat.

"You're in on this?" I asked.

He turned around to face me. "I failed to protect your sister," he said quietly. "I never should have gotten out of the car. That is what made it possible for them to surround me. That is how they got the car, and took her."

I reached over and kissed his cheek. "Don't think that." I told him. "Their entire plan hinged on getting that car and driving Sara away. If you had been behind the wheel, they would have probably dragged you out. They would have killed you. There's nothing you could have done any different, Garth. I have never, not even for a second, blamed you."

"Thank you." He smiled. "I don't think I can talk you out of this. I just hope you have a good plan. I hope Chris and I will just watch from the sidelines. But if not, as good as Chris is, when you're being chased by vampires, it's better to have a dragon on your side."

Kevin grinned. "That belongs on a tee shirt," he said.

We picked up Ethan and started driving. Nobody had much to say.

We finally pulled up in front of a tiny cabin in the middle of nowhere.

"Figures," Kevin said. "Does she have a pet owl too?"

Becca shushed him, and we went inside.

I was feeling excited now. I was thinking that maybe we could really do this.

I had made a map of the mall as I had remembered it. Becca had helped me, and I was pretty sure it was accurate. Stefan had been there that afternoon with his goggles, and he studied the map carefully.

"She's there," he said, pointing.

"That's where Friendly's used to be," I said. "Why would they keep her in a restaurant?"

"Easy," Ethan said. "There would have to be bathrooms there. Maybe even a shower."

Stefan flashed a smile. "Very good. Yes, that makes sense. There's also probably a walk-in storage, something that can be locked from the outside, so that if they are not able to watch her, they can lock her in."

I shuddered. I knew Sara wasn't claustrophobic, but the thought of her locked in a huge empty refrigerator made my skin crawl. I was starting to hate Renata Brunel.

We talked through every single step. Where Becca would wait with the car. Where Chris and Garth would hide on the roof. How Ethan and Kevin would approach. When Deanne would step in.

Ethan would drive Kevin and Deanne in his RAV4, and I would be with Chris, Garth and Becca in the van. Stefan and I would go in the service door where the Joyce Leslie used to be. It was only three stores down from where Sara was being held. We would take her back through the same door, where Becca would be waiting in the van, engine running, ready to speed off.

Meanwhile, Ethan and Kevin would be at the opposite end of the mall. Kevin had firecrackers—I didn't want to know how—and they would break open the glass doors and make as much noise as possible before running back to Ethan's car, where they would simply drive away. If anyone started chasing them, Deanne would do whatever to help them escape. Chris and Garth would be on the roof of the mall at that point, ready to prevent anyone trying to catch us as we left the parking lot. We would be in and out in less than ten minutes. On paper, it looked like the simplest thing in the world.

"We'll go in tomorrow night," Stefan said. "Comments, anyone?"

"What about the outside guards?" Kevin asked.

Stefan frowned. "They may give chase. We'll need Garth on your side of the building, just in case. And Chris will stay on the other side, with Becca." He looked at Chris. "If you wait until we are being pursued, you can act without consequence. It is not against the treaty to protect."

Chris nodded. "That's right. Garth?"

He was frowning, thinking hard. I watched him, waiting for him opinion. He was the grown-up among us. I felt like we had a much better chance at success with him on our side.

Finally he shrugged. "Yes, I suppose it might work."

Kevin grinned. "So, Stefan, can I see those goggles?"

Stefan laughed. "Sure. Out in the car."

Of course, Ethan and Chris had to follow them out. I went over to Deanne and hugged her.

"Thank you. You can keep them safe, right?"

She smiled. "I happen to be a very powerful witch. Yes, I can. I have to. If I let something happen to Kevin, Becca would haunt me for the rest of my days."

Becca nodded. "Damn straight."

We left a few minutes later. Chris stayed with Deanne, and Garth drove. He dropped off Ethan first, then Kevin and Becca. He pulled up in front of my house, turned off the ignition and sat, his hands on the steering wheel.

"What?" I asked.

"You know that I would do more if I could," Garth said.

I took a deep breath. "Yes, I do know that. It's hard for me, sometimes. I have to remember that you are a member of the Family, before anything else. I'm grateful, Garth, that you're willing to do anything at all."

He nodded. "I've grown fond of you all. Very much so. I don't want anything bad to happen to you, or your mom. And especially not Sara. Luc is going to be my king, I love him, and he loves Sara. He has chosen her. I would do anything do return her to him safely, but I cannot go against the will of the Family."

"I know. It's okay."

"This will work. You can get her out. Stefan will protect you. Deanne will protect the boys. It will be fine."

"And I've got you, willing to rain down fire if needed."

He reached over and squeezed my hand. "Let's hope that doesn't happen."

I asked Ethan to drive me to Dad's the next morning.

When I called to ask if I could see him, he seemed distracted, but when we got there, he gave me a big hug. He nodded to Ethan, then decided to shake his hand. They had met before, and for some reason did not hit it off too well, but that morning, he was all smiles.

"Where's Sara?" he asked right away.

I had the lie ready. "She's in New York with Luc. They're celebrating, I think. The Juilliard audition went really well."

Dad nodded. "Yes. I spoke to her right after she got her callback. She seemed pretty excited."

We made our way to the kitchen, and Dad poured himself coffee. I could tell that he'd been up very late the night before, probably working on one of the sites he managed. The house was pretty quiet.

"Where are the boys?" I asked.

He was putting water in the kettle for my tea. "Heather took them someplace to see trains. Electric trains. Down near Somerville, I think."

"Northlandz?" Ethan asked.

Dad nodded. "Sounds right. Been there?"

Ethan nodded. "Many times. It was great fun."

Dad was watching the kettle. He seemed more than just tired.

"Everything okay?" I asked.

Dad shrugged and glanced over at me. "She went with that client of hers," he said shortly.

I felt cold. "What client?" I asked, even though I knew the answer.

"George Brunel," Dad said. "He told her about it, and offered to take her and the boys down in his car. He's become very interested in her welfare. Told her he wants her to handle all his international business dealings. He even suggested she leave her firm and go out on her own. I don't get it."

Ethan grabbed my hand and squeezed it gently. "Maybe he's got a father complex thing going on," I suggested. "You know, the daughter he never had kind of thing."

Dad shrugged and pulled the kettle off the stove. "Lipton or herbal?"

"Lipton's good. What else could it be?"

He made quite a project of making me my mug of tea. When he finally set it in front of me, he smiled. "You're probably right. I mean, she says he's all business."

I sipped my tea. Why was Brunel still interested in my stepmother? Had he been lying to us all, blaming Renata for everything? Was he using the crazy niece as an excuse to start the war he wanted in the first place?

I warmed my hands around the mug. I had wanted to just enjoy today. I hadn't wanted to think about Brunel or even Sara. I had wanted to spend time with Dad and my brothers because in the back of my mind, I knew that what we were doing tonight was dangerous, and that it could easily go very wrong.

Ethan came to the rescue, breaking into the silence by mentioning pitchers and catchers. Baseball season was right around the corner. I had learned that Ethan was a hard-core Mets fan, and watched every game. I had inwardly groaned.

Dad, I knew, was a Yankees fan.

It had the makings of a long baseball season.

I hoped I'd be bored to tears by it.

Ethan picked me up at eight, and we drove to Burger King, where Garth and Chris were waiting with Kevin, Becca and Deanne. Mom thought we were just going to the movies. She was in pretty bad shape. We had not heard from Sara since they took her, four days ago. Mom had stopped eating. Abbott sat with her and held her hand. He had told me that Luc was in a bad place, and if they didn't hear something soon, he was afraid of what might happen.

I gave Ethan a long, hard kiss before I got out of the car. "You'd better be really careful," I told him. "Listen to Deanne. Do whatever she says, okay?"

He nodded.

I got out of the car and gave Kevin a hug as he took my place in the front seat of the RAV4. Deanne flashed a smile.

"Don't worry," she said. "I'll keep them both safe."

I hopped into the van. I was close to tears. They were risking so much. Becca put her arms around me. "They love you," she whispered. "We all do. And we'll be fine."

We were meeting Stefan at the north end of the empty mall parking lot at nine. We got there way early, killed the lights, and waited. Nobody talked. In my mind, I was going over the last few minutes I had spent at home. Hugging Mom, just a little too tightly. I had hugged Abbott. Then I went downstairs and gave Moon a kiss between her silky ears.

Stefan appeared from nowhere, and jumped in the back seat.

"Here," he said, and gave me a Bluetooth. "Sync it to your phone. Just before we go inside, call Deanne. Keep the connection open. We need to know what they're doing, okay?"

I nodded.

He turned to Becca. "Have you driven this van before?"

Her face fell. "No. Should I practice?"

He rolled his eyes. Garth and Chris got out, and Becca drove out of the lot onto the deserted access road. After about ten minutes, I could tell her nervousness was gone.

She looked at Stefan thankfully. "This was good," she said.

He smiled. "You'll do great."

We drove back to where we had left Chris and Garth. We opened the van doors, letting in the cold night air.

"How many are in there?' Chris asked as he came up to us.

Stefan frowned. "I figured no more than a dozen. "Why?"

Garth shook his head. It was very dark, no moon, and I could barely see his face, but I could see he was worried.

"There are a lot more than that," he said.

"How can you tell?" I asked.

Chris shrugged in the darkness. "The stench," he said briefly. "It's pretty powerful. If I can smell them from here…"

Stefan frowned. "It doesn't make sense." He turned to me. "Call Deanne."

I put the Bluetooth in my ear, pulled my phone from my vest pocket, and dialed. She answered right away.

"Chris thinks there are maybe more in there that we first thought," I told her.

"Chris is right," she said in my ear. "There may be a few hundred. But they are not active. I think most of them are nesting. I sense very little movement. If we follow the plan, and move quickly, we'll be gone before they can be roused."

I looked at Stefan. "What does she mean, nesting?"

"It's like a state of hibernation," he explained. "We can shut down and conserve our energy. That way, we don't need to feed."

I felt a chill at his words. "She says a few hundred, nesting."

Becca made a noise. Stefan clenched his jaw for a moment, then shut his eyes. When he opened them, they had gone completely black.

My heart jumped into my throat.

Stefan blinked, and his eyes were normal again. "We must move now," he said. "Are they ready?"

My mouth was so dry I could barely talk. "Ready?" I asked Deanne as I slid the phone back in my vest pocket.

"Yes," she answered.

Stefan looked and Chris and Garth. "Go," he told them.

They vanished in the dark.

We closed all the van doors. We watched the empty parking lot until we saw two figures come around the side. They were walking towards us, but I knew that it was too dark for them to see us. When they reached the corner of the building, they turned right and followed the empty wall. They were heading towards the front. I whispered to Deanne that they were coming.

As they turned the next corner and began walking away from us, Becca eased the van into gear. We drove down to the back of the mall. The service door was barely visible.

Stefan spoke to Becca. "Just keep the engine running. As soon as the noise starts, they'll head for the front. They won't come back this way. Make sure you're ready to go as soon as we come out."

She nodded.

I followed Stefan out of the van. It was very dark and cold. He put his hand on the metal door handle and turned it. It was obviously locked tight. He kept his hand on the door.

"Ready?" he asked me.

I nodded. "Deanne, we're ready," I said into the Bluetooth.

I was holding my breath. When the noise came, I jumped. A loud explosion cut through the air, and at the same time Stefan pulled the door from its hinges, the sound of twisting metal covered by the sounds of the blast.

"Let's go," he said.

And we went through the open door.

PART FOUR

SPRING

CHAPTER ONE

I HAD GOTTEN USED TO the dark.

I wasn't sure how long I'd been there. They took away my phone, of course, and I never wore a watch. I had no idea how long I had slept, and with nothing to do but sit and think, I couldn't judge the passing of time. Except when I played music in my head, because I knew exactly how long each piece was.

I think I had been there for five days, because five times they brought me food — sub sandwiches and bottles of water in a Styrofoam cooler.

I knew where I was, that old mall that Mom used to take me and Carrie to. Somehow, it made me feel better knowing I was in a familiar place. I was sleeping in the Friendly's. There was an iron grate across the entrance to keep me from getting out, and there was a metal door locked with a chain and padlock that may have led to a back exit. There were bathrooms, booths and tables, and the kitchen, of course. There was also a huge walk-in that had probably been a refrigerator. That's where they put me when whoever was guarding me had to leave. They'd walk me in and shut the door and it was completely black in there. That's when I would shut my eyes and play my flute. I never let myself sleep in there, because I was afraid I would never wake up.

I could sit in the front booth and look out into the deserted mall. There were no lights near me, but if I strained to look down the hall,

I could see some of those emergency lights at the end, maybe from the Macy's store. Macy's also had big display windows all along the front, and sometimes it looked brighter down that way. I figured it was from daylight trickling through. I guessed that they broke the lights at my end, so all I could see were shadows and shapes. I could barely see the faces of the vampires who were guarding me. They never spoke, just stayed on the other side of the iron gate, watching me. They opened the gates to give me food. And they opened it to come in and lock me in the walk-in.

I thought about Luc a lot. I kept imagining him bursting in, killing my captors, whisking me away. I imagined us sitting in front of Juilliard, watching people walk by. I tried to imagine what it would be like to make love to him, lying together on a wide, soft bed.

I spent a lot of time replaying my Juilliard audition in my head. The Partita was perfect. The Mozart Concerto was perfect. I hadn't made any mistakes during the Debussy piece, but I hadn't been as into it as I could have been. I'd been tired, and nerves had been creeping in. I would hold my hands up and run through the music, eyes closed, fingers dancing on the air.

I spent the rest of the time playing "What If?"

What if Deanne had come to the audition with me instead of her mother, Allegra? Allegra had been behind me as we came out of Juilliard. I had been feeling so good that I never noticed anything, didn't even think it strange when we were suddenly surrounded by bodies that appeared from nowhere and swarmed around us. I just knew that Amelie grabbed my arm, and Mr. Jenkins came up on the other side of me, and they tried to run with me down the steps, but there were too many of them. They were all beautiful, all smiling at me, and they wouldn't let us pass.

What if Allegra had been in front? Would she have seen them any sooner? Would we have been able to turn around and get back inside? I know she did something, created a wind or a force that suddenly opened up a pathway in front of us. We ran, Amelie on her cell phone, calling Garth, telling him to hurry, Mr. Jenkins swearing steadily under his breath. I couldn't find Fabienne. I couldn't find Toad. I knew they were somewhere close, they had been with me since seven that morning, ever since we had left the house and driven to the audition. But I couldn't see anything but the cement under my feet. I kept my head down and ran.

What if somebody had stayed with Garth? I was worried that Garth was dead. How else could they have gotten the limo away from him? How else could that vampire have been crouched in the back, waiting for me? The second that Amelie had opened the door, I had been grabbed and pulled in, and the car took off even though the car door was still open and I was only half-way inside. In a flash, the vampire had been on the other side of me, slamming the door shut, looking at me, smiling.

He had grabbed both of my hands in his. He began squeezing them, slowly. I could not pull away, it was impossible, he was way too strong.

And then he told me that if I tried to get out of the car, or tried to scream or attract any attention to myself, he would break all the bones in both of my hands.

He had smiled. His perfect teeth gleamed. "Do you think that callback will be worth anything if your hands are crushed?" he asked me.

I couldn't speak, so I just shrank as far away from him as I could and stared down at my hands, trapped in his, until we were on the other side of the tunnel. Then he let me go, pulled a black bag down over my head, and pushed me down on the seat for what seemed like hours.

What if it had been nighttime? Then Amelie and Fabienne and Mr. Jenkins and Toad could have turned and followed the limo, and when they finally pulled me out into the cold night air, they could have swooped down and killed them all.

What if Luc had been with me? Would they have even dared to take me if he had been there? But he had been downtown, working. He had texted me that he would meet me at home, and we would celebrate.

I had gotten a callback. That meant I would probably be accepted. Everything I had been hoping for was going to happen. All I needed to do now was get back home.

What if no one came to rescue me? What if Luc decided I was not worth going to war over?

What if I spent the rest of my life locked in a deserted Friendly's restaurant? They weren't going to kill me. Renata told me so herself.

She had been very reassuring. This was just a political maneuver, she had said. She almost seemed sad about it. I believed her. I wanted to believe her.

Because I didn't want to think about being dead.

And I really didn't want to think about being undead.

I was asleep when the explosion came.

After sitting in silence for so long, it hurt my ears. I ran to the front, and grabbed the bars of the gate. The two vampires who had been sitting outside didn't even bother unlocking the gate the way they usually did. They just broke it open. One of them grabbed my arm and began leading me back to the walk-in. I sat myself on the floor, hoping that dragging would slow him down. It didn't. I grabbed hold of a table leg with my other arm, kicking at him with both of my feet. He grabbed one foot and kept going, wrenching me away from the table leg and tossing me in the walk-in like I was a crumpled piece of paper. And then the metal door slammed shut.

Whatever was going on, it was for me. They were coming for me. How could they possibly find me locked in this huge, empty box?

I threw myself against the door and started to scream.

I was pounding on it with both of my hands, screaming, no words, just sounds, until I started crying along with the screaming, so loudly that I never heard the lock click and the bolt slide open, and I just fell forward.

Stefan Brunel caught me.

I couldn't breathe. It took me a second to recognize his face. I could see him by a thin beam from a flashlight. He looked glad to see me, relieved. What was he doing there?

"Sara."

It was Carrie. She was right behind Stefan, holding the flashlight, and I threw my arms around her and held on, crying. She has hugging me back, saying, it's okay, it's okay, it's okay...

"Quiet." Stefan said.

Carrie jerked her head up. She held a finger up in front of me, and I bit my lip to keep from making noise. There were more explosions, a different kind of noise this time.

"That's Deanne," Stefan said softly. "Something must have happened."

He was gone, moving so fast I could barely see him in the darkness, and then he was back, pushing us further back. He came to the padlocked door. He tugged at the chain and it fell to the ground, broken. Then he pulled the door out of the casing and gently set it aside, pulling us both into the empty space beyond.

It looked like some sort of service hallway. There were actual lights on, dim emergency lights, and at the far end, a familiar red "Exit."

Carrie was whispering as she followed him, and I realized she had a Bluetooth.

We stopped at the end of the hallway, where it turned a corner. Stefan peered around, then flattened against the wall.

I could hear moving. The vampires were running. Away from us, thankfully, but there seemed to be a lot of them.

"Deanne said the boys got away," Carrie said in a whisper. "But she's still here. She's trying to get them to the other end. Then she is going to get Becca. We need to get into Macy's."

Stefan nodded. "How close are we?" he whispered.

"We should be right here. It's the only thing at this end of the mall."

We turned the corner. We were in a loading area. I could barely make out the outlines of the huge doors that would open, allowing access to the trucks that would have backed their way in. To the right were a series of doors. Stefan pulled one open, and we slipped inside.

We were in some sort of storage space, with rows of empty metal shelving. Again, there were emergency lights, dim and flickering. I could see blankets on the floor, two long rows of them. A lot of somethings had been sleeping there.

"Shit," Stefan breathed.

"What?" I whispered.

"This is where they were nesting," Stefan answered. "And now they're all looking for us."

Carrie grabbed my hand. We walked behind Stefan. There was absolute silence now, broken only by a slight noise of static coming from the Bluetooth.

We went through another door, and we were on the sales floor.

Of course there were mannequins everywhere. It looked like a cheesy old horror movie, with broken plaster bodies in big piles. I looked around quickly. This had been the Men's Department. I remembered coming here with Dad to get a new suit.

"Do you know where we are?" Stefan asked.

I nodded. "Yes. Where do we need to go?"

"Deanne?" Carrie said softly.

I could hear a faint noise. Carrie's face was tight and worried. She swallowed and nodded to herself a few times. She closed her eyes and took a deep breath.

"Becca had to run," she said. "Deanne's trying to get Ethan back." Her eyes filled with tears.

I didn't understand. "What is Becca doing here? And Ethan? Where's Luc?"

There was another noise, like an eruption, and the building shook. I jumped. Stefan put his arm around me and squeezed my shoulder reassuringly.

"It's okay," Stefan actually smiled "Deanne must be having some fun," he said. He looked at me. "Luc is not here. We're going to get you out. We had to act before Luc realized that Renata had no intention of negotiating your release."

"What do you mean, we?" Who's we?"

"Stefan and I," Carrie said. "With Deanne helping. And Kevin and Ethan. Garth and Chris are on the outside. They'll be able to protect us once we're out in the parking lot. Becca was supposed to be driving us out of here, but now she's racing down RT. 287 with six vampires chasing her." Carrie laughed nervously. "Poor Becca," she said again. "We need to get to the front of the store. We'll watch for Ethan's RAV4. Stefan will have to break us out."

Stefan still had his arm around me. I had expected him to be cold, but I could feel him through the thin layer of my clothes, and he was not cold at all. I was still dressed in the clothes I had worn for my audition, a flared black skirt and white blouse. I was filthy. I knew I smelled bad. My hair was matted, and I hadn't brushed my teeth in days.

"What day is it?" I asked.

"It's Saturday night," Carrie said. She wasn't looking at me, she was looking at Stefan. He dropped his arm from my shoulder.

They had taken me Tuesday evening. Four days. And four nights. I felt the tears start again. "Is Mom okay?"

Carrie nodded. "Yes. I mean, no, but she will be."

Stefan jerked his head around, and pushed me to the floor. Carrie dropped down with us. There was suddenly smoke everywhere, and it was impossible to see. It was cold. My teeth started to chatter. As I inhaled the smoke, I felt it burn my nose and throat, and I started to cough. And then a wind started to rip though the store, driving the smoke back into the mall.

"Deanne?" I asked.

Stefan nodded. "Let's go," he said. "Get us to the front."

I stood up and started running, away from the smoke as it whirled its way out, away from the noise. Now there were shouts and voices, high-pitched and angry.

I glanced behind. Carrie was right with me. Stefan was farther behind. I slowed for a second, but Carrie pushed me ahead.

"Keep going," she yelled. There was no point in trying to keep quiet. They had found us.

I zigzagged through the empty racks and displays, heading for the front doors. Carrie was yelling into the Bluetooth," come on, come on, come on." I heard a shattering of glass and Ethan's RAV4 came barreling down the center aisle of the store.

There was a screeching of brakes. The RAV4 came to a stop. I felt like I was on a movie set. Kevin was looking out the window, screaming for us to hurry.

We were in the car in seconds, and Ethan sped through the store, trying to circle back so he could get to the front doors. I was looking out the back window, my heart in my mouth. They were following us, a hoard of them, gaining fast. I could not find Stefan.

"SHIT!" Ethan screamed. I jerked my head around and there were at least twenty of them between us and the doors. I could see the night just beyond, stars in the sky. Ethan slammed his foot to the floor and kept going. A few of them hit the hood in a series of sickening thuds, while even more somehow latched on to the sides of the RAV4. He kept going.

Kevin had opened the passenger window. A vampire was there, holding on, grinning. Kevin threw something in his face, and the vampire screamed and let go. He passed something back to Carrie and me. Small glass vials. Carrie opened her window and cracked open the vial, and threw the contents at another vampire. It screamed. Holy Water. My hands were shaking as I opened mine. I turned my head. The vampire who had been clinging to the outside of the door suddenly let go. I glanced up. They were on the roof of the car.

Ethan jammed on the brakes again, and at least three were flung forward and off the roof. Then he hit the gas and drove right over them, the wheels spinning fast, the vampires screaming. The doors were right in front of us. I closed my eyes and prayed. When I heard Kevin give a loud whoop, I opened my eyes, and we were outside, speeding through the empty parking lot.

The night sky had never looked so beautiful.

Carrie was trying to talk on the Bluetooth. "Deanne, we're out. Where are you?"

She was frowning, chewing her bottom lip. I looked back again and we were being followed.

Carrie touched the Bluetooth button and said calmly, "Call Garth." I could hear the metallic voice respond, "Do you want to call Garth?"

"Yes." She was still chewing her lip. I looked over Ethan's shoulder. He was going about seventy miles an hour. His headlights cut the darkness as he circled the lot.

"Ethan, keep left," I said. "The access road is just ahead."

"Thanks," he muttered.

Carrie was speaking into the Bluetooth. "Garth, we need to go back. Can you keep these guys off us for a few minutes?" Her voice was calm, but I could see her hands shaking as she clenched them in her lap.

"Go back?" Ethan yelled. "Go back where?"

"The Sears side," Carrie said. "They'll be waiting out front. Deanne is hurt. Stefan has her."

Ethan sped past the turnoff and started to circle back. He was still going really fast. It was so dark.

"We could use a light," Kevin said.

We got one. The whole place was suddenly bright as day. And there was a silver dragon, it's tail whipping around, hovering over us, with a stream of fire coming from its mouth, burning everything that had been running behind us.

We skidded to a stop in front of Sears. Carrie was screaming into the Bluetooth. The roar of Garth's fire was intense. So was the heat. There were more of them coming, from the other side, in front of us, where Garth could not see them.

Stefan came racing out of the building. He was cradling Deanne in his arms. I jumped out and left the door open, and as he pushed her in the back seat, I went around and jerked open the back hatch.

"Come on," I yelled to Stefan. He looked around. There were at least a dozen vampires coming towards us, moving fast.

"Come on," I yelled again. A winged lion dropped down in front of us with a savage roar, and with one swipe of its paw, threw back the vampires.

Stefan jumped into the back of the RAV4, tumbling in next to me, and Ethan took off. The hatch was open. I tried to grab something to keep from falling out the back. Stefan put his arms around me, tucking my head against his shoulder. He felt solid and strong, and I knew I wasn't going anywhere. He reached out, grabbed the handle, and brought the door down.

We were moving fast again. I pulled my head up to look. No one was following us now. They were burning. I could see them, black figures running, outlined against the flames. I could also see the lion lift off the ground, circling slowly, massive wings beating gracefully in the air.

We swerved onto the access road. I looked towards the front.

Ethan was facing forward, concentrating hard. Kevin was next to him, cell phone to his ear. He was shouting excitedly to someone, but the blood in my ears was pounding so loud that I could only hear a muffled noise.

Carrie had put her arm around Deanne.

I closed my eyes and leaned against Stefan.

The roar in my ears began to quiet down. I could hear Carrie talking to Deanne. Kevin was laughing. It was over.

"Will Deanne be okay?" I asked Stefan quietly.

I could feel him nod. "Yes. They had nested on the other side, and she was walling them in. I think she misjudged her own strength, because something collapsed and she was trapped underneath some rubble. She was conscious when I found her. She's just weak and very bruised, I think. Her mother will be able to heal her."

"How many were there?"

He shrugged. His arms were still around me in a loose, protective circle. "A few hundred. Renata's whole army was there, I think. If they had gotten out, we would have been in trouble. As it is, those who were trapped inside are the lucky ones. I don't think Garth left any of those who came out alive."

"Did we break the treaty?"

He chuckled. "Really? You're worrying about that?"

"Yes. I couldn't stand it if I was responsible for a war."

Carrie had turned around. "Garth was protecting us," she said. "He didn't do anything wrong. I think we're okay."

She was looking at Stefan. I was suddenly aware of what we must have looked like, with his arms around me. I pulled away from him and moved against the back of the seat.

Carrie handed me her cell phone. "Call Mom," she said. "And call Luc."

I held the phone to my ear and listened to the ringing. Abbott answered. I felt tears.

"Abbott? I'm okay. I'm with Carrie and we're on our way home. Tell Mom, okay? Tell her we're safe."

"Sara? My God, where are you? What happened?"

"I'll tell you when we get there. Twenty minutes. Tell Mom."

We were on Rt. 287, heading north. Ethan had slowed the RAV4. Carrie and Deanne were slouched down. It was very late, and there were very few cars on the road, but I knew that Ethan had a provisional license, and he could get a ticket for too many passengers. Just our luck, after all that had just happened, that we'd get pulled over by a cop.

I nudged Stefan. "Can you drive?"

He lifted his head. "Ethan, pull over. Let's not get in trouble now."

Ethan pulled over, got out, came around, and opened the hatch. Stefan slid away from me.

"I'll stay back here," I told him. "I'll stay low." I dialed Luc as the RAV4 began to move.

"It's me. I'm okay. Carrie and I are on the way home."

"What?" He exploded into French, speaking loudly and too fast.

I laughed weakly. "Luc, I can't understand a thing you're saying. Just meet me at Mom's okay? We'll explain everything." I hung up, turned around on my knees and stuck my head between Carrie and

Ethan.

"Okay, now explain everything," I said.

"It was Stefan's idea," Carrie said. " And it would have worked a lot better if Renata's whole damn army hadn't been camped out there. Did they hurt you? Are you okay?"

I nodded. "Just filthy and disgusting. Renata told me she wasn't going to hurt me."

"Renata was there?" Carrie asked.

I nodded. "When they first bought me in. She said I was a political prisoner, and it wasn't personal, so she wouldn't hurt me. I never saw her again." I wrapped my arms around my sister's neck and rested my head against her. "I can't believe you came and rescued me. What the hell were you thinking?"

She put her hands around mine and squeezed. "I was thinking that if Luc had to wait any longer, there'd be war in the camp. Literally. And even though you're a spoiled brat and a pain in my butt, a major war with vampires was probably worse than having you back home."

Something chirped and she hit her Bluetooth button, listened for a minute, then hit the button again.

"Chris found Becca and the van. They're on their way home."

Kevin turned around. "Yeah, she ended up going the wrong way on 287, and pulled into a rest stop and locked herself in the van. Major trauma for Becca. She may never drive on the highway again."

"Becca?" I asked in wonder. "How did you get Becca in on this?"

I could feel Carrie smile. "We had rather limited resources," she said. "But what we lacked in numbers, we made up for in enthusiasm."

Deanne made a noise. "Some of us," she said loudly, "were less limited than others."

I took my arms away from Carrie and threw them around Deanne. "Thank you," I said, kissing her on the cheek. "Thank all of you. I was so ready to just stay there forever."

"Luc would have come for you," Stefan said from the front seat. "He would not have waited much longer. I know he had soldiers of his own. He was willing to go against his mother's wishes."

I stared at the back of his head. "How do you know all that?"

Stefan glanced in the rearview mirror. "He told me. Right after you were taken, he sought me out. Asked me if I knew where you were. I lied to him, told him I needed a couple of days. He began planning right away. He was just waiting for me to give him the information."

"Why?" I asked. "Why would he do that? It would have been the wrong thing to do. He would have been risking a war."

"He loves you," Stefan said simply. "He would risk anything."

I moved back and huddled against the side of the RAV4. I was crying again, stupid, useless tears. What had I done to deserve that kind of love?

Carrie turned around to look at me.

"None of this is your fault, okay? Nothing that has happened is because of anything you did."

"I applied to Juilliard," I yelled, my voice choking. "I had to have my stupid way, and look where it got us. All of you were in danger. Mom — God, I don't even want to think about what she's been going through. And Luc was willing to start a war that could have killed half the people on the planet, and all because I needed to go to a stupid audition."

Carrie was shaking her head. "It wasn't a stupid audition. You got a callback, right? Which means everything you've ever wanted, all you've been working for, is probably going to happen. That's, like, huge. We're all fine, Mom is going to be fine, and I don't think half the world was ever in danger. Maybe, I don't know, a fifth of the world, but not half. You're not that important."

I laughed. I had to. "Stop trying to make this funny," I scolded.

"It's not funny, okay? But it's over."

I nodded and wiped my face with both of my dirty hands. Over. I hoped to God she was right.

Stefan pulled the RAV4 into the driveway. I reached over and grabbed Carrie by the sleeve.

"I need to talk to Stefan, for just a minute. Okay?"

She looked at me a little funny, but nodded.

Stefan had gotten out of the car, and came around to open the trunk. He held out his hand to help me out. I was suddenly so tired I could barely walk. I held on to his arm as he slammed the door shut.

"Wait. Where are you going?" I asked.

In the light from the streetlamp, I could see him clearly for the first time that night. His leather jacket was torn. The jacket was open in front, and I could see where something with nails had clawed through his shirt.

"I need to get some rest," he said.

"Thank you. I can't even think of the right words. But I don't understand. Why did you do this?"

He smiled tiredly. "I was trying to prevent a war, remember?"

I looked at him.

He took a breath. "I play the violin," he said. "I have for almost three hundred years."

"Wow. You must be pretty good."

He nodded, smiling. "Yes, I am. I love music. That's how I happened to be at a concert of the London Philharmonic last June. I saw you when you performed there."

My heart began to pound. "That's where Luc saw me. He said I touched him. His soul."

He nodded. "Yes. You even touched those of us without a soul."

"You don't know me. Why would you do something like this just because you heard me play the flute?"

He looked at me intently. My heart pounded. "When you played, it wasn't just about the music. There was passion there, and love. Watching you, a man could imagine taking some of that passion and love for himself." He took a deep breath. "I will not see you again, Sara. But I am forever grateful that I was able to help you. And I hope that, even for a few moments, you thought of me as something other than a monster."

I touched his sleeve. "You saved me," I said. My throat was full. "You stepped up and came for me."

He was shaking his head. "I helped your sister. She and her friends are the reason you're safe. I would never have done this alone."

There was screech of brakes and I heard a car door slam.

"Sara!" It was Luc, running towards me. My feet were moving, I wasn't even thinking, I just ran to him, and he caught me in his arms and picked me up off the ground, hugging me so tightly I thought I'd never breathe again, and he was kissing me, my matted hair and filthy face.

My heart felt so full I thought I would burst.

Someone else was calling my name. Mom had run from the house, and Luc let me go so I could go to her. She was crying hard, looking exhausted and broken in the darkness. She couldn't talk, just held me, crying. My eyes searched for Luc. He had found Stefan. They were shaking hands. Luc said something to Stefan, who nodded, then slipped away in the night.

I was home.

Chapter Two

FIRST, I TOOK A LONG, hot shower. I scrubbed every inch of my body and washed my hair four times. There was even grimy stuff under my fingernails. When I finally felt clean, I wrapped my hair in a towel, got into my oldest, softest sweats, and went upstairs.

Mom had been cooking. I had asked for hot food. She had made bacon. As I came up the stairs and she saw me, she grinned and started making pancakes.

In the living room, Abbott was having a fit.

"You all could have been killed," he was saying. Well, not saying. Yelling. His face was red and he was waving his arms around. Carrie was just looking up at him, shaking her head.

Becca was sitting on Kevin's lap, looking very small and pale. I knelt next to her.

"Thank you."

She smiled tiredly. "I was pretty useless. I sat in the van, screamed, drove away, screamed some more, got lost and screamed again. Not much going on there."

"I know," I told her. "But you were there. You were willing to put yourself on the line. I only wish I had friends like you."

Garth was standing in a corner, looking very grim. Isabeau, Fabienne and Amelie were all crowded in the dining room, looking delighted, trying not to giggle too hard at Abbott, who was still ranting. I went over and gave Garth a hug, too.

"Garth, you were amazing. And beautiful. I never knew that a dragon could be so beautiful."

He actually blushed. In the months that I had known him, and been with him almost every single day, he had never shown any emotion. Now, he was like an embarrassed schoolboy.

I looked around. "Where's Chris? And Deanne?"

Abbott turned to me. "They're in the guest room. Allegra is here, trying to heal her daughter. It's a miracle that she was the only one hurt." His face sagged. "Oh, Sara," he said, his voice suddenly soft and shaking. "Thank God you're home." Then he rushed forward and hugged me.

"Is the lecture over?" Ethan called, and everyone started laughing.

I went down the hallway. The guest room was very crowded. Deanne was sitting up on the bed, Allegra sitting beside her. Chris was on her other side. Luc was standing at the foot of the bed, arms folded, looking concerned.

"Hey," I said.

They all turned.

"She's going to be fine," Chris said. "Mostly, right now, she's weak. She had to pull together a whole lotta shit."

I grinned. "Oh? Is that the technical term for it?"

Deanne smiled. She looked exhausted. She looked up at Luc.

"I didn't even use a binding spell," she said.

I thought, what is she talking about? Then I knew. Luc wanted to make sure that whatever she did would not cause a problem for her or any other witches.

"I just built walls," she went on. "They had been nesting, and I knew they were going to be roused, so I just walled them all in. Three feet deep. Rock and concrete."

Luc was nodding. "Renata?"

Deanne shrugged. "I didn't see her. I didn't see anyone I recognized."

"They're supposed to be Jelenak," Luc said.

She shrugged. "I don't know them."

Allegra had been holding her daughter's hand. Now, she placed her palm on Deanne's chest, raised her other hand, and closed her eyes. I could feel the air move, just a little, and I felt a warm breeze. Deanne closed her eyes, took a deep breath, and her face took on some color, and the lines of strain around her eyes disappeared.

"Thanks, Mom." She said.

Allegra patted her daughter's hand, then she looked at me. "I'm sorry, Sara," she said. "I should have made it a point to not leave your side. I should not have been afraid to use a bit of Power."

I shook my head. "There must have been hundreds of them, Allegra. Don't worry. I'll never do anything like that again. I won't put any more people at risk for my own needs again."

Luc raised an eyebrow. "Don't tell me that you're actually going to change your ways?"

I made a face at him. "Ah, no. Not when it comes to you, anyway. I still expect you to bow to my every whim. But everyone else, well, they'll be off the hook."

He smiled.

"Thank you, Deanne," I said. "You too, Chris."

Chris waved a hand. "Hey, part of the job." He looked at Luc. "They're dead. We didn't go inside, of course, and once the RAV4 was on the road, we left, but I don't think we left anything out there alive."

Luc nodded. "Good. Garth said the same thing. I'm sure we're fine."

I sat down to hot pancakes. Mom even warmed the syrup for me. She sat right next to me as I ate, her hand on my knee. She looked so tired.

"So, you're okay?" she asked for the gazillionth time.

I nodded, my mouth full of bacon. Fred kept trying to climb on my lap.

"Will we talk about this?" she asked.

I nodded again. Not right away, but I would need to talk about it. I had thought I was going to die. I thought I wasn't going to die, but remain a prisoner for the rest of my life. I thought they'd make me one of their own. I was going to have a lot to talk about.

Fred started yapping as Violetta, Monroe and Toad came through the front door.

I stood up and swallowed quickly, so when Violetta came over to me, I was at least able to smile without pancake showing.

"I'm so glad you're safe," she said, squeezing both my hands. "Lucien was beside himself." She went into the living room, sat next to Carrie, and took her hand. "Tell me."

Carrie took a deep breath. "Deanne brought Stefan Brunel to me. Stefan said he would help me get Sara out so the treaty would remain unbroken, and these guys came on board because there was no one else. Deanne promised not to hurt anybody, and Stefan did most of the, well, hard stuff. He had to kill some of them. Maybe a lot of them. Whatev'. But he took care of us until we were outside. Chris and Garth said they would do what they could, and thank God, because when we were trying to get out of there, it was crazy. Of course, if Renata's whole army hadn't been there, it would have gone SO much easier."

Violetta smiled and patted Carrie's hand. "I always knew you'd be the one to watch, Carrie. But why would Stefan come to you in the first place? We were willing to negotiate."

Carrie made a face. "He said that Renata wasn't interested in that. She was waiting for Luc to start something. She was trying to start a war."

Violetta sighed. "Then it's a good thing you did what you did, Carrie, as foolish and dangerous as it was. Lucien would never have gone after Sara, and this would have ended very badly."

I glanced at Luc. His face never changed expression. He didn't know that we knew that he had been gathering an army of his own, to break in and rescue me.

Toad had been standing with Isabeau, Fabienne and Amelie. He cleared his throat. "Well done, all of you. Even though you aren't technically part of the Family, I've come to think of you as, well, mine, and I'm very proud of you."

Everyone started clapping. Carrie, seizing the moment, stood up and bowed. "I'd like to thank the academy," she said loudly, "and, of course, my agent."

Everyone laughed. Luc came up behind me and wrapped his arms around me. I leaned back against him. He was solid and warm and, for the first time in days, I felt safe.

Later, after I'd changed into yoga pants and a tee shirt to sleep in, he sat on my bed and combed out my damp and tangled hair, easing the comb through the knots, tugging gently until they were smooth.

Then he eased me down into my bed and tucked the blanket around my neck.

"Stefan told me," I murmured. I was so tired.

"Told you what?" he asked gently, his fingers on my cheek.

"That you wanted to know where I was. That you were planning to come after me."

He continued to stroke my cheek, saying nothing.

"You would have done that? You would have gone against the Family for me?"

He kissed me on the forehead. "I would have gone against the world," he said.

And then I was asleep.

The next day, it was all over the news. The White County Mall had burned to the ground. Arson was suspected. There had been reports of fire around ten p.m. The police drove by, but found no signs of life, so they left. By dawn, the place was in flames.

"What happened?" I asked Luc. We were in the living room. I was curled up under my favorite quilt, lying in the sunlight. I never wanted to be in the dark again. Luc was on his laptop.

He shrugged. "Brunel did it, I'm sure. We told him what Deanne had done, sealing in members of Renata's army. He probably burned them all. It would send a strong message. It would tell the other Clans that he would not tolerate Renataain's disobedience. It will make it that much harder for her to try again."

"Do you think she will? Try again?"

He looked up at me. "She will be caught soon. There are only so many places where she can hide. And those that might have supported her will think twice. It was a very good move on his part."

Fred was on my lap, and I scratched his ears. "You sound like you admire him."

Luc shrugged. "I do. He's a leader, and he's doing a good job at keeping peace among his people. Sometimes, that requires violence. As a leader, you can't be afraid of making tough choices."

"Like you were willing to make?" I asked.

He dropped his eyes. "I don't know what you're talking about."

I put my head back and closed my eyes.

I dreamed about Stefan Brunel. We were running through the darkness. He was holding my hand, pulling me forward. I could hear Carrie yelling for me, but every time I tried to follow her, Stefan pulled me further away. I woke up with a start, my heart pounding. I looked around. Mom was at the dining room table, reading the paper, and she looked over at me.

"Hey, sleepyhead, you okay?"

I nodded. "Bad dream. Where's Luc?"

"He said he'd be back. I think he's with his mother." She walked over and sat at the other end of the couch. "So?"

So I told her. Everything. She watched my face, and a few times, tears came to her eyes. When I was done, she nodded to herself. "We have a lot to thank Stefan for, don't we?"

I felt disloyal, hearing her say that. "Luc would have come for me, Mom."

"Yes, I know. And I think it would have gone very wrong. As angry as I am about your sister and her friends being in such danger, it was really the only thing that could have worked without all hell breaking loose."

"Maybe. But, listen. You know that I got a callback, right?"

She grinned. "Oh, Sara, that's right! Your audition! Tell me about your audition!"

Finally, something to talk about that didn't give me the shivers. Carrie came up from downstairs, with Amelie, and we sat in the sunshine and talked about normal kinds of things. Amelie was cooking a celebration dinner—did I want roasted asparagus or green beans? Spring break was coming up—Carrie wanted to drive with Ethan's family to Virginia to stay at his family's farm. Mom rolled her eyes and pretended to drag her heels. But finally said that maybe, just maybe Carrie deserved a reward for all her hard work this past week.

Carrie made a face. "Ethan's mom loves me. She says I'm a good influence. Can you imagine what she's say if she knew what I had talked him into?"

We laughed. It felt good to laugh. It felt good to sit in the sun. It felt good to be home.

Mom and Carrie both went to school the next day. I had nothing to do. My auditions were all over. There was nothing more to be done but wait to see if I was accepted or not. I tried playing my flute. Fabienne had been holding it for me, as I came out of the hall after my audition, so I didn't have it when they pulled me into the car and drove off. Thank God for that.

I thought about visiting Dad, but when I called, he was in the middle of something for work. We talked a few minutes. I'd see him the next weekend.

I napped, but kept having bad dreams. Or dreams about Stefan Brunel. I awoke from those anxious and confused. I didn't remember them, exactly, I just knew they were not happy.

Late in the afternoon, I did work in the yard. The crocus and snowdrops had popped through in the garden, so I raked and weeded. My fingers felt stiff and cold, but I was glad to be out of the house. I heard birds and felt the weak sun on my face, and I was so glad to be home.

Carrie came out of the house and sat on the ground next to me. "Do you want to talk?"

I sat back on my heels. "I don't know what to do," I said. "I feel like I'm just waiting now. I have absolutely no control over what happens next. It's up to Juilliard, or Eastman. Or Renata. Or George Brunel. I've spent most of my life planning and making things happen, and now, all I can do is sit around and let others decide what happens to me."

Carrie sighed. "That sucks. Big time. But you can't just play around in the dirt. What about Prom?"

Prom? "What are you talking about?"

She rolled her eyes. "Where have you been? Spring Thing for underclassmen is next week. But Prom is the first week of May. I figured since you had a hot boyfriend and somebody who could make you a killer dress, you'd be all over it."

Crap—how had I forgotten all about Prom? This is why I needed somebody around to remind me of the non-music-related things in my life.

"You're right. I've had my head in the clouds about auditions for the past three months. Can I get tickets on-line?

She shrugged. "Call Erin, she'd know."

"I can't call Erin, because I never got my phone back after Renata grabbed me, and I haven't gotten another. "

"Well, shouldn't you get one of your minions to start working on that?"

"You are exactly the perfectly annoying sister I need. Come with?"

She nodded, and we went inside. I yelled for Amelie, who came running up the stairs.

"What's wrong?"

"I need a new phone," I told her. "And I need to go by school and see if there's anyone still there who knows where I can get Prom tickets. Then I have to start looking for a dress. Oh, and I've got to talk to Luc tonight. I bet he doesn't know a thing about Prom."

Amelie's face lit up. "I'll call Garth, and we'll get the car.

I was right. Luc was clueless.

"It's a dance?"

"Yes. And dinner. I'll pick up our tickets tomorrow. You'll need a tux, and I have to start looking for a dress."

He frowned. "Can't Amelie make you something?"

I nodded. "Yes, but I need to at least shop around and get ideas. So I'd like to go into the City next week and do some major shopping.

"That's fine. You can drive in with me."

He had been working from home a few days a week all winter, but now that the weather was warmer, and the clocks had changed, he was driving to Wall Street every morning. He had been stopping by the house every evening, just to talk. I'd been seeing him every day for so long, if he called to say he couldn't make it for some reason, it felt like a real letdown. I looked forward to seeing him every day. I had started feeling lonely without him around. Even though my head had been full of music and practice and music theory tests, I still managed to find a connection to him that was strong. Sitting with him now, and thinking about how all that other stuff was behind me, I realized that, for a little while at least, I had nothing but time. I wanted to spend it all with him.

"Hey, do you go on vacation?"

"What has that got to do with this Prom?"

"Nothing. I'm just asking. We've never just been alone together, you know? I'd really like to do that."

He looked at me. "Being alone with you sounds like the best thing in the world," he said quietly. "It's what I've been wanting since the first time I saw you. But I could not be alone with you for very long before I'd want to make love to you. And that would be a problem."

I felt the heat rush to my face. I looked down and stared at my clenched fists. "For most people our age, it wouldn't be a problem at all," I said.

I felt him nod. I couldn't look in his eyes.

"I take this very seriously," he said. "As much as I want you, I will wait until we are married. It had been that way for thousands of years, Sara. I'll not break with tradition, no matter how much I want to."

I exhaled loudly and finally looked up at him. "If I ever told my friends about this conversation, they would never believe me."

He shrugged. "What can I tell you? I'm an old-fashioned kind of guy."

I had to laugh. I'd spent so much of my time telling guys no, and here I was, with the one I would have said yes to, and he wasn't even going to ask.

"Well, Prom also has a few traditions. Like going down to the Shore. Hurricane Sandy pretty much wiped us out, but there are some boardwalks open. Erin's parents have a shore house, and it was far enough behind the dunes that it's fine, so we're going down there right after Prom, a bunch of us, and we're spending the weekend. Girls in the bedrooms, guys on the living room floor. How about that?"

He smiled. "That sounds wonderful. Can I swim in the ocean?"

"Luc, the ocean in May is, like, freezing."

"Oh. How about a pool?"

"Nope. No pool."

He frowned. "Then, what will we do?"

"Well, there will be some drinking, I'm sure, and probably a lot of pot smoking. But there's also skee-ball and mini-golf and midway games. And rides. And we can go dancing at night, if we can find any clubs that are open. But the point is, we'll be alone together, but in kind of a huge group. What do you think?"

"You know what I think," he said. "How will I protect you?"

"Maybe Renata will be caught by then?"

"Maybe."

"Here's hoping."

I found out I was accepted at Juilliard the same day Toad came by to tell me they had found Renata. Brunel had been searching for her, but so had Toad, and Toad found her first. There had been a meeting with George Brunel, and the two of them decided what to do.

"Is she dead?" I asked. I couldn't believe those words came out of my mouth. What eighteen-year-old girl wanted anybody dead?

Toad shook his head. Mom and I sat together on the couch. Carrie perched on the ottoman. Amelie and Fabienne were hovering. Luc was on his way over. "No, she's not dead. He couldn't quite agree to that. But there's a place…" Toad shrugged. "Brunel understood that he had failed to contain her last time. So he took my suggestion."

"So what does this mean?" I asked. "For my real, day-to-day life, what does it mean? Can I walk outside without being followed? Can I meet Erin for coffee without an entourage? 'Cause, I gotta tell you, as much as I loved it before, it's getting old."

Carrie laughed. "Just like Mom always says, be careful what you wish for."

I made a face at her. "Brat."

She laughed again. "No. That would be you."

Toad spread his hands. "That's why Luc is coming over. We need to talk about what's next."

"Oh? Is that why he's coming over? I thought we were celebrating me getting into Juilliard."

Toad's face lit up. "That's great, Sara! I didn't know. Well, good for you. Yes, celebrating should come first."

"What about Jelenak?" Carrie asked. "Aren't they pissed off because we killed so many of them?"

I stared at her. We. She said we. She was already thinking of herself as part of the Family.

Toad looked thoughtful. "Actually, they're pretty angry at George

Brunel. They felt he should have honored the promises Renata made to their Clan. Garth killed in battle. Brunel set fire to a nest. Brunel is responsible for burning many more of them than Garth. There's trouble brewing, but it's not our trouble, for once. In fact, all the rumblings we've been hearing for the past few years have suddenly stopped. That's good."

Luc took us all out to dinner. I knew it was his idea of a celebration. It was also a good excuse to have lots of people around guarding me. He would give me no definite answers to anything. Isabeau, Fabienne and Amelie were still on duty. Garth would still drive me around.

Carrie told me that most of the "new" faculty members that appeared last fall were gone, and the gargoyles that had been perched on the school roof had disappeared. Mrs. Grant was still there. Apparently, the Queen liked being a guidance counselor. Who knew, right?

I finally made plans to go into New York to get my dress.

Amelie offered to make me something, of course, but I really wanted to shop. Mom had agreed to let Luc pay for my dress, so I was stoked. I was finally feeling like my old self. I was playing the flute every day, seeing Luc every night. Carrie wasn't around too much, she was spending most of her free time with Ethan. Abbott had practically moved in. Everything was shifting, but I felt pretty good about it.

Garth drove Amelie, Fabienne and I into Midtown. We'd been followed by one of the other Family cars, so I knew I was being watched. Still. But it felt okay. Besides, shopping with two French girls was the best. They knew all the latest designers, and where to find them.

"You two never go anywhere without me," I said. "How do you know all this and I don't?"

Amelie rolled her eyes. "What do you think we do all day while you play the flute? We're on the Internet. Virtual shopping. It's what keeps us from going crazy."

We were going up the escalator in Saks, when Amelie grabbed my arm and started looking around. Fabienne climbed down a few steps to do the same. I turned cold. Vampires? In Saks 5th Avenue?

At the top of the escalator stood Stefan Brunel.

He was dressed in a suit and had a Saks name tag on his lapel. I got off the escalator and stared at him.

I'd forgotten how big and dark his eyes were.

I turned to Amelie. "Can you guys just give us a minute?"

She and Fabienne exchanged glances, then moved off.

"How are you?" I asked.

He was smiling gently. "Good. I'm good. You look much better than the last time I saw you."

"You too. No shredded shirt today. You work here?"

"Yes. I have for about three years."

"Why?"

He shrugged. "Why not? I want to work. This is as good a job as any."

"Do you live in Midtown?"

"Brooklyn. How is Carrie?"

"She's good. She's still with Ethan."

"And you? I see you're still with Luc."

"Ah, yes. Prom is next week, so I'm doing a little shopping."

"Right." He'd been looking at me steadily. "When are you getting married?"

My throat closed up, and I had to swallow hard before I could speak. "I don't know. I've got Juilliard first."

"You're in?"

I nodded. "Yes"

"Congratulations. Then you'll be spending more time in the City?"

I nodded again. "Listen, I've heard that there may be some trouble for you. For your uncle."

He shrugged. "Some of the Clans are angry. There's a price on my head. My role in your escape did not go unnoticed."

"Oh, Stefan, no. God, I'm sorry."

He shook his head. "My choice, Sara. Besides, I am still George Brunel's nephew, and his heir. I feel quite safe."

"Have you seen Renata?"

His smile disappeared. "Yes. She is quite mad, now. I will not try to see her again. Her hatred is too hard to bear." He reached over, took my hand, and kissed it. His lips were cool against my skin. "Perhaps we'll run into each other. This is a city where anything is possible, right?"

I couldn't speak. And he walked away.

"Are you okay? You look very pale," Amelie said.

"I'm fine. I just never expected to see him again. Of all the people to run into, I mean. It's just, weird."

Her mouth was a thin line. "Yes. Let's go somewhere else. Okay?"

I waited until I lost sight of him in the crowd. Then we left.

I was staring in the mirror. The dress fit perfectly. Amelie had made a few alterations. Carrie, sitting on the edge of the bed, gave a long, low whistle.

"Can anyone say, 'Prom Queen'?"

Fabienne nodded her approval. "My sister did a good job," she said, somewhat grudgingly. Amelie nudged her sister, hard, and they both laughed.

Mom had not been too thrilled about the whole Shore thing, but she didn't argue as too much after Luc told her that the usual suspects would be along for the weekend. That didn't thrill me too much, but I what choice did I have?

Amelie and Fabienne left the room. I stood, still staring. Finally, I met Carrie's eyes in the mirror.

"You didn't mention meeting Stefan," she said.

I shrugged. "So? It was a coincidence. I didn't know he worked in Saks."

"Deanne told me he just quit."

Something knotted in my stomach. "Oh? I wonder why he would do that?"

"Because he's in love with you, that's why. And he probably doesn't want to take the chance of running into you again."

I turned slowly. "How could you know that?"

"God, Sara, are you blind? Or just stupid? Did you believe all that crap about keeping the treaty? You are engaged to the enemy. He not only acted against his Clan, he acted against his sister. Only a fool in love would do something like that."

I sat down next to her. "I love Luc."

Carrie raised her eyebrows. "Since when?"

"Since I asked him to go away with me, and he wouldn't because we'd probably have sex."

She made a noise. "Am I supposed to understand that? At all?"

"Maybe not." I thought for a minute. "It's not just about the fact that I want to sleep with him. I know that sex and love get all mixed up. It's about him. I've never been in love before, so I'm trying to be slow and sure about this. I want to be with him all the time. It's not just that I know how much he loves me, although, I gotta tell you, that's a pretty big thing. So is the 'Being a Queen Someday' thing, and how he can help my music career, and then, of course, there's the money and the travel and all that stuff." I plucked at the fabric of my dress. "If I push all that away, and just look at him, the kind of man that he is, I love him. He's good. He understands me, and I want to be a better person for him." I looked up at her. "Does that make sense?"

She nodded.

"I'm not going to marry him right away. I want to live alone, away from home, just to prove to myself I can do it. I know how spoiled and cared for I've been. I need to be more independent. But knowing that he's there, waiting for me—that's what's going to keep me going. That's what kept me going when I was sitting in the dark, locked in and alone. I thought about you and Mom, but it was thinking about Luc that kept me sane."

She nodded again, reached over, and hugged me. She held on for a long time. When she pulled away, there were tears in her eyes.

"I'm so happy for you, Sara. Luc is a good guy. He'll never let you down. I don't know why, but I was worried about Stefan."

I took a deep breath. "You were worried because you know me, Carrie. And as good a guy as Luc is, there's something about Stefan that's, well, intriguing. Exciting."

"Yeah, but he's a vampire. And Luc is a prince, and as exciting as Stefan may seem, in your heart of hearts, you've always wanted to be a princess."

"That's right. Not every girl gets her childhood wish, right? I'm so lucky."

She looked thoughtful. "As long as your childhood wish is enough, sure."

I stood up and shook out my hair, then reached down and grabbed my shoes. "Time to blow this pop stand. So, I'm gonna wow them?"

"Absolutely."

"Okay then. That's the important thing."

I went upstairs, where Luc was waiting. He smiled when he saw me, and swept me into his arms, and I knew, right at that moment, I was where I wanted to be.

ABOUT THE AUTHOR

Marijon was born and raised in New Jersey, which may help to explain her attitude towards charlatans and idiots. She started writing stories at an early age, her first literary influences being Walter Farley, author of *The Black Stallion* series, and Carolyn Keene of Nancy Drew fame. That's probably why her earliest efforts involved a young girl detective who solved crime on horseback.

She had a very happy childhood, did well in school, and was a fairly obedient daughter until she went away to college. The original plan was to major in journalism. She wrote for the college paper until she realized that wasn't the kind of writing she wanted to do when she grew up. So she switched to education. That was not, perhaps, the smartest move.

Then, life happened. Jobs, rent, husband, baby, another husband, another baby, until she found herself a stay-at-home mom, about to chew her foot off if she had to watch one more episode of *Barney*. So, she started to write again.

She still lives in New Jersey with her husband, daughter, two cats, and a very spoiled cocker spaniel. Her older daughter is off in Oregon, fighting the good fight for the homeless. She loves to cook —and eat—and plays RPG games on her Xbox when she needs to decompress (*Skyrim* alone cost her months of her life). During the past few years, she has lost, and tragically found again, the same twenty pounds. Life is all about trying, failing, and trying harder.

She writes in her downstairs office surrounded by her growing collection of gargoyles. *Smoke, Wings, and Stone* is her first YA novel.

Marijon Braden is the pen name for Dee Ernst, who writes adult romantic comedy and has lived an almost identical life.

Made in the USA
Charleston, SC
10 May 2013